PRAISE

"Emma Barry has been one of my favorite authors in the world for many years now, and *Chick Magnet* only deepens my already-fervent love of her writing. Her books are always crafted with exquisite care and thoughtfulness, abounding with graceful prose, extremely likable characters, rueful humor, and a thorough grounding in how good people think, work, and love. Plus, her writing is simply *fun*, not to mention sexy. With the release of this book, I expect new hordes of fans to join the Emma Barry Stan Club, but rest assured: I will always be the club's president and most enthusiastic member."

—Olivia Dade, national bestselling author of *Spoiler Alert* and *All the Feels*

"One of the chief pleasures of being a romance reader is getting to watch Emma Barry's complex, honorable characters forging themselves into stronger, happier versions of themselves. *Chick Magnet* is Emma Barry at the peak of her powers: hilarious and humane, it will restore your faith in the power of love."

—Jenny Holiday, *USA Today* bestselling author

"I could tell you all the reasons *Chick Magnet* is spectacular—the nuance of the emotional arcs; the witty dialogue; the delightful characters; the endearing small town—but really, all you need to know is that Emma Barry is about to become your new favorite contemporary romance author."

—Therese Beharrie, author of *A Ghost in Shining Armor*

"Intoxicating and deeply romantic, *Chick Magnet* delivers a riveting opposites attract, slow-burn-with-the-hot-guy-next-door small town romance. I fell in love with Will Lund from the first grumpy meeting."

—Zoe York, *New York Times* bestselling author

FUNNY
GUY

ALSO BY EMMA BARRY

Stand-Alone Novels

Chick Magnet

Political Persuasions Series

The One You Want

The One You Need

The One You Hate

The One You Crave

FUNNY GUY

EMMA BARRY

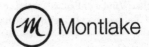

Published by Montlake, Seattle

www.apub.com

Amazon, the Amazon logo, and Montlake are trademarks of Amazon.com, Inc., or its affiliates.

ISBN-13: 9781662505034 (paperback)
ISBN-13: 9781662505027 (digital)

Cover design by Eileen Carey
Cover photography by Regina Wamba of ReginaWamba.com
Cover image: © StockLeb / Shutterstock; © Ingrid Bockting / Offset

Printed in the United States of America

FUNNY
GUY

CHAPTER 1

"Do you think it's true?"

If the woman in line behind Sam Leyland was trying to whisper, she wasn't good at it. Of all the bougie coffee shops in Williamsburg, Sam had had to pick this one, where apparently people didn't know how to mind their own business.

"I mean, he can't still think frozen cheesecake is fancy," she went on. "That's just—not possible."

"Could be," the equally whisper-challenged man responded to her. "Should we say something? Or—"

The couple dissolved into laughter, and it took every ounce of the self-control Sam famously did not have to point out they were *already* saying something. The juncture to not say something, the place where they could have all stared at their phones or the floor with the air of exhausted irritation that generations of New Yorkers had cultivated on teeming subway platforms and buses, had passed. Sam should've waved as it flew by.

But these people—loud and annoying as they were—hadn't started things. That fault rested with Sam's ex-fiancée. Over the loudspeakers, she was cooing her new single, "Lost Boy," about how Sam was such a child. Which . . . fair.

The next time he dated a pop star, it was going to be someone less talented. Someone whose latest single was less likely to top the Billboard charts with its "instantly iconic" video. And he was going to be sure to keep his secret pain buried good and deep, somewhere no one would ever find it again. Like maybe onstage in his act, where everyone just thought he was being ironic and didn't ever suspect he was telling the goddamn truth.

The bit about drawing the cool *S* on his sneakers while his piece-of-shit parents had fought in the next room that had gone viral and established him as the "voice of a generation"—had any generation needed a "voice" less?—every word of it had been true. The bits about paying for Slim Jims at the 7-Eleven with pennies, about flunking out of college, about blowing his *Comedy Hour* audition and then getting the gig anyway: all true. And none of it had felt funny while he'd lived it.

Do you think it's true? The words of the woman behind him echoed in his head. Of course it was fucking true.

The couple continued to giggle as the line clicked forward one more person. Sam closed his eyes and wished it all away. The loud gossips. The too-catchy song. The pouring rain that had driven him to stop here for coffee rather than at his regular place.

It all sucked, but he hadn't done anything in his life to enable him to complain about his luck. He'd had way more good breaks than he deserved; he knew that for sure. Part of what kept him hungry was the knowledge that he should never have escaped Leanver, Ohio, in the first place. It wasn't gratitude—hell no—but a belief that if he stopped moving, he might sink. He was going to sink someday, but every day he didn't was a win.

At last, Sam arrived at the counter.

"What can I get for you, man?" One thing that service workers in New York City could always be counted on to do was to never, ever be impressed with you. Sam would bet he was the most famous person to get coffee here this morning, but still, the kid didn't even blink. Impressive.

"Grande Red Eye with dark roast." Sam handed the kid at the counter his credit card. "And I'll pay for the order of the couple behind me too."

"Oh no. Don't start that." The kid wasn't going to say *please*, but his eyes were wide and desperate. He was staying just on this side of begging. "It's obnoxious."

"It's not to be polite. I promise it's not going to start a chain."

"If you say so."

Sam stepped to the end of the counter to wait for his drink. Up at the front, the world's loudest whisperers just couldn't believe that that guy from *Comedy Hour* had bought their caramel-macchiato-with-whip bullshits. They, of course, did not bother to extend the gesture to the people behind them—because such was the world.

It was stuff like this that made Sam unapologetic and kept him angry. The only differences between Sam and these two were that he didn't pretend he wasn't pissed and he got to say his piece on television. Deep down, the three of them were the same, and it was only a complete lack of a filter that kept Sam from being like everyone who complained about how rude he was.

Before the couple had managed to make their way down to him, the barista handed him his coffee. "Have a nice day."

"It won't be."

In the week since "Lost Boy" had dropped, Sam had barely left his apartment. Instead, he'd listened to the song about fifty times, connecting each one of the lyrics to all the various ways he'd fucked up in his brief relationship with Salem. It hadn't been healthy, he was sure, but he was convinced that anyone who said they wouldn't do the same thing if their exes wrote about them was lying. He'd only been grateful that the show had been on hiatus and he hadn't had a set lined up.

Sam was bold, but he wasn't that bold. He'd needed a chance to lick his wounds first. Frankly, he wasn't quite ready to stop licking yet. His chest was still ringing, as if Salem had taken a baseball bat rather than her lyrics to it.

The whisperers at last arrived. The woman was all fluttering eyelashes and fake kindness. In the morning, you could put on polite or you could put on rude. Sam just happened to think it was more honest to pick the second one.

"Are you Sam Leyland?"

"In the flesh." All this would be so much more awkward if it were a case of mistaken identity—and it was about to get really awkward.

For one second, Bree's face flashed before him. His best friend since kindergarten, Bree Edwards was the conscience Sam didn't have. Her brown eyes would be serious, and her red hair would bounce around her shoulders as she shook her head. *Don't do this,* she'd say.

But even if she were here, he'd barrel into it anyhow. It was his nature.

"That was so nice of you"—the woman was still gushing—"paying for our drinks."

"You didn't have to do that," the man added.

"I know I didn't," Sam said, pointing out the obvious. "I did it so that I wouldn't have to feel bad when I told you you're assholes."

The woman gasped. The man seemed to be legit speechless.

Ten seconds prior, the coffee shop had been all noise and bustle. The hiss from the milk frother. The ting from spoons hitting mugs. The bubble of coffee percolating. The low-level roar of conversations and the city outside. All it took was Sam being Sam, and the place went dead. Just fucking silent.

He knew he didn't have any special powers, but honestly, he could be forgiven if he forgot. It really did seem as if he'd made this happen.

Anyhow, he was in it now: he had to finish it.

"Look, I'm not saying, 'I'm a person. Can't you see my humanity?' or anything like that." Jesus, he'd never be so absurd. "Just, for fuck's sake, don't talk about someone when they're standing sixteen inches from you. Point and whisper from across the room like a good WASP. Or just text your friend. Everyone else was. Hey, you, sir—no, not you; you're reading the *New Yorker* so you'll pretend you don't know me— that guy." He pointed to a man of about twenty-five who was staring at his iPhone without blinking and trying to ignore Sam's rant. "Were you texting someone about me?"

A beat. Then the guy looked up and nodded sheepishly.

"See? And there's no shame in that." Sam didn't blame him at all. "But don't talk over the song." Sam pointed at one of the speakers. "It's a good song. Hell, I love hearing all about how I have daddy issues and that's why I can't commit—because I don't believe anyone can truly love me. It's great. It's like therapy I didn't even have to pay for, and the entire world gets to listen in."

The woman's eyes were huge, like the moon in that good-night book Sam's mother definitely hadn't ever read to him. The man was going red in the face, as if he were trying to decide whether he wanted to get in the first fistfight of his life. It appeared that Sam had made his point.

"So yes, I bought your coffee. But it wasn't a nice thing." Sam didn't really do nice. Not for anyone other than Bree. "And for the record, frozen cheesecake was and remains the shit."

After a silence long enough to watch *Titanic*, the woman managed to say, "You . . . are an asshole."

"Oh, absolutely. I never said any different. Enjoy your coffee." And with that, Sam headed back out into the rain.

A relatively painless subway ride later—forty minutes, and only three people shouted "you're that guy" at him—Sam emerged in Midtown. It was Friday at the end of a hiatus week, and Sam had to take some publicity photos and tape some promo spots—which was the kind of stuff he absolutely hated. He knew that it was necessary, and the bozos who thought he was good looking until he opened his mouth and ruined the illusion were central to his career, but he'd rather eat cold SpaghettiOs than take pictures.

He supposed that someone else, someone more sentimental, probably got tingly walking up to the Manhattan studio where the most famous sketch comedy show in American television history had filmed for the last fifty years. The guest hosts were sometimes saying crap like, "Do you know that so-and-so worked here," but the thing was, Sam did know and he still didn't care.

He'd been aware of *Comedy Hour* when he was a kid, but it had mostly seemed stagnant and boring to him. Sure, he was standing on the shoulders of giants, and whatever else he'd be expected to say at the next Mark Twain Prize dinner, but as far as he was concerned, comedy spent too much time looking backward.

What got Sam up in the morning was some kid on TikTok right now writing material that was fresh and could be distributed immediately, whereas Sam had to wait all fucking week. He worried his big paycheck was making him slow and complacent. You had to be a shark in this business. Never stopping. Never satisfied.

Sam rounded the corner and found more people than usually showed up for the average Mets game. Cameras started flashing, and he almost flinched. Someone must have tipped the press that he would be coming in. Sam was roadkill here, and they were the vultures.

"Sam! Sam!" one of the "journalists" shouted. "How do you like the song?"

"What do you want to say to Salem?"

"Did you really hate your father?"

"Why did you insult some fans in a Brooklyn coffee shop?"

The hullabaloo continued, but Sam managed to slam a hard expression on, the mask he used to not crack up when Roxy and the rest of the cast were really on. If his mask wouldn't crack when someone was being hysterical, it ought to be enough when many someones were being awful.

He wished he had a hat and some sunglasses, but that would make him feel like an even bigger phony. All he could do was push down the sidewalk, counting his steps and the breaths moving in and out of his lungs while they screamed at him.

Screamed the *truth*: that was the worst part. Sam was a broken piece of shit. Salem had certainly been right about that. He didn't deserve the life he had, and he'd probably wreck it sooner or later. That was the only thing that was going to even the scales.

The door to the studio opened, and one of the security guards, Derek, waved him in. "Sorry about that," he said once he managed to get the door closed behind them. "I called your agent."

Sam probably had about thirty missed calls from Riaz. This was what he got for not checking his phone. "I was on the subway."

He scrubbed a hand over his face. He should've anticipated this. He'd practically ensured it by showing so much of himself to Salem when they were together and by being snarky to so-called fans. But facing the consequences of his decisions—bad ones, neutral ones, angry ones, stupid ones—all he could manage to feel was tired.

He'd been in places like this so many times, and he didn't want to sleep in this particular bed. His own mind wasn't a great place to be in the best of times, and this wasn't the best of times. He'd made sure of that.

"Be sure to go out the back door," Derek said. "And don't go in the front door of your building neither."

Christ, Derek was right. Sam's apartment would be mobbed for the next few weeks.

"Thanks," Sam said. "I'll stay with a friend for a while."

Bree's was the only place where things made sense anyhow.

CHAPTER 2

"Wait, what *is* the best-smelling place you've ever been?" Bryony Edwards was genuinely interested in the answer, which had never happened to her on a date before. When your boss sent you for coffee with a guy she'd met at a party, insisting he's *perfect* for you, was that a date?

If not, Bree couldn't wait to get to the date, because it turned out that Carl was seemingly perfect. It wasn't only his nominal good looks or the dark hair he kept sweeping out of his eyes in a completely unselfconscious way. It was how he watched Bree when she talked and then asked follow-up questions. It was how he had been an investment broker but had left for nonprofit work. It was that he had read books (including by women!) and had traveled. That he didn't seem put off by Bree's passion for her job or her declaration that she was looking for something serious—and when was the last time a guy hadn't dashed when she'd said *that*?

No, Megan had really knocked it out of the park. Bree hadn't thought about Sam Leyland, her best friend of twenty-seven years, once so far.

Crap.

Bree refocused, pushing Sam out of her not-quite date. He didn't belong here.

Carl answered Bree's question. "Well, Paris."

"That seems obvious."

"No, look, this is going to sound ridiculous, but even the sidewalks there smell good. This mix of stone and bread and espresso. Then it rains, and—well, it's not like here." He gestured at the water streaming down the window behind Bree.

New York in the rain smelled like wet dog, with the gutters somehow filthier after having a river of sky water and trash running through them.

"Paris has the most gorgeous petrichor." Because Carl was the kind of person who used *petrichor* casually in conversation. "And you feel like a dweeb, looking at the city through rose-colored glasses, but it's perfect. Paris, no question."

Bree would've sighed if she'd been more romantic, but she was a person of straight lines and properly filed building applications and consensus-building meetings. She'd made herself into that, trusting in it to save her from where she'd come from. She wanted to sigh, though. Carl could make her sigh. Maybe.

"I'll have to take your word for it."

"You've never been?"

"Nah."

When Bree talked about how housing projects were dehumanizing, she was drawing on personal experience. When you grew up eating government cheese, international travel seemed about as realistic as finding a golden ticket to the Wonka factory. She had eventually gotten a passport, and it had felt like the most ridiculous splurge. It was still in a drawer, unused and unstamped—thank you, COVID, for taking away whatever hope she might have had to leave the continental US.

"I never had the chance," she said carefully. Bree had worked hard to scrub the working class from her accent, to dust herself with Ivy League credentials, but sometimes, people who had had access to those things from birth didn't like being reminded that not everyone did. "I've always wanted to, though."

Carl blinked—not surprised, just thinking. "Let's do it."

"Excuse me?"

"What are you doing this weekend?"

"Nothing." She didn't even have to check her calendar. Her social life wasn't exactly active.

"Everyone goes to dinner for their first date. Let's go to dinner *in Paris*." Bree had only known Carl half an hour, but he didn't seem to be joking.

For a second, she thought the buzz was coming from her head, not from the phone in her purse. But she ignored it; she let the slow smile that was spreading across Carl's mouth—his very, very pretty mouth—warm her through.

As rational as Bree was most of the time, she wished her practicality extended to love. But she'd never gotten in over her head, never let any stomach butterflies lead her astray, because when she'd been fourteen, she and Sam had been laughing together in the sad excuse for a park near his grandma's house when she'd known: *I will love you and only you forever.* It didn't help that her next thought had been, *Nooooooo.* It didn't help that she was a deeply rational person who didn't believe in fate or destiny. Nothing had ever been as sure to her as the moment when she'd looked into Sam's too-skinny face and known that she loved him. Next to that, everything else felt incompletely sketched. Sam had that effect on things, soaking up all the light. Like a black hole.

Which was unfair—she knew she was being unfair—but she did *resent* him as well as love him.

Across from her, Carl was still waiting. Was still perfect. "So what do you say?"

Bree again lectured herself about the importance of staying in the moment. While Sam might have an unholy talent for bursting into her life, it was her fault that she'd never been able to move on. Sam didn't have the slightest idea how she felt about him; he wasn't responsible for helping her not feel it anymore.

"I can't decide if you're serious."

Carl leaned his elbows on the table, bringing him closer, and then he lowered his voice, as if he were about to tell her a secret. "I think I am."

It should've sounded silly or like a line. But Bree's heart started beating wildly in her chest. She'd spent the seventeen years since she'd fallen in love with Sam trying to get into this moment, when the idea of someone else touching her made her jittery in the best way.

Carl was certainly worth getting jittery for.

"You think?" she whispered back, and her tone was the perfect blend of sexy and coy.

"Yeah, you're . . . I'm really glad Megan introduced us."

Bree's purse buzzed again. She wanted to ignore it. She wanted to tell Carl they should get an Uber to the airport now. She wanted a minute to process all this.

That last one won out. "Sorry. Let me, um, check that."

Inevitably, it was a text from Sam: Can I sleep on your couch?

Bree had received pretty much the same text many times. She quickly ticked off the time when, just before he'd dropped out of college, Sam had given up his apartment to save money for a Greyhound ticket to New York. He'd spent weeks on Bree's couch in Columbus, slept with her roommate, and cleaned out their fridge.

Then, after she'd finished college and grad school and had ended up in NYC as well, he'd crashed on her couch when he was between gigs and girlfriends. He stayed there after he'd gotten a little too drunk for even the subway during Friendsgiving, and when he'd found out that his father had died and the news had obviously cleaved him in two—not that Sam would or could ever admit that.

After he'd gotten famous, it had happened less often. For starters, his condo was about six times as big as Bree's place and infinitely nicer. He'd also gotten smarter about moving in with women—though obviously not smart enough not to propose to Salem.

But of all those requests over all those years, this was the first time Bree was tempted to say no. She could go on a first date, a first date in *Paris*. She could maybe, finally, at long last move on.

She could've chucked her phone to the moon.

"Everything okay?" Carl asked.

Bree waved her phone, she hoped airily. "Just a friend with a problem."

Another text arrived from him: Pleeeeeease. I'll get dumplings for dinner.

In the picture she'd assigned to his contact, Sam had his arm wrapped around Bree. His cheek was resting against her temple, and the memory of it was so strong, she could almost smell his deodorant across space and time. He was slightly buzzed: she could see it in his face. He wasn't so tense, wasn't performing the cool, sardonic mask he put on when he did stand-up, on *Comedy Hour*, or—hell, as he went through life.

Sam always looked about two seconds away from challenging someone to fight—except sometimes with Bree. There were moments, though they were rare now, when that fell away, and Sam was real and unguarded and anything seemed possible.

But now she was going to tell him no—no, he couldn't stay with her. She needed to get a life. Her own life.

Carl was staring at the phone in her hand. "Holy cow, is that Sam Leyland?"

"Yeah."

"You know him?" Carl's expression had gone part starstruck, part astonished, a mix Bree knew all too well. All his coolness and polish were gone. He was a child who'd just realized that he was one step away from an idol. All the flirty-ness and possibility, all the Paris, had evaporated.

Oh, damn. The tactile sense of someone else disappointing her fell through her stomach like a stone through shallow water.

"We grew up together," Bree managed to say.

"What's he like?"

Bree set her phone facedown on the table. She chafed her hands together, trying to get back some of the elated feeling she'd had a moment before, but she just stayed cold. "Complicated."

This seemed to offend Carl, which was odd given that he'd never met Sam. Bree ought to be the one who was offended here—and somewhere, under the hurt, she was.

"He must be hilarious," Carl insisted.

No one on earth made Bree feel as good as Sam did. Even with the ache—dear God, the ache—she laughed more with Sam than anyone else. But laughed *with* him, not at him. Not because of him. Sam was funny. That was what he was, what he was made of. But funny wasn't the first thing she thought of with him.

The first thing would probably be kind.

For someone with some of the world's shittiest parents and a volatile personality that torpedoed most of his relationships, Sam had always been uniquely, excessively kind to Bree.

She wished that it had been the kindness that had made her melt. How convenient it would have been if his kindness had been her kryptonite. Because then she could have transferred her affection and hopes and dreams to the next kind guy to fall into her path. But that hadn't been the entire picture.

It was the way Sam's eyes crinkled and his left cheek—and his left cheek only—dimpled. It was how he knew everything about her family without being told or needing to talk about it. It was the way he'd held her hand under the table, fierce and silent, when she'd discovered that her mom had tried to pilfer her financial aid. It was the way he'd mocked an older man who used to pester her on the city bus so mercilessly that the guy had stopped talking to her—insisting he "could've kicked his ass, but this was more satisfying"—and then had never let her take the bus alone the entire rest of the time she'd lived at home.

It had combined all together and alchemized somehow. That mix was who Sam was and why she loved him.

"He *is* funny," she told Carl. "He's my best friend in the world. But mostly, he's . . . complicated." He could be cutting and proud and excessive and petulant. But to her, he was kind. And chivalrous. And generous. And so good looking, he made it hard to see anyone else.

"I guess that makes sense. I mean, that entire set he did, ragging on his mom—"

Sam hadn't been ragging on her. He'd been trying to work through his childhood, slay some demons. When that bit had gone viral, it had basically made Sam's career.

"—and there was the time he broke up with that actress in the middle of a set—"

The actress had screamed at him backstage during the set break.

"—and you've heard 'Lost Boy'?"

"I have."

Carl paused, waiting for her to get into what was true and false in Salem's song, but of course Bree had no intention of doing that. It really wasn't any of Carl's business.

The door opened, and a blast of cold air—with none of the apparently gorgeous rain smell of France—hit them square in the face. It was enough to break whatever spell Sam's picture had cast over Carl.

"I—oh my God, I'm being such a jerk." Carl reached across the table and set his hand over Bree's.

There wasn't a single freaking jitter. Not a butterfly in sight.

Bree had been deluding herself yet again. She hadn't been on the verge of getting over Sam. As long as she stayed in New York, in his orbit, she'd never get over him.

"I am so sorry," Carl said. "I saw his picture, and I just got carried away."

"It happens a lot."

"I can't imagine how frustrating that must be."

He didn't know the half of it, but Bree just shook her head. She wasn't even upset. It felt like the oldest story in the world, or at least the oldest of her life. People saw her, and they only saw Sam. She looked at her life, and she only saw Sam.

When he'd announced his engagement to Salem, Bree had almost decided to leave. She'd applied and interviewed for jobs. She'd had *offers*. But she hadn't been able to bring herself to do it. Now, she regretted that choice, if only because it would have spared her the exquisite awkwardness of this moment.

"So . . ." Carl tried for some of the intimacy they'd had, but he couldn't get it back. He'd broken it, he and Sam. "There's a proposition on the table: Paris?"

Bree gently pulled her hand from under Carl's. It didn't even feel like a loss. She got to her feet. "Not this weekend."

"Maybe soon?" He sounded genuinely hopeful. He didn't realize they would never see each other again.

"Maybe." But she didn't mean it.

In the doorway of the coffee shop, she pulled out her phone and sent Sam a single-word reply: Sure.

Because even though Sam made an outrageous mess of his life on a regular basis, aggravating her and seeming to make half the world hate him, she loved him. Always had, and always would.

His reply arrived almost instantly: You're saving my life.

Sam probably did need to be saved, but if there was one thing Bree had learned over the years, it was that she couldn't do it. No one could. Sam had to save himself.

Just like she had to save herself—from him.

At seven, after her failed quasi date with Carl and overseeing a playground inspection, Bree returned to her apartment and began to peel off her work clothes. She climbed into some sweats and her favorite T-shirt (**You Had Me at Mixed Use**), removed her contacts, washed off her makeup and the dirt of the city, and put on her glasses—because she never had to pretend with Sam. It was a relief and a sucker punch at the same time.

Her phone buzzed with a text from him: Will be there in five minutes. With dumplings.

Well, at least there would be dumplings.

Bree spent the next few minutes straightening up her apartment, which didn't take long because it was simply too small to get really messy, and finding her extra bed linens. Then the buzzer sounded, and she pressed the button to let him in.

The funny part was that when he swept in, his arms filled with take-out bags and his mouth already moving—Sam began every conversation as if they were in the middle of things—it didn't hurt. Being in love with your best friend wasn't like having the crap kicked out of your heart every time you were together. It wasn't as if her heart skipped a beat every time he smiled.

Being together was the easiest thing in the world. Being apart was impossible.

"So I got some shumai and jiaozi, and three orders of bao. I didn't get any xiaolongbao, because you have terrible taste—and also, they don't travel well."

Sam looked bad. Or at least as bad as an objectively hot guy could look. He had shadows under his eyes so purple, they almost looked like bruises. His cheeks had hollowed, and his hair was messy, and the energy radiating off him was rancid. But Bree could say absolutely none of this. Sam hated pity.

She greeted him. "Hello to you too. Feeding an army?"

"No, I'm apologizing for the short notice."

"Well, the joke's on you, because the radiator is on the fritz again."

Sam rubbed his arm. "It is pretty cold. You've called the super?"

"Of course." She attempted to turn the subject back to him. "Why don't you have any luggage? Are the paparazzi at your place?"

It wouldn't be the first time. Frankly, Bree had been expecting it after Salem's new single had dropped last week. She'd tried texting and calling dozens of times, but of course Sam had ignored her. When you thought he might be in pain or have need of a friend and reached out, you might as well have been flashing Morse code at the International Space Station.

If the situation had been reversed and Bree had needed him, Sam would have been there instantly. But she wasn't allowed to be there for him in any way that suggested she thought he needed to commiserate or receive comfort. Sam had to feel like he was in control, not you. Never you.

"You haven't seen what happened this morning?" Sam asked carefully.

As if it wasn't enough that he was already global news. Of course Sam had gotten himself into more trouble.

"No. What?" Bree grabbed some plates and set them on the bar. Then she added a bottle of wine while Sam went to the drawer for the corkscrew. It featured the logo of a snobby wine bar where he'd worked for a few months before he'd started at *Comedy Hour*.

"I was perfectly behaved. I bought some fans coffee." He set it on the table and scratched his cheek. "Don't check Twitter."

"Jesus, Sam, what did you do?" Bree turned to the cabinet to get some wineglasses.

"You sound like my mother. Oh, wait, no you don't."

Sam didn't speak to his mother, which Bree understood. Bree didn't think Sam's late father had actually hit him, but she wasn't sure. Close as they were, there were aspects of Sam's childhood she didn't ask about. Seeing the shadows it had cast over Sam's life was enough; you didn't have to know everything about the tree that had cast them. It was why Sam had vowed long ago to never, ever return to Leanver, Ohio.

"No, you sound like my agent."

"I'm sure he'd stick a *fuck* in there." Riaz, Sam's agent, was notoriously foul mouthed, and Bree couldn't stand him. Not because of his language but because he didn't seem to have Sam's best interests in mind. He ought to have known Sam was going to have a meltdown as soon as the song dropped and stashed him in a spa or at the bottom of the Mariana Trench or something.

"Not anymore. I think he's lost all affection for me."

"If he has, it's only because you're his worst client."

"Not possible. He also represents Roosevelt Austin."

"Who had two Videon specials last year."

Every comedian wanted a Videon special. After the bit about his mother had swept the internet—part of a set where he'd ranted about the various ways in which parents could psychologically damage their children, using examples from his life—Sam had gotten one, and it had basically made his reputation. The tone was somehow as corrosive as battery acid and screamingly funny at the same time. Bree had no idea how he'd pulled it off. But the bit's success had made Sam himself the main subject of his own comedy, and Bree knew he hadn't counted on that. No one could be blamed for not realizing that putting yourself out there could earn a global audience for your dirty laundry—and require you to keep hanging it out there forever.

Sam curled his lip at the thought of Roosevelt Austin. "What a hack."

"How are your negotiations with Videon going?" She knew Sam usually got what he wanted, but yelling at fans in coffee shops wasn't going to help matters.

"They're dragging their feet, but this isn't about that." Except that it most likely was, since everything Sam did affected his career one way or another. "No, here's the thing: I think I might really have fucked up this time, Smoosh."

Whenever he called her Smoosh—a ridiculous childhood nick-name—Bree knew things were serious.

Sam sagged against the back of the chair. He closed his eyes, and his head fell back. Bree could have drawn his silhouette in the dark. The slope of his nose, the jut of his chin, the line of his throat. They were more familiar to Bree than her own.

"With Salem or with whatever you did this morning?" she asked.

"With all of it. I think I've broken things beyond fixing."

"You haven't. You're too talented for that."

He smiled, faintly. Softly. The kind of smile that he never gave anyone except her. "You're the best liar. That's why I had to come here and ply you with meat wrapped in carbs."

He had to come here, because whatever Sam was for Bree, she was the same for him. The thing they shared, the affection they had for each other, was real and valid. Just friends? She and Sam weren't *just* anything. They were everything. If this was all they could ever be for each other—and she was sure it was—then it was enough. Her stupid hormones were exactly that. Stupid.

"You're here because you don't want to see sad pictures of yourself in the *Post* tomorrow. And because you probably have a crowd of people outside your apartment waiting to blow smoke up your butt. Here, eat." She scooped some dumplings onto his plate.

He shoved a dumpling in his mouth and sighed appreciatively. "I don't, but I should hire some. That sounds like a service Goop might offer."

"Sycophants are us?"

"I'm going to write that up, thank you very much. Roxy will love it. But no, seriously—I don't trust anyone but you." He was looking straight at Bree, his face sober and his body tight.

Bree knew he did love her, in his own way. In a course in college, one of Bree's English professors had talked about slant rhymes in the poems of Emily Dickinson. It was so close to the real thing, you could almost be mistaken for thinking it was.

That was what Bree had with Sam: a slant rhyme.

"Then you should know that you'll be brilliant. Well, first you'll be an ass, but then you'll be brilliant."

"What if someday I'm not anymore?" This question was sincere.

Sam had demons—larger, scarier ones than Bree did. They came out of trauma, and they came out of personality, and they came out of working in a terrifying industry where success was almost impossible and frequently short lived. Bree would have vanquished those demons for him if she could, but only Sam could do that.

"Then you'll go be something depressing, like a plumber."

"I'd be a great plumber."

"You'd be a terrible plumber, but you'd charm everyone, and they'd pay you anyway. Except for the people you decided to fight, and then you'd get fired. But that's it, Sam: that's the worst thing that could happen. Your time on *Comedy Hour* will eventually end, which isn't an appalling outcome. I've never been on *Comedy Hour*. My life has gone on anyway."

"That bluntness is why I trust you." He gave her a faint smile, which he followed with a gusty sigh. "But you know the most galling part? Not about *Comedy Hour*, about Salem."

Oh, good. They were moving on to other things.

Bree had mixed feelings about Sam's ex-fiancée—a title that felt ridiculous since Bree had known the engagement had been unlikely to turn into an actual marriage. She and Salem had only met a few times as it had been a whirlwind relationship, which pretty much summarized every one of Sam's interactions with people. But Salem had seemed warm and kind. She was ten years younger than Sam, but she wasn't wide eyed or naive. She'd been around The Industry (a phrase that Bree felt silly just thinking) for longer than Sam had.

No, Bree knew her jealousy was ridiculous, but there it was: Sam would never look at Bree and think they could have something fresh and untainted together, which she was certain was what he'd seen when he'd looked at Salem.

"The most galling part is that it's a catchy song?" she guessed.

"Oh my God, it's so catchy. I like it—until I remember that it's about me." He dropped his face to his hands, and Bree had to cackle.

When someone at work had played it for her, Bree hadn't been able to find the humor. She'd first been worried that Sam might freak out over how Salem had pinned him so specifically and devastatingly. Sam might well be the "Lost Boy" Salem had labeled him, but he was also proud.

"And see, I thought the worst part was that everything she said was true." Bree framed this as a funny jab, but she also meant it. With Sam, it was better to frame anything touchy as a joke and wait to see how he responded.

Hamlet had been onto something with that play of his.

"Hell no," Sam blustered. "I'm not a lost little boy. I know exactly where I am."

But he didn't.

As intimately as Bree knew Sam, even she had never bothered to put into words everything that Salem had crammed into three minutes and forty-six seconds of an infectious pop beat. But it couldn't all have come as a shock to him, right? Repression was the name of his game— and perhaps the name of the game that she had mastered too.

"Here's to my next ex being into roller derby and not music," he said, raising his glass.

Bree raised hers and clinked it gently against his, but she didn't want to contemplate a world in which he had yet another ex.

CHAPTER 3

The expression "as easy as falling asleep" was bullshit. Sam never found falling asleep to be easy. His mind couldn't turn off; it didn't even have airplane mode. He couldn't stop chewing on the stuff he'd done right and, more often, what he'd messed up. The jokes he'd told and how he should've told them. What he wanted and would never get. How hard he was running away from the person he'd been born to be and where he wanted to get to, which kept reconstituting itself and slipping away from him.

Wait, maybe "as easy as falling asleep" meant something was *difficult*, and Sam had been using the phrase wrong his entire life.

Shit, now he definitely wasn't going to be able to sleep.

"You're tossing and turning." Bree's voice came from her bed not ten feet away. He could hear the smile in her tone. She sounded fully awake; maybe she didn't have an airplane mode either.

"That's because it's fucking freezing, Smoosh." Which was true. He'd offer to have her over to his place, but—paparazzi.

He could hear her shift, the movement of her limbs against her covers. "Do you want another blanket?"

"I already have one."

"Which doesn't mean you can't have another."

She turned on the lamp by her bed. Her hair was tousled, and her thin cotton University of Pennsylvania tank top was falling off one of her shoulders, revealing one of those sports bras with the complicated twisting straps, the kind that seemed to be designed to catch and hold your attention.

To catch your attention *generally*, not with Bree specifically.

She raised a single eyebrow at him. Their entire lives, he'd always wanted to know how she did that. It was one of those tricks he probably ought to learn for the show. But the expression had its typical effect on him, and he huffed out a laugh.

That was the real reason why he was at her place. It wasn't about the jerks with cameras in front of his apartment. It was about how, for the first time in a week, since "Lost Boy" had cracked his life like an eggshell, he felt okay because he was with Bree.

"Why aren't *you* cold?" he asked.

"Duvet." She slid out of bed and padded over to her closet. "Sadly for you, I only have one, but . . ." She trailed off as she popped up on her toes to reach the top shelf. In the process, her tank top hitched up, revealing several inches of fine-grained skin, painted gold by the light from her lamp. The swell of her hip was perfect. Her spine was in a shallow channel down her back, disappearing into her PJ bottoms.

For a minute, Sam quite simply couldn't breathe.

He'd dragged Bree to the beach before. Had seen her in a bathing suit more times than he could count. But this was different somehow.

It was—he was unsettled. That was it. Like when you shake a snow globe, and all the fake snow swirls around: the last week had done that to him.

Except for the space of a heartbeat, the explanation didn't quite convince him. For twenty years, Sam had the occasional moment where he noticed Bree not simply as the warm center of the universe but as an embodied person—emphasis on the *body* part. He'd gotten exceptionally good at shoving those moments back under the bed where they belonged.

Frankly, Sam ought to stop noticing anyone in that way. He was basically a tornado in human form. Him and bodies? They didn't mix . . . not for long, anyhow. For the sake of humanity, he ought to take a vow of celibacy. He needed to stop inflicting himself on anyone, let alone someone he liked and respected as much as he did Bree.

He let himself take another peek. She'd twisted, and he could see her stomach now. The dip of her belly button. She was soft in the best way. The way you wanted to sink into and never come up for air.

Fuck.

He rubbed his hands over his face. For the love of mashed potatoes, it was just skin. Okay, objectively beautiful skin. But still, his best friend's skin.

"Will this work?" she asked.

He almost said no, but of course she wasn't talking about whatever pothole his brain had tripped into where it was okay—inevitable even—for him to think about her that way. Sam was a disaster person who broke everything and everyone. Bree was the literal best and deserved the world. He couldn't give it to her, so he couldn't, wouldn't, notice her skin.

But he still had to give her an answer. He cracked an eye open. Bree had tugged her shirt down—thank Christ—and was holding a pilling blue blanket he was fairly sure had once been her mom's. That gave him something else to focus on that wasn't her.

"Yeah. That's fine."

She crossed to the couch and settled the blanket over him. "Better?" she asked. "Or do you need some warm milk too?"

Neither of them drank milk, which of course she knew. What he *needed* was to get back to being his normal self. In a bid to do just that, he flipped her off, and she laughed as she went back to her bed.

The lamp clicked off, leaving Sam a little warmer but still with the conundrum of how to fall asleep. Especially now that he was doubly stirred up.

Go to sleep, motherfucker.

But profanity didn't help in this particular situation, and he couldn't bully his brain into quieting down.

"If you don't stop sighing over there," Bree said, "I'm going to make you talk about your feelings."

"Oh God, no. Not *feelings!*" he whined.

A pause. Then she said, "You could, you know. Talk about your feelings."

That wasn't happening. "Nah. Let's talk about why you have this blanket."

Sam had well-documented problems with his mom. He blamed her for subjecting them both to his father. Blamed her for still loving the bastard after what he'd done to them. But at the end of the day, he could see how his mother had cared for him, at times. She'd been selfish and immature and bad at parenting, but she hadn't been the actively malevolent one, not toward Sam.

Bree's parents were another story. Her father had never been in her life. While she and her mother hadn't been *close* close, they'd gotten along better than Sam and his mom had, at least until her mother had—intentionally or unintentionally, Sam had never been clear on that—taken out a number of college loans "for" Bree, keeping the money for herself.

When Bree had discovered it, her mother had denied what she'd done. Bree confronted her with the paperwork before she pulled out some bullshit about being confused. Sam actually hated her for it.

It wasn't as if he cared about credit scores, but the woman had almost ruined her kid's financial future and then lied about it. That Bree wasn't actively bitter toward her, that she'd cut her mom out of her life and then had moved on with trying to improve the world—it was like witchcraft.

"Damn, I shot myself in the foot there," Bree muttered.

He pressed on. "You heard from her?"

"You know I haven't."

He couldn't decide if that was good or incredibly sad.

"You talked to your mom?" she asked.

"Nope." Not since his early days on *Comedy Hour* when she'd made some noise about reconciling that he interpreted to be all about anticipating a fat payday. He might have more perspective on his mom today, but he wasn't about to forgive her. Some shit was too deep to contemplate.

"All this talk about blankets isn't helping me fall asleep." Bree was making a joke, but they both knew she meant it.

"Where we come from isn't a good bedtime story."

Except it was a fairy tale, wasn't it? Two kids from an Ohio trailer park making good. Getting out. Maybe it was a different kind of fairy tale, one in which the peasants saved themselves, not by becoming royals or even slaying dragons but by clinging together and moving on.

"We're okay, though," he said. "We're . . . safe." That was, honestly, more than either of them might have hoped for when they were twelve.

"Yeah," Bree said, softly. "We are."

That thought was enough to settle Sam's mind and finally let him find some peace.

"You didn't have to come." Bree was arranging a lumpy brown scarf around Sam's neck.

Sam didn't have the heart to tell her that rather than disguising him, she might make him go viral: he was approaching the Lenny Kravitz blanket-scarf meme here. It would undermine the entire point of him staying at her place if he ended up trending on Twitter for the second time in two days.

"Yes, I did," he told her, trying not to laugh at the way she was chewing on her lip while she worked. She was taking camouflaging him *very* seriously, but she ought to know that a hat, scarf, and sunglasses weren't going to make Sam invisible. He was still him. "I'm a guest. This is what guests do." Sam hadn't exactly grown up with Emily Post's rules, but it would've seemed rude to send Bree off while he moped on her couch. Ruder than he was comfortable being, that was.

Bree took a step back and surveyed her work. "But you hate historical-architecture walking tours."

That was . . . true. Leave it to rich people to make walking complicated. He was fairly certain he and Bree could take a stroll in any neighborhood in the city, and, off the top of her head, she could come up with as many interesting facts as this yahoo they were paying to lead them around.

"What's this one about?" he asked.

Over the years, Bree had dragged Sam on so many of these things: the development of tenements, the way Robert Moses had destroyed the city, the construction of skyscrapers, the design of Central Park. As big and old as New York was, it was difficult to believe they hadn't taken all the walking tours.

"The history of Forty-Second Street."

Sam almost groaned, but then he remembered how his dad would shit on anything he or his mother expressed interest in, and Sam stifled his response. He didn't want to be that guy. He didn't ever want to be that guy.

But Bree, because she knew him better than he knew himself, picked up on his loathing anyhow and gave him an apologetic look. "You can still leave."

"Not a chance, Smoosh. Wild horses couldn't drag me away. I'm *obsessed* with the history of Forty-Second Street. Ask me anything."

"How much revenue do the billboards take in annually?" She pointed to one of the gigantic, gaudy lit-up things.

"No idea. But I've *appeared* on one." Several actually. "So—"

"Shh." She put her hand over his mouth to quiet him. Her wrist smelled like her perfume, some combination of vanilla and flowers that made his head spin. "You're supposed to be flying under the radar here."

She took her hand away, and he had a sudden, ridiculous urge to tug it back.

Before Sam could figure out what *that* was about, the tour guide clapped his hands to get the group's attention. "We're going to get started, everyone!" He proceeded to tell them about what they had to look forward to over the next three hours: the lions at the New York Public Library, Grand Central Station, and the United Nations. Oh joy. Then he got started on the history of Times Square.

Sam might not be a "real" New Yorker, but even he knew these were the crappiest five square blocks in the city. Overdeveloped, overpriced, and overcommercialized, the area was a Kraft Single in real estate form. No, that was unfair. Sam enjoyed Kraft Singles; he didn't enjoy Times Square.

But next to him, Bree was smiling and nodding. She loved this more than anything. More than bagels, even. Approaching how much she loved dumplings. So Sam let her happiness buoy him over the chatter.

As they started walking toward Bryant Park, the tour guide dropped back and gave Bree a grin. "You from out of town?" His question was as bland as mayonnaise, except the way he said it was anything but.

The tour guide was hitting on Bree. He probably did this all the time: picked up tourists, offering to show them something special after dark. He likely saw that as a perfectly acceptable bonus for what was objectively a crappy job.

Sam chewed on the inside of his cheek to avoid telling the guy exactly where they were from.

"Oh, no." Bree was all friendly cheer. "We live here."

Sam almost draped an arm over Bree's shoulder to help her repel this creep. She didn't need some failed architect who led walking tours on the weekends trying to get her number and into her pants.

Except she also didn't need a college dropout who appeared in comedy sketches on TV to shield her.

"I work at Innovation X," she explained.

"Megan Davis's firm?"

Bree's boss was *not* Sam's biggest fan, but she'd always done a good job shepherding Bree's career. Sam had to give her that.

"That's the one."

The guy whistled. Now he was an entirely other kind of impressed with Bree, and Sam didn't like it one bit.

Before Sam could stage some kind of emergency disruption, maybe fake a heart attack or at least a blister, the tour guide dropped his voice to the conspiratorial range and edged closer to Bree. "You know, I just finished an MArch at the Pratt Institute, and I've been looking—"

Sam was so annoyed that he couldn't even enjoy that he'd clocked this guy's entire biography at ten paces. He couldn't believe this booger was trying to take advantage of Bree like that.

"See," Sam interrupted and didn't even try to keep his voice down to maintain incognito mode. "I knew he'd have the answers to all your questions about Tudor City."

The look Bree gave Sam—the astonished tilt of her head, her brown eyes wide, and her brows arched—was textbook flabbergasted. She wasn't surprised Sam was blowing his disguise. No, she couldn't believe he'd remembered the name of that richy-rich apartment complex she'd dragged him to see a dozen times.

Sam ought to be offended, but he was mostly aggravated with the tour guide, who was still patiently waiting for Bree to turn her attention back to him. He didn't know that he'd climbed into the ring with the champ. Sam didn't lose, not where Bree was concerned.

Sam knew he was being selfish, but he needed Bree this weekend. Needed all her attention. Besides, this guy wasn't worthy of her.

Like clockwork, when she did turn back to the tour guide, Bree's tone was apologetic. "I *am* really interested in the development of Turtle Bay. That's mostly why we're here."

Sam was unequivocally only here for Bree, but sure, she could tell this goober that if it made her feel better.

The guy's smile faltered as he realized he wasn't getting her number, nor was Bree going to take his résumé into Megan. "Well, I'll answer all your questions when we get there. Enjoy the tour!" And he drifted away to try to find some midwestern rube to ply his lines on.

"Can you believe that guy?" Sam asked. "Trying to get you to rec him to Megan like that?"

"Can you believe that guy?" Bree matched Sam's tone. "Calling attention to himself like that when someone was just being friendly to me?"

Sam snorted. "You should audition for *Comedy Hour*. You're a pretty good mimic."

"Know anyone in the cast?"

"For you, baby, heck yes." He intended it as a joke, but somehow, it didn't land right. Some of Sam's comedian friends would want to unpack that. Figure out why the audience—Bree, in this case—didn't laugh. But Sam wasn't really one for introspection.

"Seriously," she said, "try to be low key for once."

"He was hitting on you!"

"So?" Bree demanded, and there was something genuinely angry under the question.

Sam didn't know why the idea of the tour guide asking Bree out made him want to kick the curb, and he didn't know why Bree was borderline pissed at him for intervening, and he really didn't want to tease out those emotions.

Instead, he dodged and told her the truth: "I need you. I can't share right now. I'm very brokenhearted." He was embarrassed more than brokenhearted, at least in the classic sense, but he 100 percent needed Bree to get through it.

Whatever aggravation had been building in Bree's eyes popped like a bubble. "You want to leave this tour and get ice cream?"

"No, I want to learn all the secrets of Grand Central Station and *then* get ice cream."

She snorted. "You don't care about Grand Central."

I care about you. But something kept the words in his mouth.

Instead, he rammed his shoulder into hers and said, "It was built in 1850, you know."

A pause. Then she bumped him back. "It was not. It was built between 1903 and 1913."

He knew she'd never let a bad architectural or design fact stand. "My bad. It's an example of bozo arts—"

"Beaux arts."

"—and the whispering gallery is how they caught Bernie Madoff."

She cackled. "You should be leading this tour."

"I really should. It'd be so much more interesting."

Anything involving Bree and him always was.

CHAPTER 4

Bree's weekend with Sam had been like walking into Bloomingdale's and, without guilt, buying shoes at full price—which she'd never managed to do. On the rare occasions when she did buy something full price, she felt bad about it for weeks.

When Sam had gone on the Forty-Second Street walking tour with her and patiently waited while she'd asked twenty minutes of questions at the end? When he'd talked to her as they'd both struggled to fall asleep every night? When they'd played Ticket to Ride and she'd laughed so hard her stomach ached? Bree was going to have to start giving herself stern lectures about the dangers of indulging impossible fantasies. Forty-eight hours of him on her couch, and she was already stuck in the Sam-shaped trap that had kept her in the same place for so many years. There was no way for this to end without pain for her.

Bree wove through the cubes to her desk. She'd spent most of the last decade working her way up the chain at Innovation X, a small urban planning firm that her college friend and mentor, Megan Davis, ran. Bree had bounced between roles that were design focused and ones that were more regulatory. While she loved the creative side, she was also good at ensuring the i's were dotted and the t's were crossed. She had a talent for paperwork.

Across the aisle, her coworker Jeff Sharma looked up from his morning routine of drinking coffee and reading the sports news before diving into a fun day of spreadsheets. "Your famous friend is having a *moment.*"

Everyone loved giving Bree crap about Sam. When she'd moved to the city, Sam had been the only person she knew, so she'd always wrangled him into coming to work karaoke nights and being her plus-one at holiday parties. As he'd gone from being that part-time bartender trying to break in to stand-up to a legitimately famous, successful comic, no one had stopped teasing her about Sam. Jeff and Megan could be especially scathing. They had to suspect Bree's feelings, even if she'd never confirmed the truth for them.

"Moments are kind of his specialty," she told Jeff wryly.

"I can't wait to see this week's show."

"I doubt it'll come up."

"How could it not?"

She felt like snapping, *Because maybe he doesn't feel like mining his personal life for material,* except that would be a lie. Sam used his life for material all the time. Sometimes, she felt like the only person who understood how painful it must be for him to publicly laugh at himself. But she didn't want to get into all that with Jeff—whom she liked, but not enough to betray Sam's privacy.

Bree scrolled through her email inbox, and then froze at the subject line Principal Consultant Position at Hutchinson-Baker.

When Sam had announced his engagement to Salem, Bree had looked for jobs away from New York City. If he were going to get married and be permanently, absolutely, irrevocably someone else's, Bree had to go. She wanted him to be happy, she did, but she didn't know if she could see it every day. It would've dissolved her heart from the inside out, and honestly, a lifetime of friendship with a man who didn't and couldn't love her back had already done enough damage. When

Sam and Salem's engagement had fallen apart, though, leaving hadn't seemed as crucial anymore.

Still, she knew leaving would be good for her career. She'd gone as far as she could at Innovation X. Because of its size, it tended to take small jobs, mostly in New York and the surrounding area. Ten years of that, and Bree was ready for something else.

A principal consultant position would fit the bill. They led teams to bid on and manage projects, and Hutchinson-Baker had them all over the country—and even the world. They were one of the most interesting urban planning firms in the country. She loved their approach to design, their business philosophy and ethics, and their focus on accessibility, the environment, and community consensus. This was her dream job.

With jittery fingers, Bree opened the message. They were looking to start a new team focused on sustainable design, and they'd heard great things about her. *Her. Bryony Edwards.* This was a head-hunting email, one that mentioned an eye-popping salary and emphasized the quality of life in Ann Arbor, Michigan.

All the variables and the cost-benefit analysis she'd considered last year came rushing back. Sure, putting six hundred miles between her heart and Sam could be a good thing. For three years in college, he'd been in NYC and she'd been in Columbus and then Philadelphia, and it had helped. It had been easier to *see* other men, to be present in the threads of her life that didn't include Sam.

But also, this was what every choice she'd made in her career had been aimed at. If she wasn't going to leave for this opportunity, she'd never do it.

Yes and *no* rushed inside her like the push-pull of a tide. Bree rubbed her fingertips together. This had gone from being a perfectly normal Monday morning to one of those crucial moments in life.

"Not to change the subject," she said to Jeff, even though that was exactly what she was trying to do, "but do you ever think about leaving?"

"Innovation X?"

"And the city."

"You're reconsidering moving?"

She'd needed letters of recommendation for her previous round of job applications, and so she'd talked to Jeff and Megan about the possibility of moving on. They'd been enthusiastic, wanting bigger and better things than this firm could give her at this point in her career, and they seemed willing to shove her out of the nest so she would go get them.

"Is this about Mr. Leyland?"

Oh, damn, another illusion shattered. Jeff had figured out how Bree felt.

Shoving the mortification of that aside, Bree said, "It's about me. I got a recruitment email for a gig at Hutchinson-Baker."

"Holy shit. Really?"

"Yup."

Bree closed her eyes and took a long, deep breath. She tried to imagine what Sam would say, and—no, for once she wasn't going to think about him. This had to be about her. About what was good for *her*.

She knew that she was risk averse, a gift from her childhood. Trusting people was hard for Bree. Not worrying about money was even harder. She always wanted to have enough in her bank account to be okay for a few months, she preferred stability to possibility, and she always needed a backup plan. Two backup plans was even better. It was probably a big part of why she hadn't been able to take any of the jobs she'd been offered last year. It was also why she hadn't told Sam how she felt about him.

Bree held a breath until her diaphragm burned. Then on her exhale, she started quickly drafting an email saying that yes, she was open to starting the interview process with Hutchinson-Baker. A few clicks, and it was done. "I'm going to talk to them," she told Jeff. "It's just an interview, right?"

He snorted. "They'll love you and make an offer inside a week. Congratulations!"

"Let's not get ahead of ourselves." Even if Hutchinson-Baker did offer her this job, Bree wasn't obligated to take it. She was testing the waters here, exactly like she'd done last year.

Except this time felt very, very different. This time, it was her dream job.

Jeff took another long sip from his coffee. "When are you planning to drop this information on a certain *Comedy Hour* star? Because I might want to vacate the tristate area first."

Oh yeah, Jeff definitely knew. "We're not as close as we used to be."

Before this past weekend, Bree and Sam hadn't spent an entire weekend together in maybe a year. He'd deny it with everything, but Sam mostly hung out with rich, famous, beautiful people now, and she was none of the above. It stung, sometimes, until Bree reminded herself that things were better that way. If they grew apart, he'd be willing to let her go. And the distance—literal and emotional—would let her move on.

"Half the year, the show's in production, and he barely has time to breathe. The rest of the time, he's traveling." Sam still did a lot of stand-up, and long term, he cared about that more than he did about *Comedy Hour*. "We mostly just text or call now. If I were offered this job and took it, none of that would change."

In the abstract, what she'd said made so much sense. But life wasn't abstract. Sam could be terribly, dramatically literal. When Sam found out Bree was interviewing for a job in Michigan, he would almost certainly think she was betraying him.

Sam didn't let people leave him. Most of the time, he pushed them away first or never let them get close in the first place. But on the few occasions when a girlfriend beat him to the punch and dumped him first, Sam simply couldn't handle it. The mess with Salem was the perfect example. If Bree moved . . . well, what was happening right now might seem like a sweet little prelude to the storm.

He'd get over it. He'd have to get over it. But it would suck first.

Bree purposefully didn't look at Jeff until the silence became unbearable. His gaze was boring holes in her skull. She finally twisted in her chair to face him. "What?"

Jeff could've been a fabulous college professor. He didn't even have to say anything. He just watched through incredulous eyes that said, *Would you like to try that again?*

"I've gone as far as I can go here." She'd stayed put for eight years. Leaving was about unsticking herself. About literally going someplace else. "In Michigan, I'd be able to afford to buy a place—which is never going to happen here. And maybe I'm just ready for something else."

"Uh-huh." Mr. Sharma was absolutely not convinced by her tepid rationalization.

"I'll tell him," she said, chopping at the air with her hand. "When this Salem thing blows over, I'll tell him I'm doing this interview."

But oof, she didn't want to. Wounded Sam was her least favorite Sam. Imagining it made her queasy.

Even setting aside his abandonment issues, the reason she hadn't told him she'd applied for jobs last time was because she knew she'd also have to tell him that she loved him. It was the only way to explain all of it.

She tried to imagine looking into his eyes and finally, finally telling him the truth: *I can't get over you when I'm here.* Nope, the very thought made her fingers and toes feel as if they were only loosely attached to her body. As if her insides might come spiraling out of her belly button. She was going to have to do it, but she simply did not want to.

"How did things go with Carl?" Megan, who'd materialized behind them, asked.

Megan Davis had been a senior in the city-and-regional-design program at Ohio State when Bree had started there. She was that student all the professors bragged about, the granddaughter of one of the most prominent architects in the country—he had an actual architectural style named after him, for crying out loud. At twenty-two, Megan had been pretty and brilliant, with Reese Witherspoon's wardrobe from *Legally Blonde*. Frankly, she had scared the shit out of Bree.

Then someone had introduced them, and Megan had become Bree's mentor. Bree, who had felt as if she probably shouldn't be cleaning the classrooms at OSU, let alone studying in them, had been overwhelmed until Megan had taught her that she shouldn't be.

Bree had worked her ass off in school. She'd earned everything she'd achieved. But Megan had taught her how to fake the entitlement. How to not feel inferior when some jerk in a suit tried to act like you should. Megan had convinced Bree to follow her to the University of Pennsylvania for grad school and helped her get a paid summer internship before basically forcing the firm's old boss to hire Bree.

She'd been encouraging Bree to apply for other jobs and, Bree realized with a start, had been gently shoving men at her for years. She'd wanted Bree to leave Innovation X and to get over Sam, which was some kind of ride-or-die friendship.

"It wasn't a match," Bree said. Carl had been great right up to the part where he had fallen into the Sam-shaped trap in Bree's life.

"Too bad." Megan's tone implied she wasn't going to stop trying to set Bree up with someone, though. "What are you two talking about, then?"

Jeff gave Bree a speculative look. He wasn't going to push her to disclose her thinking to Megan before she was ready.

"I had an email from Hutchinson-Baker," Bree explained. "They need a new principal consultant, and they'd like to talk with me about it."

There was a beat of silence. Then an all-too-familiar light came into Megan's eyes, like when a carefully laid plan with ten different moving parts involving fifty meetings and convincing a dozen people of two dozen different things suddenly flowered and a permit came through.

"And you told them . . . ?" Megan asked.

"I mean, what's the harm in chatting?"

Megan beamed. "Right. Well, they'd be fools not to make that offer, so congratulations to you and boo for me. I guess the only thing left is for you to tell me how it is I'm going to live without you, because I have no idea."

Why was everyone so convinced that this was a done deal? "No, there are *lots* of things left! Like the fact I don't have a real offer from them. Or the issue of whether I would want to take it if they made one. Plus the logistics of when they might want me to start, and how much notice you want me to give, and oh gosh, I might have to give up my apartment and move halfway across the country, and—"

"Cake. We need a cake," Megan said, breaking into Bree's realization that this was going to be as complicated as mastering the 12-00 Rules for Construction of Language regulations.

"And one of those ridiculously large cards," Jeff added.

"And maybe a music dance experience?" Megan asked.

"Defiant jazz." Everyone at the office was obsessed with the show *Severance*. It used design *really* well.

"You two are putting the cart before the horse. Counting my chickens before they're hatched." And probably several other clichés Bree couldn't think of.

"No, we're not. We believe you are awesome, and we know they'll see it instantly." Megan toasted Bree with her **WORLD'S BEST MOM** mug, and didn't that just say it all? Bree's personal and career growth had been limited by Sam. Meanwhile, Megan had become the boss but had also met an investment banker and married him. She'd had two kids, cut back her hours, and remodeled a co-op.

Bree couldn't do that or anything like it. Not if she were turning down dream jobs to carry a torch for Sam for another few decades.

"Nothing will be the same, though," Megan told Jeff.

If Bree decided to go, that would be the best part about it.

CHAPTER 5

Monday morning, Sam slipped in the back door of the *Comedy Hour* studio. The pitch meeting was almost an hour off, and the offices should've still been quiet. But given the complete shit that was his life of late, Sam wasn't surprised when he nodded to Louise, the receptionist, and she gave him an apologetic smile.

"Where are you headed, youngster?" Louise couldn't have been more than ten years older than Sam, but she called everyone *youngster*. She had the attitude to pull it off, though; he'd give her that. She managed comics and writers who were way bigger assholes than Sam, and producers and promoters who threw around their weight like a sledgehammer, all without breaking a sweat.

"My office."

"*She* wants to see you."

"*She*, as in Marie Antoinette?"

"Nope." Louise didn't even crack a grin, which was fine. It hadn't been very funny. "Get in there."

This was what he got for coming in early.

The door to Jane Feeley's office—the largest suite in the studio and the only area that could honestly be described as swanky—stood open, and Sam walked right in. "Louise led me to believe that I'd find Santa Claus here. I have to say, I'm disappointed."

"Have a seat," Jane said without looking up.

Sam knew he was supposed to kiss Jane's ass. He was supposed to find Jane scary and intimidating, and on some level, he did. But the way everybody tiptoed around her, acting as if she were some kind of leading light, when really, she was a showrunner and producer—it rubbed Sam the wrong way. It always had.

Jane wasn't an expert in comedy, as in, she didn't *do* the comedy herself. She didn't have to face a dead audience week after week. While she occasionally made a cameo or got name-checked in a review, it was the performers who dealt with the majority of the pans.

Sam's respect was rare and hard earned, and Jane had never bothered to try for it. In exchange, Sam never bothered to suck up.

"Samuel." She twisted in her ergonomic desk chair that probably cost as much as a double-wide back home and regarded Sam over the top of *Variety* and her single-vision glasses—no bifocals for her.

Okay, so the one thing that did frighten him about Jane: the woman didn't age. The studio was filled with framed pictures from the show's history, going back to the 1970s. Any one of Jane could've been taken today. She still had the crown of extravagant, penny-colored curls. Still had the sharp chin and the unlined face and the Lilly Pulitzer wardrobe. It was uncanny. Did she sleep in formaldehyde? A coffin? One day, he was going to be really bold and really stupid and ask.

"I have to get to the writers' room." Which was a lie. The pitch meeting was still a ways off, and Jane would be there for it too.

"Humor me."

Fuck. That was a devastating line read.

When Sam's latest breakup had become tabloid fodder, Jane hadn't forced Sam into a meeting. He'd been expecting a call from her—or someone at the show—when Salem's single had dropped last week, but maybe Jane had been trying to up the suspense.

Sam threw himself into a chair, letting himself take up as much space as possible. Bree would say he was being a dick and that not everything had to be a power play, and she would have been right. Only about 40 percent of things were power plays, and this happened to be one of them.

Jane started to fold the newspaper, getting every crease right. She took her time about it, showing Sam that she could and that he would sit there and take it. That was how things were between them.

He had to respect the display the way you had to respect a peacock's tail or a baboon's scarlet ass.

"So you're trending on social media," she finally began.

"Whatever I can do for the show."

Jane gave him a bored look. "Do you think you're the first petulant child in the cast?"

"No, generalissimo. Petulant children are your bread and butter." They were the majority of people in comedy.

"Mm-hmm. So a word of advice."

"Only one?"

"People expect a comic to be a jerk, but no one likes an asshole."

"Both our careers seem like evidence to the contrary." Sam absolutely meant that as a compliment.

Jane snorted. "I'm not talking about *my* preference. Just the audience's. So she wrote a song about you. So she laid your soul bare—"

"I don't have a soul to bare."

"It's right here, kiddo." She set *Variety* aside and rifled through a pile of other papers—seriously, who knew they still printed so many of them—before she found the *New York Times*. She flipped to a page that she'd labeled with one of those sticky paper flags. "'Salem's newest hit isn't just a perfectly poppy confection made for the dance floor; it's also an astute analysis of Sam Leyland, one of late-night's most popular and mercurial faces.'"

Sam released a long breath. "I always knew it, but now I have proof: the *Times* is garbage. The Bee Gees tried to warn us. Heed now the counsel of disco, ma'am. We should all probably avoid Waterloo too."

"Don't be cute." Jane gave him a look that could have frozen magma. "This is a career-defining moment for you. The next few weeks, you have to be perfect. Funnier and looser than you've ever been."

Sam wanted to say something snide and cutting, but Jane was right. Damn. That was disappointing.

"I know, I have to show it's all a lie."

"No." Jane famously rarely raised her voice. These days, she didn't need to. She'd won her battles fifty years earlier, when women never ran network television shows, when the kind of diverse cast that she'd insisted the show needed was still unusual on television, and she'd built an empire, or at least that was what the profiles and biographies of her always said.

Yet the precariousness of Sam's situation was making her . . . talk pretty loudly. That was how much trouble he was in.

"Who cares if it's a lie or if it's true?" she went on. "I sure as hell don't. No, you have to show them that it doesn't matter. That you're a goddamn professional and that, even when some pop princess returns your ring and kicks you in the head, musically speaking, you're still the funniest fucking thing on television."

Sam might not have put it the same way, but—no, he probably would put it the same way. There were things Sam wanted: to have enough money to never risk living in a trailer or only eating those desiccated ramen packets again. To get another special on Videon. To know, really know in his bones, that he was good at what he did. When he did dumb shit, he endangered all that, bringing him closer to the inevitable end of his career.

There were probably two ways to feel when you knew in your soul you were going to fall off a cliff someday: avoid cliffs with the force of everything in you or dance on the edge of them as frequently as possible. He was in the second group. He was pretty much the king of the second group.

Ashes to ashes, right? Piece of shit to piece of shit was Sam's version. There was no avoiding the inevitable, and he couldn't seem to stop pushing the envelope, wondering whether this was the time when he'd gone too far.

Jane was saying he was right on that line.

He appreciated that someone had been honest with him about how fragile his position was, even if that person was Jane.

"Well, admiral, I have to hand it to you: that's the first thing you've ever said that I agree with."

"You hide it so well." A pause. "Get out of here."

"Make that two things."

Feeling perversely better, Sam strolled down to the writers' room. All it would take to kill the mystique of *Comedy Hour* would be to post a few pictures of the writers' room on Instagram. It looked like a middle-school cafeteria: a bunch of cheap folding tables arranged in a U shape with whiteboards ringing the walls. There were a few nice chairs up at the front for Jane and the guest host, and a small separate table for the writers of the standing current events segment, "News Minute." Also a plastic plant. That was it. There wasn't any glitz or glamour. They didn't even have trash can liners. Sam had played nicer truck stops.

A few of the junior writers were milling about, probably waiting for Dennis Drummond, the show's head writer and a first-rate jerk, but as soon as Sam came in, the conversation went dead. Most of them were smart enough to inspect their nails or phones, but one woman was watching Sam with the kind of wide-eyed pity that made him want to change his name and take up alpaca farming.

Briefly, Sam considered ignoring their heavy silence and annoying attention, but he never ignored anything. Even if Sam could be quiet— and he probably couldn't—that wasn't going to end the gossip.

"Stop it," he instructed them. "Who among us hasn't been publicly flogged by a pop star?"

That at least got a laugh. How many other self-deprecating and not-at-all-funny jokes was he going to have to tell in the next week? The next year? The rest of his life?

Jane was right. There was only one answer for critics, only one answer for humiliation: good work. Being funny was Sam's shield, his superpower, and the only thing he'd ever been good at. Maybe there were people with more than one trick up their sleeves for a moment like this one, but Sam had never met such a person. Most people were as limited as he was, and when things didn't go their way, they could only fall back on the horse that had brought them there.

This week's show was going to make or break Sam's career. That was clear.

Sam had done two good things in his life: he'd made people laugh, and he'd been a friend to Bryony Edwards. If he couldn't do the first one anymore, if he flamed his career out like he'd always assumed he would, the only person who would still care about him would be Bree. Bree was funny and smart, and she wanted to make the world better for other people than it had been for kids like the ones she and Sam had been. She was so much better than almost everyone else on this forsaken planet, and eleventy billion times better than Sam. Even more than losing this job or his chance at another Videon special, he worried about losing her.

Just then, Roxy Warren swanned in the door of the writers' room. If Bree was Sam's lifelong best friend, Roxy was his work best friend. In pleather pants and a crop top, which were either designed to intimidate this week's guest host or were what she'd worn out last night, and with a perfectly kept fade, Roxy was responsible for many a middle-aged straight *Comedy Hour* fan questioning everything she'd ever assumed about her own sexuality. Roxy was, in a word, hot. She was also a perfect mimic, a damn fine writer, and as hardworking as Sam. He loved her dearly, and if she'd have considered it for more than half a second, he would have asked her to marry him.

But he was not her type, and he was done proposing. He'd tried it once, and look where it had landed him.

Roxy dropped into the chair next to his, then crossed one ankle over the other on the table in front of them. "Did you see the Knicks last night? I've seen you make better passes." Somehow, Roxy was able to give him crap that always felt like she was ruffling his hair in the nicest way. Like the world's best butch big sister.

"You oughta know, I have a very good conversion rate." Or at least he did back in the day when your performance on the neighborhood basketball court was important for having some kind of street credibility. He wasn't tall enough or big enough to actually be *good*, but he'd willed himself to be decent. Faking it till you made it was pretty much his thing.

"They should have put you out there, then." She took a long sip from her MOO Bottle. Roxy didn't believe in coffee, which went to show that no one was perfect. Then she asked, "Everything okay?"

He appreciated how she'd given him plausible deniability. *Everything* could be politics or whatever he was watching on Videon or what he ate for dinner last night. But he knew she meant that he hadn't responded to her texts last week, and she wondered where he was at in terms of the inevitable breakdown that would follow having every one of your numerous character flaws exposed to the world.

"It wasn't exactly the best week of my life. And then I endured an architectural walking tour."

Roxy immediately pieced together what he hadn't said. "You're staying with Bree?"

"Yeah. Just for a few days."

"Why didn't you call me? I have an actual guest room."

As much as he loved Roxy, he wouldn't go to her place to hide out. They weren't that kind of friends. He only had one of that kind of friend. "Nah, I'm okay. It should blow over soon."

"If you're sure. But we should all get together soon." One of Roxy's many good qualities was that she liked Bree.

"Game night?" he asked.

"I've never understood your obsession." From Roxy's perspective, the correct number of board games to play was none.

"Childhood friends. It comes with the territory." It also helped when you were trying to avoid going out in public. The last thing either he or Bree needed was some ridiculous story that they'd gotten together when he was on the rebound from Salem.

Which would be ridiculous not only because it wasn't going to happen but also because he and Salem's breakup had occurred months ago. Everyone seemed to think the engagement had crumbled last week when the song came out, not realizing Salem was rehashing what already felt like ancient history to Sam.

"So who's going to propose a 'Lost Boy' sketch first?" he asked.

"Alan," Roxy answered without hesitation. Alan Murray-Smyth would propose a sketch in which he shanked his own grandmother if it would get him on the air. He hated Sam with every fiber of his being, which was only fair, because Sam hated him right back.

"See, I think it'll be Joya."

Sam had always had trouble getting a bead on Joya Perez. She didn't seem to have a sense of her voice or what material worked for her. She was relentlessly in touch with social media trends and youth culture, though. Some of the cast couldn't have worked harder to stay away from that stuff.

Alan was terrified of being original—as if good comics were original—but Joya only wanted to be topical. And at the moment, there was nothing more topical than Sam's love life.

"Fifty bucks?" Sam asked.

"You're on. You're lucky this week's guest host is Devin Mackey and not some pop star."

"Small favors."

Gibson Long came in, and as soon as he spied Sam, he made a sour face. A critic had once called Gibson "Sam Leyland when the printer is low on toner," and, well, it wasn't an inappropriate comparison. They looked alike: white guys in their early thirties with brown hair and slim builds. But the similarities stopped there. Gibson had played tennis at Harvard, which he both wanted everyone to know and didn't want to take any crap about. He was a piece of work.

"What are you going to pitch this week?" Roxy asked.

"I was thinking an appearance by Rich White might be in order." "The Adventures of Richard White" was Sam's most popular and longest-running *Comedy Hour* sketch. He'd meant it to be a one-off during his first week, but now it was legendary. Depending on the situation, Rich White could be a frat boy, an investment broker, a lawyer, a real estate agent, or a crypto dude. Rich was a relatively flexible concept, designed to let Sam insult many different kinds of his least favorite people.

It was one of life's great ironies that Sam could so easily disappear inside the trappings of something he hated so much. It should've made him feel like a chameleon. Instead, it made him loathe himself, but, well, everything did.

The rest of the morning passed in a blur. Devin Mackey came in to halfhearted applause. Some hosts were easy to write for. Some were super game. Mackey, a former football player who was trying to make the difficult transition into superhero movies, wanted them to think he was, but he wasn't. The man grimaced more than a newborn figuring out how to take a shit.

"Don't you think it would be funnier if I played the superhero?" Mackey asked Roxy at one point when she pitched a sketch in which he would have played an inept criminal getting caught by a series of even more inept superheroes.

"But you . . . I mean, you play a superhero. In the movies. Don't you want to not be super for once?"

He blinked at Roxy as if the question literally didn't make sense to him. Someone had inhaled a little too much of their own PR.

Jane stepped in smoothly. "Go ahead and write it, Roxy, and we'll try it at the table read."

That was the *Comedy Hour* schedule: Monday was for pitching, Tuesday for writing, and Wednesday for the judgment of the table read. Sam knew some of his success on the show came down to how willing he was to throw down on Wednesdays. He was passionate about his work, passionate about what was funny, and he had absolutely no compunction about stepping on anyone's toes. For reasons Sam didn't quite comprehend, this had won him respect . . . and also made him a lot of enemies. Then they rehearsed on Thursday and Friday, before taping the show in front of a live audience on Saturday evening and partying until it aired a few hours later. One day of rest, then they did it all over again, twenty-two or so weeks a year.

Sam had a grateful tingle in his stomach that this was his life, at least until he finally and inevitably fucked up and they kicked his ass to the curb.

CHAPTER 6

Sam rolled into Bree's apartment at seven on Tuesday. He'd texted midafternoon to check in and tell her that they were ordering food to the studio, but as soon as he'd hit send, something had felt off.

Maybe Roxy was right and he should go back to his own apartment. The paparazzi situation outside the studio had been better today, Derek had told him, though Sam had gone in through the back and hadn't seen it for himself. His assistant had swung by his place to put together a bag for him and had confirmed that there had "only" been two photogs waiting outside. There was so much going on in the world, it seemed like most people were content to wait until Saturday's show to see what, if any, response Sam might have to "Lost Boy."

The day had gone downhill from there. The writers and the cast sorted into cliques. There were the people who wrote for "News Minute" and the writers who specialized in the host's monologue. And then you had the rest of the cast, who were roughly divided between those who got a lot of airtime and those who didn't.

Look, Sam woke up hungry, and he went to bed the same way. Ambition was a flavor he knew well. No one at *Comedy Hour* was untalented. Even the people who weren't his particular brand of beer—say, Alan—wrote some good bits. But good wasn't enough, not here. It was a cold-blooded and political place, and frankly, Sam sucked at the game playing that was required, so he often bludgeoned people until they agreed with him.

After lunch, when Sam had been sliding into his regular seat, Jane had come in with her assistant trailing her. She'd consulted the list from yesterday morning's pitch session. "Who's taking the superhero piece?"

"Which one?" Roxy had asked.

Devin had heartily approved every superhero idea that anyone had pitched. If they could have done an entire superhero hour, he would've been happy.

"Roxy, you take the first one," Jane had said. "And Alan will take the second. I'm going to cut the third now. I'll manage Mr. Mackey."

And would she ever. Mackey was going to think it had been his idea to cut that piece by the time Jane was done with him.

Jane had continued to briskly distribute the rest of the pieces. Some sketches had an obvious genesis and were written by the people who had pitched them. Others were born on the fly during Monday's meeting, and Jane had to figure out who was going to do what.

"This sounds good," she'd finally said, surveying her notes. "I do have one final request, though. Sam." She'd speared him with her gaze. "A 'Lost Boy' sketch."

It had been like that moment when the guy in the black robe stabbed Frodo with the Morgul sword. Jane's words were a puncture of boiling, scalding shame, going straight through Sam's gut.

Neither Alan nor Joya had been brave enough to put that idea forward on Monday, even though it would've been topical, Mackey would have loved it, and it would've gotten under Sam's skin.

Jane, though, clearly didn't lack for boldness.

"I don't have a problem doing such a sketch," Sam had said, though his tone said he clearly *did* have a problem with it. "But I don't have a hook, and I can't figure out how to work Mackey in."

That had been the best excuse Sam could come up with since his pride was still hollering. Even his improv skills deserted him when he felt exposed. He'd rather ditch his clothing.

"You can't figure out how to work him into the sketch you haven't written yet?" Jane had said, skeptically.

"Yup."

She'd narrowed her eyes at him. It had been a weak defense, and they both knew it. But he didn't want to write the sketch. He wasn't going to be able to avoid it forever, but he needed one more week. And, honestly, he needed a better idea. When he talked about what had happened with Salem, he had to be funny, or else what would be the point? Hadn't Jane said he had to be the funniest fucking thing on television? Well, he wasn't ready yet.

"Fine. Have it your way." Jane's sigh had been resigned or livid or some other emotion Sam didn't care to figure out.

The expressions of half the people around the table said that they would rather die than be the object of such a sigh. But Sam didn't give two tepid fucks.

"I cannot believe that didn't freeze your eyeballs out," Roxy had muttered.

"I'm immune to her dirty looks." Roxy probably didn't believe him, but Sam had known actually terrible, abusive people in his life. Jane might make a lot of noise, but she didn't frighten him. If all it took to neutralize her was thirty seconds of irritable silence, then he was up for it.

In short, it had been a crap afternoon, and that was why Sam didn't go back to his own place. The only solution for his mood was Bree.

She buzzed him up, and when she pulled the door open after he jogged up the stairs, he could breathe for the first time since he'd left that morning. He was going to keep sleeping on her crappy IKEA couch because Bree felt like home.

Bree had the newspaper in one hand, folded back to the crossword, and a pen clenched between her teeth. "What's a four-letter word for *whimper?*" she said around it.

She'd ditched her work clothes—faux-preppy things he hated—for worn pajama pants, fuzzy socks, and a tank top. She looked relaxed, so much like herself, and completely unworried about the world and what people thought of her: God, he would have given anything to learn the secret of that. To be able to feel it and do it for himself.

Deep down, he'd always known Bree was a thousand times more confident than he could ever be. Where he always felt the need to prove himself, to thump his chest, and to get praise, Bree's confidence came from someplace magical inside her. She'd always had it, even when they'd been the type of kids whom the world humiliated every day.

"It's a little late in the day for the crossword," he said.

"No such thing. I nicked the *Times* from Jeff."

She loved the crossword, but she wasn't willing to spring for the paper often, which he totally understood. Poor habits die hard.

He followed her back into her apartment, locking the door behind them. "I dunno. Oh, wait: *mewl.*"

"Hell yeah it is." She wrote the answer in and gave him a smile so bright, it could have powered one of those billboards they'd seen in Times Square. Getting that smile from her made him feel ten feet tall. It was better than when he'd really nailed a joke today.

The remnants of her dinner were in the kitchen—tomato soup and grilled cheese, which made his heart ache in a different way. It was their comfort meal, his and hers. Okay, and probably most millennials, but still. She'd turned on the twinkle lights she had strung above the couch, and it made the place look warm and cozy, like Christmas mornings in the movies.

He hadn't been surprised when Bree had become an urban planner. She'd always had a sense of design and an ability to make a place *better* just by touching it. He felt like someone who only saw things as they were—and mocked them mercilessly. She could see what things could be and had the patience to make it happen.

"You ate?" she asked.

"Yeah, you don't have to feed me. I'm just . . . I dunno. I don't want to be on my own right now."

He'd thought she was only half listening to him while inspecting her crossword, but when she shifted her eyes up to meet his gaze, he knew that was wrong. She was weighing what to say and how to say it.

Sometimes, people made him feel like a minefield, and he knew that he was—even though being reminded of it made him doubly twitchy. Bree realized that, and while she couldn't always manage to smother the pity impulse, she tried.

Finally, she said, "I'm not upset you're here. And you're a big boy, Sam; I know you can feed yourself. I'm just lazy and haven't done my dishes."

She was absolutely not lazy. She'd left the stuff out in case he decided that he wanted to take a trip down food memory lane. She'd been thinking about him.

No one ever thought about him. Not like Bree did.

"You crossword. That's more important." He dropped his bag by the bar and began scooping her dishes up and depositing them by the sink. "What are you stuck on now?"

"*Nurses*, five letters. *Health*—that's six. *Cares*? Nope. The second letter is *i*. *Nightingale* is way too many letters. I don't know any other famous nurses. Come to think of it, why aren't there more famous nurses?"

He glanced at Bree's chest—which he'd tried not to do ever since she'd grown breasts, a confusing and surprising turn of events that had temporarily thrown his world into turmoil when they'd been eleven. Since then, he'd tried very hard not to think about Bree as having a body, let alone breasts. He . . . mostly succeeded, the other night with her skin excepted. Honestly, Sam tried not to stare at anyone's chest. It was such an obvious, asshole move. He had flaws, but that wasn't one of them.

He soaped the pot she'd used for the soup and considered how to phrase his answer. "Babe, it's *sip on*."

"*Sip on*?" Her expression was adorably befuddled. "What the . . . oh yeah, it is." She snorted. "A pervert wrote this."

"Not necessarily. What do you do when you nurse a beer?"

"You think this is about beer?"

"Yup."

"You're hopeless. *Sip on*? Why not just go with *jugs*?"

"It doesn't have five letters."

She threw the crossword across the bar at him, and it fluttered to the ground. "Ew! I don't think I can finish that crossword."

Grinning, he rinsed the pot and set it on the drainboard. He wanted to keep bickering with Bree. For her to keep his mind off everything, and for him to keep making her laugh. They couldn't go out, so that left: "Movie night?"

"Movie night," she agreed. "I'll get the popcorn."

By mutual agreement, they never watched comedies. He'd spend the entire movie critiquing the jokes and performances, telling her how he would've written it differently, would've read the line better. He was so grateful she was letting him stay, he didn't want to piss her off, at least not any more than was necessary. He'd go on ten more walking tours with her if she'd just keep leaving out the fixings for tomato soup and grilled cheese for him.

She flipped open her coffee table, the interior storage section of which had about as many nineties action movies on DVD as your average Blockbuster had stocked. "Are we feeling more *Enemy of the State* or *Heat*?" She shifted a few cases around. "Oh, or what about Arnold? And if yes, which Arnold?"

"I see you're omitting Nic Cage from this conversation."

"I've tried, Sam, I have, but I don't get the appeal. *Face/Off* is ridiculous, *The Rock* is illogical, and I hate the constant threat of rape hanging over *Con Air*."

She'd voiced that opinion a time or ten, and he'd had to admit she was right. "Fair enough."

She held up a case. "*Hard Boiled*?"

"Chow Yun-Fat is always a good choice."

She put the movie on and fell onto the couch next to him.

"Long day at work?" he asked. He didn't want to talk about *Comedy Hour*, but he liked hearing about her work.

She shrugged. "Not too bad. The City of Yonkers Department of Planning and Development, though—they're going to have a bad day soon. Well, no they aren't, but if I were a different kind of person, they would."

While Bree could hold her own with him, she was way too kind and deferential with everyone else. Something about how you caught more flies with honey, but why on earth would you want to catch flies? You just needed to kill the bastards.

"So what are you going to do about it?" he asked.

"You say that as if I have a lot I can do about it."

"You always figure something out."

"Well, I thought I'd go insult them in a coffee shop."

"Unf." He thumped his chest as if she'd struck him.

"You know, we never really talked about your breakup with Salem," Bree said carefully.

"What's there to tell?" He gave a twitchy shrug. "She said it wasn't going to work, and then she was gone. It was months ago. I don't really think about it much." Or at least he hadn't until she added a seriously danceable beat and broadcast it to the entire world. He'd known on some level that he and Salem weren't going to work out, but he'd really known it when she'd left him and he'd been fine after a day or two of heartburn.

"You were going to get married," Bree said skeptically.

"Eh, I don't think either of us believed that."

Marriage—at least the only kind of marriage he was interested in having—had been like having a birthday at Disney World. It wasn't fiction, but where he came from, how he'd grown up? Well, it might as well have been.

His parents had split up before he could remember, and it was truly a crime that they'd been together at all. Then his father had periodically smashed back into their lives, demolishing everything in his path, like a vindictive human wrecking ball. Sam's mother had her own set of issues, and Sam had repeatedly been the flotsam, tossed around and between them, until he'd made himself strong enough, prickly enough, that they stopped using him.

It hadn't been a hardship. His parents had lots of other ways to hurt each other. They didn't need Sam for that. Frankly, they didn't need Sam for anything, which was fine, because he didn't need them right back.

As he'd grown up and had begun falling in love—or at least stumbling into bedrooms and into liking women if not loving them—Sam had resolved not to be his parents. Oh, he knew that he bruised egos along the way; he was too much of a jerk not to. Sam wasn't going to become some totally new, nice person. There were limits to his resolve.

Even still, he tried not to cause intentional harm. While Salem looked innocent, with her blonde hair and blue eyes and retro-doll style, she knew the score. She hadn't fallen any more than he had. They'd been playing together for a while, and it had been fun to pretend with her. But that was all it had ever been. It had kept both their hearts safe.

"You bought a ring," Bree pointed out. "You asked her a question. She apparently said yes. What would belief look like if not that?"

He picked at something on the couch cushion, avoiding Bree's gaze. She saw too much, and it made him want to squirm. He didn't like feeling seen, and somehow, both Salem and Bree had managed it. "I can't seem to keep a relationship going for more than about three months. There are probably bottles of buttermilk in people's fridges older than that."

"So why did you propose?"

"It was really stupid." They'd been in Vegas—thank Christ they hadn't actually gotten married. He'd wanted, at some level, to stop playing games. To have something real. But when he'd asked the question, he'd all but had his fingers crossed behind his back. It had been okay because Salem had been doing the same.

"I didn't say that," Bree countered.

"You didn't have to."

"Sam." She waited until he looked up. "Loving someone isn't stupid."

He almost said, *How would you know*, but he bit the words back just in time. If his own love life was a series of half-cocked schemes that he only partially engaged with, Bree's was a lukewarm bath. Setting aside the attempts of the city's tour guides to pick her up, Bree's relationships didn't last long, but only because neither she nor the guys she found seemed to be fully in them. If Sam tended to burn through every stage with his girlfriends in weeks or months, Bree was hesitant. Tentative.

He knew why he kept his own shriveled and pitted heart out of the way. But Bree, she was better than him in every way. She could have that Disney vacation. She ought to have it. She should have everything she wanted.

"Who are you loving these days?" he asked.

"No one." Oh, now who wouldn't make eye contact? "I'm talking in the abstract."

"Why is it abstract, Smoosh?"

As far as he could tell, Bree was the total package. She was pretty, feisty, and very smart. Every time she went out with someone else, he gave himself a little talk: *We're not going to be an asshole to this one.* But all too often, the men she dated weren't worth being assholes to—and they certainly weren't worth being nice to. He couldn't remember the last time she'd had a boyfriend who provoked him, or apparently her, to remember.

"You've spoiled me for all other men, of course." Her tone was wry, but she was blinking too much for him to entirely believe it. She turned to the TV. "Oh boy, Tequila's gonna regret that." She gestured at the screen, trying to get their normal pattern of rollicking banter going on.

But something was off, something that even a John Woo movie couldn't fix.

He reached up to touch her, to make her look at him, but that felt even more off. She squished herself into the farthest corner of the couch and pulled her knees up like a wall. She was shooting off some kind of force field he knew he wasn't supposed to cross. She'd tried to get him to talk about his feelings the other day, but this was different. These were *her* feelings.

"I'll show you mine if you'll show me yours," he said.

"My what?" She still wasn't looking at him.

"Sad, broken heart."

"I don't have a sad, broken heart." She was firm about that. Certain.

"Oh, me neither. I was just trying to get you to talk."

"You voluntarily exposing weakness was clearly a ruse." She rolled her eyes. "You're gonna have to do better than that."

"I'm working on the fly here." Fuck it. He reached across the couch and wrapped two fingers around her wrist. Her skin was so pale, and her bones so fragile, compared to his. Hers were like bird wrists . . . if birds had wrists. "If you did want to talk about it—"

"I'd call Megan. She doesn't judge like you do."

She did, actually. Megan was very judgy. "I do not—"

"You were going to kick Ryan's ass when he forgot my birthday."

"Because it's your birthday!"

Okay, Sam had been an asshole to Ryan, but only because he'd been totally unworthy of Bree. For starters he worked on Wall Street, which—just no. Sam could understand wanting financial security after where they'd come from, but *investment banker* was taking it too far. And then Ryan had forgotten Bree's birthday even though they'd been dating for months, and Sam had made it very clear to him that, as far as he was concerned, Bree's birthday was a federal holiday. Sam had done nothing but rejoice when Bree and Ryan had broken up.

After a second, Bree set her free hand over Sam's fingers and squeezed. "You really can be sweet."

"That's a fucking lie." But he liked that she said it. Even with everything that was brewing under the surface and confusing him, it was still the right choice to be back here with Bree. "Let's watch this movie."

CHAPTER 7

Bree was jumpy. She'd updated her CV and sent it to Hutchinson-Baker after she'd gotten the first email about the job, and they'd responded by scheduling her interview on Wednesday morning. In ninety-two minutes, to be precise. They were giving every indication they were *really* interested in hiring her.

It should've been flattering. Triumphant. But Bree still hadn't shared any of this with Sam, who was leaning on her counter, drinking his morning coffee a thimbleful at a time. So all she could feel was guilt, plus a burning desire to get Sam out of her apartment so she could call Jeff and tell him how to cover for her this morning.

Sam raised his mug for another sip and then—obnoxiously—lowered it without taking a drink. "How'd you sleep, Smoosh? You seem edgy."

Subterfuge didn't become her. "Fine."

"You're almost growling."

From the twinkle in his eyes, she knew he was about to tease her out of what he supposed to be a bad mood. But because she was some kind of masochist, she wasn't going to let him. She deserved to feel bad about this. It was bad.

"Don't you have to get to the studio?" she said sweet-tartly.

"We don't recognize Dolly Parton's nine-to-five schedule at *Comedy Hour*. But you're probably in a rush. Megan seems like she'd be a schoolmarm about those kinds of things."

She wasn't, but if Bree got sucked into defending Megan, she'd lose valuable minutes. "I'm working from home this morning." That was true—it just wasn't the entire story. "I have some meetings around the city later, including one in Midtown at four. Maybe I can drop off dinner for you." Wednesdays tended to be wickedly long for him, and Sam wasn't always good about taking care of himself when he was working, or really ever, especially if he was still trying to avoid going out in public.

"That wouldn't be a pain?"

"I don't mind."

"Okay. Roxy would be glad to see you." He took a minuscule sip. Since Bree had banned him from going to coffee shops for the moment—obviously he couldn't be trusted—she'd picked up several different bags of grounds for him. "I dunno. The French roast tastes exactly like the private reserve to me. Maybe we should brew another pot."

She didn't have that kind of time. "Nope, the world can't handle you on more than one pot of coffee."

"The world should be so lucky."

The smile he gave her was an invitation—or what she previously would have taken to be an invitation. In the past, she would've playfully insulted him. He would've defended himself. She would've countered. And all the time, her heart would've been tap-dancing in her chest while some sliver of her mind pretended that they were really flirting. That he was as affected by the tug between them, by her smiles, her proximity, as she was by his.

But it would've been a lie. She *knew* letting herself play this one-sided game was poisoning her life. She had to stop. Did she want to move on or not?

Him essentially living with her since Friday had been dreamy, but Bree had to wake up. From now on, she had to put on her own oxygen mask first in the swan-diving plane, which was why she was going to interview for her dream job in—she checked the clock on her oven—eighty-nine minutes.

She let Sam's pitch whoosh by her as she drained her cup and set it in the sink. Sam's eyes were hurt, like a kitten's when you stopped playing with the yarn, but Bree could live with that. She had to.

She went over to the table and got her laptop and a notebook out of her bag and began fumbling with them. Sam's attention was still on her, heavy as a dumbbell.

She needed to say something. "Who's the host this week?"

"Devin Mackey. It's basically a multiverse of superhero sketches."

"Nice." Which . . . it wasn't.

She used to know how to be with Sam and compartmentalize her feelings for him. Be neutral. But being together the past few days, having him in her space, taking care of her, making her laugh—she'd lost the knack of it, and she couldn't pretend anymore. The wall had fallen, and all her feelings were scurrying across into no-man's-land.

Bree's phone rang, and it was Jeff. "Hey," she answered. "Thanks for going to this meeting for me."

"No problem. I want you to get this job!"

Good gravy, was Jeff normally so *loud*? She glanced at Sam, but he'd picked up her unfinished (dirty) crossword from the night before and was filling in one of the blank rows. He didn't seem to have heard Jeff's gigantic yawping.

"Sam and I are finishing coffee—" she said.

"He's there?" Oh, so now Jeff had learned to talk at a normal volume.

"—so I'll make this quick." She found the page in her notes. "This meeting is for the redesign of East One Hundred Twenty-Fifth Street. Innovation X was brought in after another firm really messed up the coalition building." The first urban planners had absolutely stepped in it, trying to rush deadlines and skipping the painstaking work of getting people on board. So now Bree had been trying to manage the project, plus clean everything up.

"Yup, I read your memo," Jeff said.

Sam was still looking at the crossword, but Bree could feel his attention, as if it were a tangible force in the room. He was still attuned to her. He probably still thought she was pissy, which, she realized, she sort of was, but not at all in the way Sam thought.

She stalked over to the window and pushed aside the flimsy curtains to watch the flow of traffic down in the street. So many of the things they were going to try to fix on East 125th were playing out down there: a bus stuck in the intersection because a delivery truck was blocking the bus/bike lane, scaffolding from an ongoing renovation project hindering pedestrians, and poorly designed curb cuts making it all inaccessible. It calmed her, seeing those problems, because she knew how to fix them. She could diagnose the obstacles—and she could make them better.

"So I've been having all these meetings with groups like the Harlem Preservation Collective, where I ensure people feel like they get heard, because they weren't before. You need to apologize for someone else's errors, and that's hard because the folks in the neighborhood don't really trust the city or us after what happened." She didn't blame them. "Then you can get into the logistics, but this is delicate, and their feelings, their *buy-in*, is more important than when the scaffolding goes up, you know?"

"I should listen to their concerns, present the new timeline, show them the pretty art, answer their questions, and apologize for what the other guys botched?" Jeff summarized.

"Yup. And I know you're careful about this, but pay attention to your vocabulary. This is tricky, because we want them to think we know what we're doing, but avoid using jargon if you can. You can't afford to come across as arrogant, because they think we're there to destroy their neighborhood."

The history of urban planning was filled with people using the field to rip communities apart. Progress for one person often came at a cost for someone else. What was a "blighted" neighborhood, and who got to decide? If Bree came along and fixed a park or the traffic flow on a street, could that attract new businesses, leading to rent hike and displacing the exact people she'd been trying to improve things for? The unintended secondary and tertiary consequences of her work hurt her mind, sometimes.

Over the phone, Bree could hear the keys of Jeff's computer clatter. "Got it. Thanks for reminding me."

She flinched. She was doing it again: trying to micromanage when she'd sat in a million meetings with Jeff, and she knew he was great at the political side of their jobs. "I'm sorry. I know you know, but I've been slowly trying to tidy this up for months, and I just . . ." It was hard to hand it over to someone else. She wouldn't have done it for anything less important than this interview.

"You realize if you take this . . ." Jeff trailed off, probably trying to decide what to call it now that he knew Sam was around. "If you take this *bagel*, you'll have to trust someone else with your stuff." That was vague enough.

"Yes." She blew out a long breath. This was hard for her.

"Well, you go get that bagel, Bree. I'll handle this meeting with all required delicacy and contrition."

"Thank you; you're the best."

"So true."

Bree hung up and went back to the table. When she'd opened Slack and her burgeoning inbox, she finally let herself look over at Sam.

He was fidgeting with the pen in his hand, but he wasn't pretending to work on the crossword anymore. He was staring at her, his expression inscrutable.

Bree held his gaze. Her cheeks were heating, and she wanted to bury her hands, her face, in her hair, but she resisted the impulse. "What?" she finally asked when she couldn't stand the silence any longer.

"You're really good at your job." He didn't sound surprised. Just . . . impressed. The kind of impressed that made her feel exposed. Self-conscious.

"Um, thank you." She hoped Hutchinson-Baker was going to agree in, um, eighty-two minutes.

"I'm such a jackass, but you're, like, making the world better and thinking about people's feelings and shit."

She had to laugh, and it gave her some cover. "You make that sound like a terrible thing."

"I mean the opposite. You're so—good." He held her eyes for another three or four seconds. Then he drained his coffee, washed his mug and hers, and gave her a wave as he headed out the door. "See you later."

After he'd finally, blessedly left, it took several minutes before Bree felt composed.

She had to go. She knew she had to go. But leaving was going to be a loss.

CHAPTER 8

Sam loved Wednesdays. After the relative calm of Tuesday's writing day, Jane made decisions on Wednesday. Sam didn't have to be nice; he just had to be honest—brutally, intensely honest in the way that was his specialty. It was like gladiatorial combat, but with comedy.

The cast and the writers were arranged around the table in the writers' room, with Jane and Devin Mackey up at the front. The guy was smiling blandly as if he were going to enjoy this. Clearly he had no idea what to expect.

"I see you didn't bring your boxing gloves," Roxy muttered to Sam.

"I can take everyone here."

"Listen, if someone *did* write a sketch that you didn't want to do on principle, are you in a mood where you could consider it on its merits, or are you disconnected from reality?"

This didn't sound like a theoretical question. He narrowed his eyes at her, and she blinked back at him, sweet and guileless.

"What sketch are you talking about?"

"Never mind, I can see you're unhinged."

"I am never—"

But before he could finish his thought, Jane called out, "Let's get started."

Sam continued to glare at Roxy. He was not above taking her out into the hallway to continue this conversation, but she shook her head.

What the hell was she up to?

That thought was going to fester, but it might have to take a number. He was still getting over seeing Bree in full urban planner mode this morning. He'd never doubted that she was awesome at what she did, but the way her voice and posture changed, the way she became authoritative but so careful? It was amazing and made him feel . . . things.

Luckily, the Wednesday mess was there to distract him. The first part of the read-through was fine. They started with Mackey trying out the draft of the opening monologue, which consisted of football and superhero jokes. He loved it.

Then Gibson read a sketch parodying a detergent commercial. There was a long history on the show of people trying to sink the sketches of others by not laughing during the table read. Sam refused to indulge in that bullshit, but he didn't laugh during Gibson's draft because it wasn't funny.

"Hmm," Jane said in response. She could save them all time if she just said no. "The ad emphasizes it removes blood, and so you play up that the intended audience is serial killers. Is that actually amusing?"

"I was thinking about the popularity of true crime, and—"

"But is true crime in the draft?"

"It's not, no, but it could be. I could—"

"And didn't we do a true crime sketch, what, four months ago?"

"But I thought if—"

"No. We're going to pass." She glanced at her list. "Ashleigh, you're up. The NFT grocery store."

That was how it went. Jane bounced from cast member to cast member, you gave your pitch and read what you had, and she gave you the thumbs-up or thumbs-down. Sometimes, she'd say, *Let's come back to it*, but that was never a good sign. If you couldn't sell Jane immediately, the piece didn't belong on the show. End of story.

It was all going great—she'd accepted Sam's Rich White sketch—until Jane glanced at the list and said, "Roxy, 'Lost Boy.' Let's go."

A ringing started in Sam's ears, and by the time it had cleared, Roxy was already describing the setup.

"So it's the set of the 'Lost Boy' video, and Sam's auditioning for the part of himself. The idea is they're going to add a Sam look-alike to the video, and you're auditioning to play yourself."

"Am I?" It was the only thing he could think to say other than, *What the fuck do you think you're doing?*

"Right, and it's down to the final two, you and Devin."

Devin clapped. He actually fucking clapped. "Classic! Oh my God, that's perfect. Would I get to wear a wig?" Devin's buzz cut didn't look anything like Sam's hair—but that was only the fiftieth objection Sam had to this sketch.

Roxy was still going. "So then the director says, 'I'm sorry, but I think—'"

"Yeah, I'm going to stop you right there. I don't like it." Sam was proud of himself that he didn't holler that, because he felt very much like hollering.

Roxy's expression was fixed. She'd been on the receiving end of Sam's recalcitrance before. The only difference was this was absolutely nothing like the previous occasions. Those times, she'd proposed stuff he didn't like or get or think was funny.

This was a violation of his goddamn life.

"What don't you like?" she asked.

"First off—"

"I think it's genius." This was just about Jane's highest compliment. "It's funny, it's topical, it uses the host—"

"It humiliates me. There's also probably a licensing issue with the song." That was a silly objection. Salem would probably be delighted by the sketch. "And Devin and I wouldn't be up for the same part."

"That's . . . the joke?" Roxy said.

Which was sort of funny. Damn it.

"Great," Sam declared. "Then someone else in the cast can do it. Gibson, you've always wanted to be me. Now's your chance."

Gibson looked as if he'd just discovered a shit in the punch bowl.

Roxy's brows went up, and her mouth curved. She didn't smile, but he knew she wanted to. She thought his reaction was amusing.

"All due respect to Gibson"—by which Roxy meant no due respect to Gibson—"it has to be you, Sam. Look, I know you don't want to do it—"

"I have no objection to doing it."

"So then, what's the problem?"

"I don't want to do it now. Or like this." Really, ever. He didn't want to do it ever. Sam didn't have an objection to doing pieces that were self-deprecating—he'd pretty much built his career on that—but something about this moment had him feeling way too exposed. It was one thing to pick on yourself when you were feeling decently strong. It was another when your skin felt so thin, it was a miracle all your blood and organs were staying inside.

"You haven't even heard the sketch. So the director says—"

"Let's come back to this later," Jane said.

Sam fumed for the next hour, shooting down everything bad with even more bluntness than normal . . . which was saying something.

Then Jane waved him and Roxy back to her office. Sam knew he was basically breathing fire, but he didn't see how it benefited him to pretend that he wasn't.

Jane took her seat and tossed her glasses carelessly on the desk. "What's the problem?"

"I said I didn't want to do a sketch about it."

"No, you said you didn't have a hook and you didn't know how to use the host. Roxy has a hook, and she knows how to use Devin. So I'll ask again: What's the problem?"

The aggravating part, the part that had him grinding his molars into gravel in his mouth, was that she was right. Jane might piss him off, but she was so often right.

He growled, which he knew made him sound about twelve, but he *was* feeling fucking petulant.

Jane's pitying smile only added to it. "I know you don't want to do the sketch, and I know *why* you don't want to do the sketch. But as soon as you do the sketch, the conversation will move on."

"How do you know that? Maybe the next single off the album is about me too." He hadn't even realized the possibility until he said it—but now it was all he could think about. Holy flaming bags of dog shit, there could be eleven more Sam dis tracks coming down the pipe.

Jane snorted. "What did you *do* to the woman?"

"Argg."

"Sorry, that came out wrong." She waved her hand to apologize.

"Sam," Roxy interjected. "I sincerely thought you were stuck, and I was trying to unstick you."

"You did this for me?"

"I did!"

"No, it was for you. You knew Jane wanted the sketch, and you wrote it to get on her good side."

"You think I'm trying to suck up to Jane? You think I'm that desperate to get on the air?"

"Yes." Which he knew was a lie—a hurtful, stupid lie—but he said it anyhow.

"Fuck you, Sam. I don't need to score points off your personal life. I do just fine mining my own. And kissing Jane's ass is pretty low on my to-do list, which I think is clear from the last two years. I know you're hurting and this isn't even really about me, but for the record, if you're trying to prove Salem was wrong, this isn't how you do that."

He felt so completely like shit. He might as well have been watching some movie of his life—maybe the sketch version written by

Roxy—and not been able to fix or change anything. He could see what he was doing, could see how he was fucking up, but there wasn't any other, better way for him to handle it beyond him saying, "I'm talking about what you did to me, Roxy."

"I didn't do *anything* to you. I did my job."

"By mocking me?"

"Yeah, you know, sometimes. It isn't as if you haven't done the same thing a hundred times, and you'll do it a hundred more. And when you take your head out of your ass, you'll realize I'm right and you'll thank me."

"I won't ever thank you for this." He ran his hands over his face, trying to talk himself down.

At her desk, Jane had watched this exchange with calm equanimity. "Are we done here?"

Roxy gave him a dirty look and then nodded. He wanted to make more arguments, but he had gone way too far earlier, so he capitulated.

"Fabulous," Jane deadpanned. "Sam, will you do the sketch?"

"You're not going to order me to?"

"Contrary to popular belief, I never order anyone to do anything." She didn't need to. Anyone who wanted to go toe to toe with Jane realized the risk wasn't worth it.

Sam knew either he could stick things out at *Comedy Hour*, or he could leave. There was no point in challenging Jane any more directly than he had—which had been pretty damn direct.

"I don't like it," he said.

"That's not what I asked. Will you do it?"

Sam glared at Roxy, and she stuck her tongue out at him. He almost guffawed before he remembered how mad he was at her.

"Fine. I want to go on record saying I think it's crap. But I've done crap sketches before." Not ones that had mocked himself, but he could sell the heck out of crap material.

"We're all so grateful for your sacrifice," Jane said. "Can we rejoin the others now?"

"But everyone I like is in here." Which was true, and it made it doubly ridiculous that he was fighting them.

It was a good thing he'd never claimed to be rational.

When Bree entered the *Comedy Hour* writers' room carrying a bag of subs, the first person she saw was Roxy.

Roxy stooped to give her a buss on the cheek. "You are the best."

"No, I was just in the neighborhood." And she was trying to apologize for the interview Sam knew nothing about. It had gone *extremely* well, which just made her feel even guiltier. "Where's Sam?"

Roxy had unwrapped her grilled buffalo cauliflower sandwich and was digging in. "Pouting somewhere. Probably in the stairwell."

"What's he pouting about?"

"We're doing a sketch about 'Lost Boy.'"

"Oh." Oh. "He didn't write it?"

"Nope. Jane asked him to write it, and he declined, so . . . I did."

Bree grimaced. She could imagine how that had gone. Sam did material about himself all the time, but that was the point: He did it. He wrote it. He planned it and decided what to put in or not and what the tone would be.

He probably felt as if Roxy had been disloyal or something. Honestly, Bree didn't love the idea of the show doing the sketch if Sam hadn't written or at least endorsed it, but she was equally sure he was being melodramatic. Sam could never manage to respond to the silly kinds of adversity with anything like restraint. When the chips were down, when you were actually near hunger or homelessness, Sam was stunningly calm. Stunningly resourceful. Maybe he'd used up his entire store of poise as a kid, and so now he indulged in tantrums over little things.

She didn't want to think about how he'd feel if he knew about the interview, or that they'd said they'd reach out about a second interview soon. Nope, Bree didn't want to contemplate how he would take that news at all.

"He was pretty awful about it, but he agreed in the end." Roxy paused. "Do you think I shouldn't have written it?"

"That's not my call," Bree said quickly.

Comedy Hour mocked people and institutions all the time. They often mocked them for good, to criticize serious social problems. But there was an ethic to what they did that Bree didn't understand at all. She could parse the power dynamics of design: how you identified and reached out to the stakeholders, how you got everyone on board in a way that was fair, how to be transparent to reduce corruption. When it came to writing—who could write what and why, when it was okay to punch and when you needed to check yourself—well, she enjoyed debating all that with Sam, but it wasn't Bree's world.

"He's so . . . proud," she said to Roxy. And most people didn't understand how bruised he could get.

"I wouldn't have written it if I didn't think it would make things better for him. No one's going to shut up until he says something."

"I'm sure you're right. Where's the stairwell?"

"Take a left. It's at the end of the hall."

"Thanks."

Bree found the entrance to the stairs easily. They were the typical cinder block tube, designed to withstand a tornado, so Sam would likely be unable to demolish them.

"Sam?" she called. A grunt came from two flights up, and Bree jogged up the steps to find him in a heap on the landing. "Come here often?"

He pursed his lips, and it was unfair how kissable that made his mouth. "Don't joke. This isn't funny."

"I have it on good authority everything is funny." That was what he often said, anyhow, but she wouldn't be surprised if he didn't or couldn't extend that to himself.

Or maybe it was "Lost Boy" specifically. He'd insisted he was over Salem, but it seemed more like a gaping wound to Bree. She tried not to be jealous of his obvious ongoing feelings for another woman. She did not succeed.

Sam shifted those intense eyes of his to her, and her knees went weak. If Sam hadn't been funny, he could have been a dramatic actor or a model, she was certain. He never would have been able to keep a straight face, but he had the looks, the energy, to pull it off.

"What did Roxy say?" he finally asked.

"That you were pouting."

He growled. "I'm not—okay, I am." He was, and they both knew it. She wouldn't put it past him to keep arguing out of sheer perversity, but that wasn't his normal style. "Did she tell you what happened?"

"Roughly, that Jane asked you to write something, and you didn't, so Roxy did. And now you're pissed." Bree omitted that "Lost Boy" was the subject. It wouldn't help matters to remind him that all this was playing out in the larger context of Salem flaying him for the amusement of seemingly everyone in the world at the moment.

"Pretty much, yes. But with more betrayal."

"Do you have to be so over the top?" Bree was trying to drag him back to reality, which she had to do not only because she wanted him to forgive Roxy but because someday very soon, she was going to need him to see that she wasn't betraying him either.

Her self-interest was making her sound more desperate than she wanted to.

"Yes, actually. I'm an entertainer." He let one arm drape across his face, hiding his expression from her. "It hurts, Smoosh."

"What hurts?" She sat down several steps from the landing where he was sprawled, which put their faces level. She would have touched him if she thought it would help, but he didn't like that kind of comfort, as much as he offered it to her freely. And with how everything between and around them was changing, she didn't think it was a good idea to add physical contact to the mix.

"I don't think I'm vain. Well, not *that* vain. I can laugh at myself. But usually I choose that, you know? I put myself out there or up there, and I decide where to put the knife."

"Is it the engagement ending, or—"

"No." He whipped his arm off his face so that she could see how serious he was. "I'm really not mad at Salem. Before last week, you wouldn't believe how little I thought about it. I'm over her."

"Good." Bree didn't know whether she meant that it was good for Sam that he wasn't walking around carrying a lot of anger at his ex or whether it was good for her to know that he wasn't still emotionally hung up on his ex.

"It just feels like the world is pointing and laughing at me."

"When normally you're the one doing the pointing and laughing?"

"Yes, I'm a hypocrite."

"That's not actually what I mean. Though—maybe a little." Because it was difficult not to see that element of it. "But I'd guess the loss of control is . . . a lot."

"Yup."

"That's maybe not a thing to process at work."

"God"—he curled up, pressing his hands onto his ears—"I have to apologize to Roxy."

"Yes. And Jane too."

"Never her." A pause. "Maybe her. Why do you put up with me?"

I love you.

As they so often were, the words were in the back of Bree's throat. All she had to do was push air through them, and they would emerge right here, bouncing around the stairwell, making it nova bright.

Or at least it would be for one second. One brilliant moment of truth and feeling until Sam responded.

He would let her down gently, as gently as he knew how, but everything between them would shift. Become strained and awful, smothering what they had and cheapening every moment of the past. He'd never believe that she treasured their friendship as it was.

"Habit," she said instead, which was true.

He sat up and dusted off his T-shirt. It was fitted and strained against his biceps. In addition to the exercise bike, he was also a fan of the pull-up bar, and she had to say, it all worked for her.

"Damn it. How much I don't want to do this makes me feel . . . sensitive." He said it as if it were the worst thing in the world, the same way he might say *tech bro*.

"It's not silly to be touchy about this."

"But to get so pissed about what I do to other people all the time? *I'm* the fucking joke."

He rolled his eyes, and Bree knew that he'd shifted from rage at Roxy and Jane to at himself, which was always what he did. Sam felt things deeply, but all that anger eventually turned to himself. Even what he felt toward his family: it eventually became self-loathing. It was Sam's way.

"Okay, enough." He stood up and offered her a hand. "Come on, Smoosh."

"Where are we going?"

"I'm going to apologize to Roxy. You can watch."

"Perfect. I even brought sandwiches."

He linked his fingers with hers. "You're amazing."

If Bree hadn't heard that from him so many times, and if she didn't know that he absolutely meant the words even though he would never mean them in the way she wanted him to, it would have hurt so much.

As it was, her heart only throbbed when she replied lightly, "I really am."

When they got to the door on the floor where the *Comedy Hour* rehearsal space was, he dropped her hand and pulled the door open, holding it for her. Then Bree followed him back into the writers' room.

He dropped into a chair across the table from Roxy. She arched her eyebrows as if to say, *Well?*

"Roxy, I am sorry I said you betrayed me. You—didn't." He obviously didn't believe that 100 percent, but he said it anyway. "I'd be honored to do your sketch."

Roxy's expression conveyed that she was either trying not to choke or trying not to laugh, and Bree couldn't tell which it was.

"And why did you say that?" Bree prompted Sam.

"Because I'm an ass who can't articulate his feelings. Sorry." He shifted his attention to Bree, who just shrugged. It wasn't her place to forgive him; he hadn't hurt her.

Roxy snorted. "Apology accepted. Don't be such a butthead next time."

"That I can't promise, because I don't want to lie. But when I fuck up, I'll admit it."

"He will," Bree put in. Sam was hotheaded and screwed up a lot, but he did take responsibility and do reasonable things to make up for it. At least he always did with her.

Roxy popped up onto her toes so she could reach across the table and give Sam's shoulder a light punch. "You gonna apologize to Jane?"

"Nah, she'd get insufferable." He twisted so he could face Bree. "You want to stick around? We're almost done. We could catch a ride together."

"Nope, I'm going to demolish this sandwich and then head home. I'm exhausted. Try to be quiet when you come in."

"Why are you still mucking up Bree's life?" Roxy demanded. "I told you, I have a guest room. And there are something like a hundred thousand hotel rooms in this city."

"No," Bree said right as Sam said, "Nah." They'd both spoken too quickly. Pathetically quickly.

After an awkward second, Bree added, "It's fine." Sam staying with her was torture in some ways, but she wanted a few more days with him, especially knowing that they might be some of her last ones in New York.

Sam grinned. "She's not ready to kick me out."

Wasn't that the sad truth?

Roxy let it go then.

After they ate—it was amazing how Sam's apology had cleared the air, leaving no hint of stress or discomfort between him and Roxy—Sam walked Bree to the studio door. "You'll be fine getting home? I can call an Uber."

"I have my bike, and besides, I'm a big girl."

He gave her a long, questioning look, and it was unfair that his eyes had this much power over her. The irises were so brown, they were almost black. It made her search for the places where they were shot through with bronze. She knew she was staring too long, and she was certain her cheeks were coloring with embarrassment, but she couldn't look away.

She'd spent two decades wanting things to change between them, but now that they were—now that she was changing them—she was getting cold feet. It was silly.

Sam surprised her when he reached out and touched her hair. "There's some fluff," he explained. With painstaking gentleness, he disengaged it, and then he held it out to her on his index finger. "Can you make a wish on these, or is that only eyelashes?"

How are you like this, she wanted to demand. One minute, he was being petulant, profane. The next, he was inviting her to make wishes on fuzzies. It should've been contradictory, but the pugnaciousness and precociousness twisted together into the pretzel of him. She just loved him so much.

"Sam." It came out as a whisper, and something flared in those mesmerizing eyes of his.

"Bree," he whispered back.

But before she could do something stupid—such as tell him she'd interviewed for a job in Michigan that morning or, even worse, touch him—there was a crash in the street. It was probably just a truck with terrible shocks, but it was enough to make Bree jump straight back into reality.

"See you," she said, and then she was waving and dashing out into the night as fast as her legs could carry her. Out there, she would definitely *not* be wondering what might have happened if she'd told Sam that her only wish was him.

CHAPTER 9

Bree's head hurt too much for this meeting. She'd woken up with a cold brewing in her body, but luckily, even at reduced capacity, she could handle the disgusting "not in my backyard" attitude of Peyton Hale, the lawyer sitting across from her.

"I understand," she said, interrupting his latest screed, "that some of the stakeholders have objections—"

"All the stakeholders have objections," Hale bellowed. But by *all*, he meant the ones who owned property and whom he was representing—which was a tiny percentage of the stakeholders. He didn't know or care about the renters Bree had met or the terms of the development agreement his firm had signed. How insolent of her to remind him of the legal exigencies that they'd agreed to, and on a Saturday, no less.

Bree really hoped that if she got the Hutchinson-Baker job, people outside New York wouldn't lose their minds about the possibility of low-income housing. But she suspected that landlords the world over hated the possibility of poor people showing up and hurting their property values.

"Regardless," she said, trying not to put all the disdain she felt into her tone, "while the owners you represent might not have understood the contract they signed, they did sign it. At least thirty percent of the units in the development need to fit the city's definition of affordable housing. The rest can be sold at the market rate. That was the city's condition, and that's why they granted the permits. Your clients' legal obligation is clear."

It was also Bree's and the architect's vision for the space, and it was the right thing to do. The city was for everyone. It wasn't some playground for millionaires and celebrities. If they were going to avoid that particular nightmare, then low- and middle-income New Yorkers needed a place to live. Compact, integrated, diverse neighborhoods should be the goal—and these people had said it was their goal, or else they wouldn't have been allowed to develop the land in the first place.

Bree rubbed her temple. If this meeting went on any longer, she was going to get nauseated. Wouldn't it serve this guy right if she puked on his shoes?

"I have a letter, signed by twenty-five property owners—"

"It wouldn't matter if it was signed by two hundred of them. It doesn't negate the contract!" Okay, that had been sharp, rude, and not at all like Bree. It sounded like something Sam would say, which was more evidence that she needed to get him out of her apartment.

The more time they spent together, the more often a dangerous thought poked its head up: *Maybe.* Maybe Bree could tell him how she felt. Maybe Sam wouldn't freak out. Maybe there was a chance— fleeting, small—that he felt the same way. Maybe they wouldn't break their friendship in pursuing something else.

Her stomach twisted itself into a braid. Nope, she wasn't feeling well enough to contemplate that subject. The last week had proved Sam had an almost supernatural power over her. Nothing and no one else made Bree that vulnerable.

But this meeting was reminding her that she *wasn't* helpless. Across from her, Hale kept running his fingers over the edges of his letter, as if he expected strength or power to enter his body from the no-doubt-very-expensive paper. He hadn't expected her to push back, and it clearly had rattled him.

"I took this meeting as a courtesy," she told him, her tone firm but more professional, "because it's important for everyone to be on the same page. But I don't want you or your clients to mistake that for wiggle room. There is no wiggle room."

He harrumphed and then launched in on a new litany of complaints. But Bree had burned through her remaining energy. She was too sick and too tired to argue, so she took notes mechanically and said, "I appreciate your feedback," until he was done.

Hale had to know at some level that this meeting was pointless. His clients wanted to be heard, and so she was hearing them. Unpleasant as it was, it was his job, and it was her job. After another half hour, he finished, and she was able to escape.

It was late afternoon, and the light painting the sidewalk was the shade of pale yellow that always reminded her of birch leaves. The air had started to go crisp, and everyone except Bree seemed to have an extra snap in their step.

Bree checked the time. *Comedy Hour* would start taping soon. She had a text from Sam reminding her about the location for the after-party, but frankly, she wasn't sure that in her current state, she could face Sam in full famous-person mode. It would simply be too hurtful when she was clearly nursing—*ha!*—a cold and after they'd spent so much unguarded time together.

Not wanting to compose a long text to Megan, Bree called her.

Megan answered on the third ring. "On a scale of Jane Jacobs to Robert Moses, how bad was it?"

Bree considered. "A five. So James Wilson Rouse?"

"Sure, that seems right. 'Will no one think of the poor landlords'?"

"You know it."

"I'll think of the poor landlords," Megan said, "all while holding them accountable for the contracts they signed."

"It's as if you could've taken this meeting."

"I'm certain you were more polite than I would have been."

"Hmm." Not really. "I'll email you a full summary by Monday, but that's the TL;DR version."

Something crashed in the background of Megan's apartment. "Sorry, party prep is so much harder with preschoolers. You sure you don't want to stop by?"

If Bree were up for it, she was certain that Megan would have shoved another man at her since things with Carl hadn't worked out. She didn't need another man, though. She needed to get over Sam.

"I'm sure. I have dinner plans, but I may cancel and go to bed early."

"Can I join you?"

"What would Jack say?" Megan's husband needed her the way Sam needed Bree, but, presumably, more romantically.

"He and the landlords can both shove it."

Bree offered a half laugh. After she stowed her phone, she dug her water bottle out of her bag and took a long drag. She had been planning to stop by a new exhibit on reclaiming gentrified spaces at the Tenement Museum before meeting Sam, but she simply didn't have the energy, physical or emotional, to do either.

She was going to spend this Saturday late afternoon and evening in a less bewildering fashion: on her couch with ramen and Gatorade, not confused and tempted by men who didn't want her and glitterati types who made no sense to her. She was an expert at design; she could arrange the pieces of her night to protect herself.

As Bree walked to the subway, she was glad she hadn't taken her bike. There was no way she would have been able to make it home. Descending into the station, she dug out her phone and texted Sam: Sam, will you hate me forever

Someone bumped her elbow, and she accidentally hit send.

She hastily typed the rest of her thought: if I skip dinner? Need to sleep. Then she buried her phone in her bag, took the subway home, and finally, gratefully, collapsed onto the couch when she got there.

"Mr. Ley-lahnd, is it?" Alan asked, and the studio audience tittered.

"It's Leyland," Sam corrected.

"Whatever. Let's try it again, but you need to try a *little* harder to act like him. Think cocky. Uncaring. Immature." Alan couldn't help but smirk—and frankly, Sam didn't blame him. "Take two from Mr. Ley-lahnd!"

Sam wanted to retract every time he'd said he loved his job. Well, he hadn't actually ever said it out loud, because that would've been dorky. But he'd thought it, clearly in moments of weakness and delusion.

Now, he and Devin Mackey were dressed identically for Roxy's "Lost Boy" sketch, which was going to be the show's cold open. Because of course it was.

Sam had wanted to fucking scream the entire time they'd worked on it, but now he was trying to channel all that rage into his perfor-mance . . . as himself.

He looked at the camera and delivered the line: "I thought we were just having a good time."

It was exactly as he was quoted in the lyrics for "Lost Boy." The truth was that Sam hadn't actually *said* that to Salem; he'd texted it. Which— looking back on things, he understood why Salem had written the song.

"No, no, no," Alan interrupted. "That's entirely too much empathy coming from Sam! Make it colder!"

And the audience—damn them—howled.

Sam had hated every moment of preparing for this sketch, but the reality of people laughing twenty-five feet from him about his life was almost more than he could take.

He'd tried to get Bree to come to the show itself. God, he wished she had. He would've felt better knowing that at least one person in the audience wouldn't have been guffawing at him, would've actually con-sidered his own feelings about the whole thing. But Bree had begged out because she had some meeting with a developer bigwig. She'd promised to meet him for dinner, though. At least he had that to look forward to.

"Mr. Smith." Alan turned to Devin Mackey. "How about you give it a whirl?"

Next to Sam, Mackey was holding it together, but barely. They were going to break the record for the number of times the host fell out of character—if anyone had ever bothered to make a note of that statistic.

"Sure thing. Thank you for the opportunity." Mackey steeled himself, and then: "'I thought we were just having a good time.'"

Sam could only hope this guy had saved his football money, because he couldn't act for shit.

"Yes!" Alan intoned, sounding as if he'd wandered out of the Globe Theatre. It wasn't clear whether he was trying to sound British or whether that was just a by-product of his faux-snooty accent. "That's the spirit of it! Callous, *harsh*. Try again, Mr. Ley-lahnd."

Sam didn't actually think of himself as a *performer*, or at the very least, he didn't consider himself to be an actor. He wrote and told jokes. It had been part of why he hadn't been certain if *Comedy Hour* was for him in the first place. He'd slowly changed his mind, seen the way that the sketch form could be an extension of his stand-up, but it was a label that fit him like a suit: awkward, as if he'd stolen it from someone else. The fact that he wasn't putting a fist through the wall while letting hundreds—soon to be millions—of people laugh at him: that was real acting.

He repeated, "'I thought we were just having a good time.'"

The resulting laughter was like an ocean wave in November—freezing cold and bigger than you thought it would be; it cut him to the bone.

He knew that Roxy had written the sketch to help him. That she wanted all this to be over for Sam and assumed that him acknowledging it in public was the only way to stop the story.

Maybe she would be right about that. But to find out, Sam was flagellating what shreds Salem had left of his pride.

"We should've skipped the after-party," Sam muttered to Roxy. The taping of the show had been a success, especially the "Lost Boy" sketch.

"Hey, it's free food." This week, the party was at the priciest, slickest Thai place that Sam had ever seen. The show always rented out an entire restaurant, but there was a clear hierarchy of who sat where. Jane would always hold court at some massive table in the corner that screamed, *Behold my importance.* He had no idea how architecture or design or some shit could communicate that, but Bree would've been able to explain it.

Everyone else radiated out from Jane in order of rank: the host sitting close to Jane, the cast in a ring around them, then the grips and such who actually made the show happen toward the edges. They tended to start at a restaurant so everyone could eat, and then they moved to a bar or club. Though rumor had it that they put on the best party in town, you couldn't really party with your boss looking over your shoulder.

"Free food is less of a draw now than it used to be."

"We could revolt," Roxy said. "Relocate to a taco stand."

She'd been so nice to Sam since his temper tantrum, he felt doubly bad about losing his shit.

Gibson walked by their table. His postshow outfit resembled a motorcycle club by way of Brooks Brothers or maybe a designer version of Nic Cage's costume in *Ghost Rider.* Okay, Bree might have a point about Cage.

"Roxy." Gibson gave her a nod.

"You didn't say hello to me," Sam said to his castmate's retreating back.

Gibson flipped him off, and Sam snorted. "I'm beginning to think that guy doesn't like me."

"You remind him of what he'll never be."

"Talented?"

The server showed up. Roxy asked for whiskey and Sam for water. He was always dehydrated after a show. He tried not to drink alcohol more than a few times a week—it was hard to grow up like he had and still think having a serious relationship with booze was a good idea—and tonight he didn't feel like he had much to celebrate.

"Did you give Bree's name to the bouncer?" Roxy asked when the server had left.

"Yup." He dug out his phone. "Wait, she texted me."

Sam, will you hate me forever

There was no period, which wasn't like Bree. She always punctuated her texts properly, which he found strangely endearing.

I could never hate you, he texted back. Are you okay?

"What's wrong?" Roxy asked.

"Bree sent a weird text. She should be here by now."

He hoped she was okay. If she'd been hurt, she would've written more. He was listed as her emergency contact, right? Maybe he ought to leave, to go check on her—

His phone dinged, and it was, thankfully, another text from Bree: The rest of my message didn't send. I'm not feeling well. Can't face food.

Some tightness in Sam's chest released. He was sorry she was sick, but he'd rather that than something else. "She's not feeling great," he explained.

"Is she okay?"

"Just sick." Or at least he hoped that was all it was.

Sam hadn't seen Bree since she'd dropped off the sandwiches Wednesday evening. He'd been coming in late and leaving early. The show just absorbed all his time; it wasn't about trying to avoid her or anything—at least that's what he kept telling himself when he'd remember the moment he'd held that bit of fuzzy up on his finger, and she'd stared at him, wide eyed and . . . something.

"You need to leave that poor woman's apartment," Roxy was saying. "After tonight, the paparazzi should forget about you. I mean, as much as they normally forget about you."

Which wasn't much.

There had been a big swarm of press around the restaurant entrance. The details of the party were supposed to be secret, but somehow, they always leaked. At least Sam could comfort himself by knowing some of this was about Devin and the rest of the cast and the general aura that surrounded *Comedy Hour*. His scandal had only amplified it this week.

"Bree doesn't mind having me. And don't kid yourself. Your sketch wasn't that good." It was, he could now admit, pretty funny, but it wasn't going to solve all his problems, in part because he would probably continue to make more problems for himself. "Plus, I can't leave Bree when she's sick."

"Or maybe that's exactly when you should leave her. No one likes houseguests when they're under the weather."

Bree would have told him to leave if that was what she wanted. She'd never, ever lie to him. Besides: "I'm not a guest. I'm me."

Roxy snorted.

The server materialized. "Water, a bottle of single malt whiskey, and two glasses."

Sam wasn't certain if Roxy had intended to use both those glasses herself, but he didn't want to stick around. The idea of these after-parties didn't thrill him in the best of circumstances, and he couldn't imagine sticking around knowing that Bree was sick. He should be with her, feeding her chicken noodle soup or whatever shit she always did for him when he was sick.

He stood up. "Actually, I need to go."

Roxy watched him steadily while the server cleared away Sam's water and the empty glass. "You know I really like Bree."

"I do too." Everyone liked Bree. She was extremely likable. "What does that have to do with anything?"

"Oh, Sam. Sammity, Sam, Sam, Sam." Roxy gave him a pitying look. She started to say something, then she stopped herself and shook her head. After a beat, she said, "Someday, it'll all make sense to you."

Sam would've pressed her to explain what precisely she meant by that and what she was implying, but he just didn't have the time. "I kinda doubt that. I'd say make my apologies to Jane, but I have no apologies for Jane."

"I'll make them anyway, and mine will be better than yours could've hoped to be."

He blew her a kiss, and then he left before anyone could try to bog him down.

Outside, the valet apologized because the car service wasn't ready yet. The studio had decided at some point to arrange a fleet of town cars for the after-party, because nothing would be more embarrassing than if a cast member got a DUI leaving what was nominally a work event.

"I'll grab a cab. No sweat."

The man looked shocked, and once again, Sam was forced to internally—okay, partially externally; he'd used up his store of tact and repression this week—curse out some of his lovely castmates.

Fifteen minutes later, Sam got to Bree's apartment, where he found her sprawled on the couch. Her hair was in two short pigtails, her cheeks were flushed, and her eyes were watery. It was such a relief to see that she was okay, he wanted to hug her.

"Damn it," she huffed out, "you're supposed to be at the party."

"I wanted to check on you. Your text kind of freaked me out."

"Sorry. I typed more, but I guess the subway ate it. I'll move to my bed. I was just watching—" She gestured at the TV and began grabbing her blankets, several used tissues, and a massive container of Gatorade. "I'm sorry you came back early. You're supposed to be celebrating." She swiped at her nose with everything balled up in one hand. "You may want to go home. I'm a germ factory."

"I don't want to be anywhere but here."

He didn't want to think about why those felt like the truest words he'd said all day.

CHAPTER 10

Bree felt like shit. Her nose was running, and her head was pounding. She knew Sam had seen her looking worse—and that he didn't care how she looked—but she'd rather have the floor of her apartment open up and suck her into the air ducts than stand there and face him for another moment.

That instinct only heightened when he said, "You don't look so good."

Right, she assumed this wasn't her finest moment. She lifted her chin as regally as she could and tried not to sneeze. "Samuel Leyland, you sweet talker."

He stalked across her apartment. He did at least look concerned. "You're red. And pale."

"I can't be both."

"You're splotchy." He set a hand on her forehead. It covered most of her face—good goodness he had big hands. "Fuck, you're freezing. Get in the shower."

She hadn't really known she was cold until he touched her, and the contrast was alarming. Maybe she *was* cold, but even still: "Excuse me?"

He removed his hand from her forehead, and she almost fell into him. "Take a shower. Get warm."

"Jeez, you're bossy."

"Which is good, because you look like hell."

She didn't want to talk about how she looked anymore. "Did you do the sketch?" Because of the tape delay, she didn't know.

"Maybe if you take a shower, I'll tell you."

"Hmm." She wiped her nose again. It had started leaking like a faucet a few hours before. "Fine. Have it your way."

Bree stumbled into the bathroom. To her eyes, she was less red and white than green and yellow, but maybe she just needed a better bulb in the light fixture. As she removed various items of clothing—she'd added layers throughout the evening—and her teeth started to chatter, she had to admit that maybe Sam was right and a shower was a good idea.

She hadn't wanted to admit that she was getting sick, but the water pressure against her skull made the pounding in her head worse.

The door to the bathroom opened.

She clutched her loofah to her chest. "Sam?"

"Don't mind me."

But she did mind him. She minded the fact that he was only a thin sheet of vinyl away from her naked body very much.

There was some shuffling, and then the door closed again.

After Bree finished an indulgently long shower, she stuck her head out from behind the curtain and found a clean towel folded on the toilet, along with pajamas and panties. She didn't want to contemplate him digging through her underwear drawer, but even still—he could be so sweet when he wanted to be. Sam had even measured NyQuil into one of those plastic cups that come with the bottle and had set a glass of water on the vanity.

"You didn't have to do all this," she called through the door as she stumbled into the PJs.

"Yes, I did," he called back. "I'm a houseguest. This is the hospitality code."

Bree quickly dressed and took the meds—then chugged the water because ugh—before she emerged into the bedroom, where Sam was straightening her duvet.

"You changed my sheets?" She most definitely sounded stunned.

"Someone once told me nothing feels as good as clean sheets when you're sick."

She had said that. Well, someone else might have also said that to him, but she definitely had.

"You going to brush your hair?" he asked.

"I . . . I'm too tired to put my hands over my head." The shower and dressing herself had taken whatever measure of energy she'd had.

He went into the bathroom and came out with a towel and a comb. "On the bed."

Feeling foolish, she sat. Then, far more tenderly than she would have thought him capable of, Sam began to brush her hair. That was always her favorite part at the salon, not just when they shampooed your hair but when they brushed it for you. There was something so luxurious about it.

She closed her eyes. It felt impersonal when the hairdresser did it. It didn't feel impersonal when it was Sam's fingers brushing her scalp and the back of her neck. It was very much the opposite of impersonal.

Softly, she asked, "Where did you learn to do that?"

He paused, three of his fingertips pushed into the wet hair at her temple. Those three points of contact might as well have been the center of the universe. "I've never actually done it for someone else before."

Bree didn't want to be pleased. She didn't. But she was. "You're good at it."

"Maybe if I practice my sweeping, there's a salon assistant job in my future."

"Never. You'd offend too many customers."

"Probably true. There, all done." He rubbed the towel over her head to soak up the excess moisture, and then he peeled the blankets back. "Get in."

It really did feel good, but . . . she began to shiver again.

Sam had gone to hang the towel up, but when he reemerged into the bedroom, he was scowling. "Do you have an electric blanket? Maybe a hot-water bottle?"

"No-o-o." Her teeth chattered.

"We'll have to go with plan B, then." He shucked off his pants.

She almost said, *I'm not in the mood*, but he might not have understood it was a joke. She was too sick and too tired to parse it herself. So instead, she just asked, "Wh-what are you doing?"

"I'm not going to wear my outside clothes in bed, Smoosh. I was partially civilized." His sweater joined his jeans, leaving him in only boxer briefs, a white undershirt, and white athletic socks.

She knew, positively knew, that she'd seen him in less before. At the beach. When he'd taken off his shirt while playing basketball or hiking. But there was something electrically intimate about this being his underwear. It made her feel like a character in a Lucy Maud Montgomery novel.

"You d-d-don't have to do that. I'll warm up soon."

He clambered in. "Come 'ere."

She scooched away from him. "I'll get you sick."

"I don't care."

He had a public job. A public *demanding* job. A job that required him to be able to write and think and perform starting just a day and a half from now.

She should say no. She should shiver in bed until she warmed herself up—and she really ought to insist he leave her apartment before she infected him. But he'd already been here for days as her symptoms had worsened. If she was going to infect him, she'd probably already done it. And honestly, she was really cold.

They'd hugged many times, but vertical hugging and horizontal cuddling were not the same thing. This might be her only chance to try the second one with him.

She slid her head and shoulders onto his chest, and his arms came around her, and she had to squeeze her eyes closed against the emotions building there. But two tears slid out anyway and ran down her cheeks. He was just so warm, and he smelled so good, and it felt so right, his body wrapped around her, with one of those big hands rubbing her back.

"You're like an ice cube," he said. "How is that possible? You were in the shower two minutes ago."

"Sick" was all she managed to say. She didn't trust her voice any further than that, and she would have no explanation for why she was crying. *I love you, and you've never held me like this before, and you probably never will again.* Nope, she wasn't going to explain any of that. Not now and maybe not ever.

"Do you want to go to the doctor?"

She shook her head.

"The show has a doctor who makes house calls. I could—"

"No."

"I know, it's such a stupid rich-person thing."

It was actually extremely kind of him to offer, even if it would make her feel silly to accept. "That's not . . . I just know it's only a cold."

He ran his hand down her back again. Her shirt had scrunched up, and his fingertip brushed over the exposed skin on her hip. She bit her lip to keep from whimpering.

"I *am* going to order some chicken noodle soup," he whispered. "And some ginger ale."

"Will you stir the bubbles out?"

"Of course."

She was warming up, half degree by half degree, and she let herself uncurl enough to set a flat hand on his stomach. She could feel the scoring of his muscles through the fabric. The year before, he'd done a spread in *Vanity Fair* wearing next to nothing. She'd given him a lot of crap—and spent more time than she would ever admit ogling him. Evidently it had *not* been computer enhanced in any way.

"What's in your shampoo?" He sniffed her hair.

"Tangerine."

"I like it."

I like you. But she couldn't have this conversation with him while she was on cold meds. While he was still staying here.

After she moved, maybe she'd tell him. Once she'd established some independence. Once he'd forgiven her for leaving.

"You warming up?"

"Yes." She cleared her throat and added, "Thank you." Her voice sounded prim and unnatural, but that was better than teary, she supposed.

"Just a second." He squeezed her shoulder to indicate that she should move. When he slid out of the bed, she did whimper. He was so warm.

He chuckled. "I'll be right back." He found his phone and then got back in. She retook her spot on his chest.

He opened YouTube and began typing in the search box.

"What are you looking for?"

"Something better than NyQuil."

"There's no such thing." She hated how it tasted. Hated it. But it was so powerful, she still couldn't believe people could buy it without a prescription. That just couldn't be a good idea.

"You just watch." He opened a video, and it was *The Price Is Right*.

"Oh, shit."

"I won't even say, 'I told you so,' because you're sick."

Because they'd known each other basically from the womb on, he knew that she didn't have a sick day movie; she had a sick day show, and it was Bob Barker or, if pressed, Drew Carey and the scraggly army of folks who lined up to correctly guess the prices of various retail items.

The Price Is Right quite simply felt like the purest, most honest distillation of America.

She settled further into Sam's arms and let the warmth of him and the pleasant routine of the show relax her. After Contestants' Row filled, the first item was a blender.

"Two hundred dollars," Sam said confidently.

"Jesus, what bougie kitchen stores are you hitting?"

"My assistant does that for me. What are you bidding?"

"A hundred and ten dollars. And I still can't believe you have an assistant." Normally, Bree would rib him louder and longer about that, but, well, she was feeling under the weather—and he was very warm.

On his phone, the host revealed the actual price: $130.

"Ha!"

"Okay, okay." The closest guess—$120; the guy had actually done even better than Bree—advanced to the pricing game, which was the big wheel.

"We both know I'd do better at spinning it," Sam said.

"Only because you're taller."

"I don't see why that matters."

"The higher you grab, the more likely you are to get it to go all the way around."

"That's why I flunked out of school."

She should have pointed out that he left college because of different priorities, not a lack of brains, but the NyQuil was starting to hit her, and she didn't feel like arguing with him. So she sank further into his chest and said, "Pfft."

"Not going to swing at that one?"

"Even I know to"—she yawned—"skip the ones in the dirt."

"If I watched baseball, that would probably have been pretty funny."

"Ask Jane. She'll explain it to you." Jane was a devoted Mets fan.

"Ouch." But he said it in amusement, not anger.

He rubbed Bree's back again, down the fabric of her shirt . . . and up over her skin. She could almost, almost believe it was on purpose— and almost, almost believe that the way she shivered under his touch might be mutual.

After a few more strokes, he whispered, "Go to sleep."

"You can leave for home or the couch." She didn't want him to stay in her bed if he didn't want to be there.

"Never."

And for once, she believed him.

Under the soft motion of his hand, she closed her eyes and drifted off.

CHAPTER 11

When more and more light poured into the room—seriously, the sun was such an asshole—Sam finally forced his eyelids open. Bree was still sprawled on his chest, one of her hands clutching his shirt tightly. Carefully, he touched her forehead. She was a little warm, maybe. She was snoring, so he suspected she was congested, but she'd slept soundly. Either because she was sick or because of the NyQuil, she'd gotten rest.

He had . . . not.

He couldn't explain what the problem had been, but he had spent the night about ten times as aware of his body as he'd ever been in his life. The brush of the sheets against his shins. The scent of Bree's dryer sheets. Her febrile heat making him seem cold.

She sighed and pushed her face against him, and for a second he was terrified she was about to wake up. But then she relaxed, and her breathing evened out.

It was because she wasn't feeling well. That was why he was concerned. Bree didn't get sick often, but when she did, it flattened her. A few years ago, she'd had pneumonia, which had scared the shit out of him. She hadn't ended up in the hospital, but he'd kept thinking about how many people died from walking pneumonia. So he'd checked on her, in person, every day for two weeks. She'd started greeting him at the front door, middle finger extended.

When she woke up, he was going to take another swing at letting him call the doctor. He would have texted to see if they had any availability, but he couldn't reach his phone, and he didn't want to move Bree. He was certain she'd never settle back on his chest if he moved her, and she was clearly sleeping well there.

Thank God Sunday was his one day off a week when the show was in production. Since the show had gone so well last night, his agent would probably send over a roundup of reviews and anything that went viral. That was their arrangement because Sam was supposed to stay off social media, as he got involved in too many flame wars.

He liked reading reviews, even bad ones. He did comedy to get a reaction, and he wanted to hear it. The *Comedy Hour* studio audience tended to be overly kind and indulgent. They were so jacked to see the taping that they weren't representative of how a bit was going to land.

Bree stirred—and he held his breath. She arched her back like a cat's, then relaxed, settling back into his chest.

He blew the breath out, low and long.

It was just instinct, the way the line of her body revved something up in him. That was all.

It was probably too soon, but he needed to start dating again. He hadn't been on a date, let alone in bed with a woman, since Salem had dumped him.

He hated the rebound phase. The pity. The questions. But he loved the moment when his cynicism would fall away, and he would notice someone else, and suddenly he could not only see the possibility of having another relationship but could feel like, *Maybe this time it could be different.*

He enjoyed the rush of infatuation. Of falling into bed with someone for the first time. Of wanting to be with them all the time. The bubble of falling. It would burst. But like trick-or-treating on Halloween, love was a heady rush. Maybe he was being greedy and indulging in wishful thinking to make up for all the shit that he'd never had. But he was only just soft enough to be able to slip into infatuation a few times a year.

The relationships were catnaps from reality, and they lasted about as long.

Bree's fingers on his shirt went slack and then contracted again. She was getting restless; she probably wouldn't sleep much longer.

He let himself straighten her hair, the strands filtering through his fingers. It stirred up the citrus scent of her shampoo, which was spicy this morning, probably mixed with his own deodorant.

"Mmm," she murmured.

"You awake?"

"I feel hungover."

For a long minute, she didn't move, and then finally, softly, she slid from his chest onto the bed. She kept her face pressed against the mattress for a beat, and he was glad he had a chance to straighten up his expression, because Bree moving away felt like—like a loss.

She sat up, keeping the comforter pulled around her and rubbing her face. "Thanks for keeping me warm. I hope I didn't drool."

"Nah. A little snoring, though."

"That's why my throat is dry." She shuffled on the nightstand for her water bottle and took a long drink.

She was . . . pretty. It struck him sometimes, and then he felt like a dweeb because it wasn't debatable. Bree wasn't simply the best part of him. She wasn't only brilliant and kind and funny, and she didn't make any space she designed or worked on better simply by touching it.

She was also pretty. Somehow, he had forgotten it again, and he had to remind himself: *This is Bree. You couldn't live without her, and she's pretty.*

He was going to remember it this time, so that he wouldn't have to deal with the shock of it again. It always made him feel as if the world were off kilter for a while afterward.

Maybe him relearning this was what was wrong between them. Because something wasn't right. He couldn't look away from the line of her shoulder, stark against the exposed brick wall next to her bed.

He shouldn't think about Bree that way. He didn't think about Bree that way.

"I'm sorry I stood you up last night." She gave him a soft, regretful smile.

Stood up? Oh, dinner. "Don't mention it." His voice sounded as if he'd just woken up, when he'd been awake for hours. "I should be thanking you. You got me out of that thing."

"You love those parties. You told me once it was the best part about the show."

"I was being ironic. Or maybe I was younger then."

She snorted. "It was last year. You sounded pretty serious."

"Maybe I was drunk." He tried not to get drunk often, but it happened sometimes. "How are you feeling?"

"Not cold, but my head hurts, and I'm just . . . off. Achy and blah. I shouldn't have let you sleep with me." She blinked rapidly, as if she were flustered. "I mean . . . you know. I should've sent you home."

"I wouldn't have gone." He'd never leave her when she needed him. But since she didn't need him anymore, he could leave now. Maybe he should.

"You're so stubborn."

"Always have been."

He ran his hand through his hair. Maybe he *was* coming down with something. He felt . . . odd, and his chest was tight.

"What are you doing today?" he asked.

She flopped down onto the bed. "You're looking at it. I need to try to shake this thing. I have about six meetings scheduled on Monday. I can't take any time off."

Right, this was his cue. He'd bothered her long enough. "I should jet, then."

Jet? What the fuck? He'd never said anything so ridiculous in his life—and he'd done a set high once.

For a second, Bree looked troubled, but then she flattened her expression out. "Of course. You'll be back tonight?"

"No." Tempting as it was, they both needed space. "I assume Roxy's sketch worked and the paparazzi are gone. You've put up with me long enough."

A pause. Then, "Okay. Well, thank you. For last night. You were really . . . nice."

He hadn't meant to be nice, and something about her interpreting him taking care of her as *niceness*—such a flat, anodyne word—made him angry, which made absolutely no sense. "I'll just get out of your bed. And your apartment."

"Yeah, yeah. Sure."

There it was again: something about this was so *weird*, but he didn't know what, and he was terrible at fixing things even if she could explain it to him.

He attempted to hop out of bed, but his foot was tangled in the sheet, and when he'd kicked once, twice, to get it out, he realized any attempt at finesse had passed. "I normally do that better," he said.

"I'm sure you do." Bree's words were sarcastic, but he simply didn't understand the joke. He was gripped by another impulse to run.

As quickly as he could, he splashed some cold water on his face and climbed back into his jeans. He made a quick circuit of her apartment, shoving his stuff into the bag his assistant had packed for him.

Then Bree walked him to the door, wrapped in a blanket. For one tense moment, he wanted to . . . hug her. But come on, the woman had just spent twelve hours touching him. She probably had no interest in doing it more, so he kept his hands to himself.

"Bye," he said, but Bree didn't even answer.

Halfway down the stairs, he collapsed and put his head in his hands.

What the fuck? What on earth had he unleashed the night before?

That afternoon, after Sam had scrubbed the smell of Bree from his skin and ridden his exercise bike until he was so sore he couldn't think about anything troubling, his agent called.

"Sam! Fucking great cold open last night. I loved it."

Riaz would've had a cow if he knew that Sam had resisted doing the sketch, which was one of the many reasons Sam didn't share the day-to-day dramas of *Comedy Hour* with him. "I thought you would."

"The reviews are stupendous. Everyone's calling it an instant classic."

"Just like Salem's video?"

"Imitation is flattery!" Riaz spoke primarily in misapplied clichés. He was an otherwise very good agent, but it took a lot of self-control not to write a character based on him.

He was still talking. "And Videon finally made the offer."

The holy grail in comedy had become the Videon special. It was what everyone wanted and not everyone got. Sam had done a special very early in his career, before he'd been on *Comedy Hour*, and it had pretty much made him. They'd wanted to do another—a sort of return to form—in the early days of the pandemic, but it had fallen apart and never happened. Riaz kept saying Sam's press problems had contributed to them dragging their feet, but based on who else Videon had had on, Sam wasn't convinced. The controversy ought to have been a selling point.

"Finally. I was beginning to feel like the last mushy tomato in the bin." Because of COVID, Sam hadn't done much outside of the context of *Comedy Hour* in a while. It made him feel tetchy and too dependent on the show. Getting his own voice back might help him regain his sense of security.

Nah. There wasn't anything in the world that could do that. Sam knew he was basically fucked in that department.

"We'll finalize the details soon, but first I need you to do two things: attend an art exhibit, and do a set."

"Yes to the second; hell no to the first." Sam didn't like art. He didn't get art. He tended to walk around the gallery loudly heckling the art. Really, no one wanted him to go to a museum.

"Come on. It's on Thursday. It's a launch party for some new show of Videon's—the next great critic or some shit. There will be all sorts of Hollywood executives there."

Few words got Sam's temper up like *executive*, but everything was a business. Comedy was no different. He could say what he wanted to say, or he could have a Videon special, but he couldn't do both.

"Son of a bitch. Well, I guess I don't have a choice."

"There's a catch."

There was always a catch. "What?"

"Salem's confirmed to attend too."

"Fuck."

He didn't do movie premieres. He didn't go to the Grammys. He tried to avoid The Scene™ as much as he possibly could. And so he'd hoped he could avoid seeing Salem, oh, for forever. He didn't have hard feelings toward her. He really didn't. But he also didn't have anything to say to her.

"They're doing this on purpose, aren't they?"

"Yeah, I didn't want you to go in blind. They want you and her basically to be the entertainment."

"But in exchange, they'll give me a special?" They were presumably giving Salem something too. Material for her next album, probably.

"Yes—if you also do a set at some club a week later."

"You told them no because I am too big to audition, right?" Sam wasn't being an asshole. He really was too big to audition. Besides, it wasn't as if they didn't know what he was capable of. He wasn't exactly an unknown quantity where Videon—or anyone—was concerned. Sam was pretty much a what-you-see-is-what-you-get kind of guy.

"It's not an audition. I have the offer right here. But some billionaire is coming in from Silicon Valley, and they're trying to woo him, get him to invest. You're his favorite comedian."

Sam hated how often he heard that. While he wanted to have fans, he didn't want to have rich-asshole fans. What on earth did rich assholes find to laugh about in his sets? He needed to find and rip out the billionaire bait from his material.

"Are they going to pay for this separately?" Sam asked.

"Yup."

"What a bag of shriveled donkey testes." Sam felt like a ping-pong ball sometimes, being slapped around the table by people who didn't understand or appreciate what he did. And of course, Sam now had money and was on a big-time television show; plus he was a white man. He could only imagine how much worse the feeling of being a bottle at the mercy of an ocean current would be if he didn't have those advantages.

"I don't like it," Sam said. "I want you to tell them I don't like it. But I'll do it." He would loathe himself for it, but that was pretty much his default mode.

Riaz laughed. "Fine, but I also have some suggestions."

"Yeah?" Usually, Riaz just handled whatever messes Sam had made and dealt with money and contracts. Sam still couldn't believe he had an agent—and an assistant and a cleaning person. It made him feel like the worst kind of dirtbag. He rubbed his forehead. "What are they?"

"Don't go bringing some supermodel to the art thing. You'll look like a jerk, like you're trying to out-hot your ex."

Salem was superhot; there was no way Sam could beat her at that game, and he wouldn't even want to try. Besides, Sam didn't generally date models. That was more Gibson's bag than his.

"Go early, shake some hands, avoid your ex, and leave," Riaz said.

Which sounded great, but Sam knew he wouldn't do it. He needed a minder. "No models, got it. Can I bring a friend?"

Riaz pondered this. "Who?"

"Roxy. Or maybe Bree." If he could figure out what had happened last night, maybe he could make that ache in his chest go away, and then Bree could shield him from his ex.

"Yes, they'll keep you out of trouble."

"I mean . . . they can try." If Sam got into trouble, it certainly wouldn't be Roxy's or Bree's fault. "You said 'suggestions,' plural?"

"Yeah, don't fuck up the set."

"You said it wasn't an audition."

"It's not. But you're still coming back from this Salem thing. You got to crawl before you can run."

"I just biked for, like, forty miles."

"Figuratively."

"So I can't bring a real date, I have to avoid my ex so I don't fall back into the tabloids, and I can't screw up."

"Think you can handle it?"

"Probably not. Send me the details."

"Will do."

Sam knew he should be relieved. This was a huge thing that he'd wanted for a long time. But the first text he sent after getting off the phone was to Bree, checking in and seeing how she was doing.

CHAPTER 12

Scheduling a Second Interview: it was one of the most exciting email subject headers Bree had ever seen. Her first interview had gone great. The job really did sound perfect, everyone from the team was lovely, and they all clearly adored Ann Arbor and the firm.

Bree had slept through Sunday, and then she had canceled her work schedule on Monday—despite her protest that she couldn't cancel things, she wasn't well yet. But when she got the email from Hutchinson-Baker, she promptly emailed Jeff and Megan, who made a big show of celebrating on Slack. The whole time, Bree could only manage muted happiness. She blamed her cold, but she knew that wasn't it.

When she got off the huddle with her coworkers, she looked around her apartment. All 545 square feet of it was quiet, empty. Because Sam wasn't there.

Yes, he'd sent a delivery of soup, ginger ale, and cold meds a few hours after he'd basically run from her bed to the door, but he wasn't there to stir the bubbles out. He wasn't there to hold her. He wasn't there to tempt her to shatter the rules she'd made for herself where he was concerned.

If he'd had any interest in her, any interest at all, it would have come out the night they slept together or the next morning. Instead, he couldn't seem to run away from her fast enough. They were friends, good friends, and that was all—which was why she should tell Hutchinson-Baker yes if they made the offer. She needed to restructure her life, and she couldn't do it here.

So in the middle of perusing apartments in Ann Arbor, just to get a sense of what was out there, when Sam texted to see if she was free on Thursday to go to a museum opening, Bree did something unprecedented. She said no.

Well, technically, she said, I've got some stuff going on.

She could picture his reaction. He wouldn't be shocked; he wasn't the kind of person to assume that she was sitting around waiting for him, but he was going to ask what, and she didn't have a good answer—at least since she couldn't tell him what she was actually doing.

The point of no return was approaching, but she wasn't ready to cross it yet.

You still feeling sick? Should I send more soup?

Her problems were so much bigger than a lack of soup. Just some work stuff. That was true enough. Why are you going to a museum?

Sam and art didn't get along. He walked around saying, *I could paint that!* to everything. Once, during a particularly bad trip to the Met, he'd insisted a Mondrian was there only because it had appeared in an episode of *Sesame Street*. The guard had audibly groaned.

Some Videon thing, he replied quickly. Roxy can't come, and Salem will be there.

Damn it, Bree didn't want Sam to have to face his ex alone. She'd resolved to help him through the Salem fallout; this was part of that.

Did Videon finally come to their senses and offer you the contract? It made absolutely no sense to her that they had dragged their feet on the negotiation. One thing that could be said for Sam was that he was funny. Him doing another special for them was the biggest no-brainer in the world.

Yup. But I have to do some stupid shit for them.

Like see art?

I said it was stupid shit. (Sorry, I know you like it.)

She shouldn't do this. She should let him find someone else to keep him in line, but he was going to be livid if she moved. The only thing that could make it easier was being a good friend to him before she left.

This wasn't him sleeping on her couch and making her ache for days. It was one night. She could handle one night of hors d'oeuvres and free cocktails and art, right?

She texted him, What's the dress code?

Fancy.

Like tux fancy or suit fancy?

I don't do tux fancy.

He'd look amazing in a tux, so it was probably good for her heart that that was something he'd avoid at all costs. She couldn't be responsible for keeping herself in check if he wore a tux. Surely she'd built that escape hatch into her rules about him?

Okay, she replied. I'll make it work.

You are my savior and too good for this world.

No, I'm just trying to offset you taking care of me.

You don't have to pay me back for that.

He'd truly never think of it that way. Their friendship had never had a balance sheet. Sam might ask a lot from her—and he might give a lot to her—but he was never counting or keeping score. It was another thing she loved about him.

I'll meet you there.

Thank you, Bree.

Anytime. And wasn't that the truth?

Bree turned back to Zillow, but the pictures blurred together until she closed her eyes tight. It did hurt now. Not just that Sam wasn't with her, but that she'd had the barest taste of what it might be like if they were together—and it wasn't something he would ever want.

Bree took several deep breaths, but it didn't help. She was going to love him forever. And it was going to cleave her in two.

Monday meant another guest host, another show to write, another set of battles to fight. Sam generally felt invigorated by the grind. He absolutely hated not having something to do. He was twitchy and fidgety in the best of circumstances. When he wasn't in demand, he got himself in trouble. But he could've taken a pass on this particular week.

"Lost Boy"—both the song and the sketch—had exposed all his flaws to the world, more completely than he had managed to do. But it had also awakened something in him that just didn't seem to be going back to sleep. That was why he'd gotten all mixed up when he'd been staying with Bree. It wasn't her; it was the larger upheaval in his life.

He was all done with change and emotional turmoil and all that silly stuff, thank you very much. He wanted normalcy: guilt-free, introspection-free normalcy. Which was probably why he'd told one teeny, tiny white lie. He hadn't asked Roxy if she could go to the Videon thing with him. He'd skipped right to Bree.

He should feel bad about this. He did feel bad about this. But not bad enough not to do it.

If he was going to have to see Salem again and, equally importantly, behave himself while doing it, he wanted Bree by his side. Only she really got him. Only she really understood what upset him so bad about the whole "Lost Boy" situation. She was the person he needed.

Once Bree agreed to go to the Videon event with him, Sam went to work. He'd managed not to insult anyone while obtaining caffeine, and the cloud of paparazzi outside the studio was down to a more normal size. Things were looking up.

But in the writers' room, he came up short when he realized someone was sitting behind the very large, very fake plant in the corner. The plant's name was Larry, of course, and it had appeared in more on-air sketches than Gibson had, but that wasn't the point. People didn't normally sit *behind* Larry.

Sam set down his coffee and bag; then he took one of the roll-y chairs and moved it over to the corner next to the person who was trying to hide.

The kid—because he couldn't have been more than twenty-two, which now felt like an impossibly young age to Sam—was clutching a notebook. He had high cheekbones and a perfect jawline. Half the women and a quarter of the men on the cast were going to fall instantly in love with him.

He also looked like he was about to hurl.

Sam would've laughed, but he didn't want the guy to bolt. "This your first day?" Sam was going to feel like a butthead if he had been hiding here for weeks and Sam hadn't noticed.

"Yeah."

Sam had the sense the guy didn't want to be noticed and would rather turn into a ghost complete with clanking chains than have a conversation, but, well, it wasn't going to get any easier once the rest of the circus showed up. Sam could at least try to break down the guy's discomfort before fifty other people appeared.

"I wasn't sure what the seating arrangement was. I started up there, but I kept moving back and back . . ."

That sounded like Bree at age five. While Sam had never been shy a day in his life, knowing Bree helped him understand that not everyone went through life wanting everyone to look at them at every moment of every day.

Different strokes, different folks, and all that.

"I'm Sam Leyland."

The kid's eyes went round and wide as bagels. "I, um, know. I'm Marc. Marc O'Moore."

"Welcome to *Comedy Hour*. How long you been sitting here?"

If Marc's expression had been embarrassed before, it was downright mortified now. "Two hours."

"Because they didn't tell you when the call was, and you thought this was a normal workplace and things probably started at nine?"

Marc grimaced.

That was actually something of a rite of passage, whether by plan or accident, and Sam hated it. It had always felt like a fuckboy move to Sam. If you knew you were good, then you didn't have to kick other people in the chin to make your point about how the show was cool and newbies were going to have to pay their dues here. It made him want to stomp down to Jane's office to yell at her, but, well, she probably wasn't in yet.

"It happens all the time," Sam assured Marc. "Jane has a—unique management style. Let me tell you how things really work around here. We're lucky to get started by noon on Monday, or really any day. The host is generally obnoxious and needs their ass kissed. The same goes double for Jane. You're a writer, right?"

Marc clearly didn't have the personality to be on camera, despite having the looks for it, and almost no one joined the cast midseason anyhow.

"Yeah."

"So you'll need to think about who you want to write for and with so you can get some stuff on the air and build your portfolio."

"I didn't—I mean, I just figured I'd keep my mouth shut and get the lay of the land."

"You could do that, sure, or we could write something together, and you could have a sketch on the air this week."

Marc seemed on the edge of a coronary event of some kind. Sam would have sworn he could see the guy's pulse going up, and he hadn't seemed exactly Zen to start.

"W-w-why?" he finally managed to stammer out.

To make a point to Jane. But Sam wasn't going to explain the politics of the show more than he had. He didn't want to scare Marc, and the guy ought to have a chance to decide what he thought of everyone without having to hack through Sam's forest of resentments, biases, and grudges. He should have a chance to decide he hated Alan all on his own—the way apparently everyone and God intended.

"Well, we're the only ones here. We should write something." Sam gestured to the notebook Marc had clutched to his chest. "What do you got?"

He fumbled with it for a minute before opening the cover and flipping through a few pages. This seemed to calm him, made him sit up a little straighter. "So there are these aliens," he finally started.

"Uh-huh."

"And when they land, they're like, 'Take us to your leader.' Everyone's like, 'No, take us to your planet.'"

Aliens were classic on *Comedy Hour* thanks to a couple of famous sketches from the show's early years. It made sense for Marc to start on well-trod ground to see if he could do something original.

"Great, let's write it."

For the next twenty minutes, Sam and Marc bounced ideas back and forth until they had several pages of a sketch roughly written. Sam would never say it to Marc, but he didn't love it. It was fine, but not brilliant, not hysterical. But here was the thing: while lots of people thought the secret to success was raw talent, raw funniness (however you measured that), Sam knew something could be funny enough and work. He'd done many okay sketches on the air, and he'd thrown plenty of legitimately good material in the trash. Those were the breaks.

Marc could pitch this and not get laughed out of the room. He'd nail it later.

"Can we move up to the table now?" Sam asked. "My neck is killing me."

Marc gave him a sheepish smile. "The plant was a bad idea."

"Under the table would've been worse. Come here. Roxy and I generally take this corner."

By the time Roxy showed up, Sam and Marc had written the skeleton of three different pieces, one of which was actually good. Sam had explained that his theory of *Comedy Hour* was to find the biggest asshole on the front of the *Times* every Monday and make them the center of the show.

"Who's this?" Roxy tossed her bag on the floor and slid into the chair next to Sam.

"This is Marc. He's new. Read her the one about the *Is It Meat Loaf?* show."

As soon as Jane showed up, Marc went silent as a statue, but Sam was confident in a few weeks, he'd be slugging with the rest of them.

"Which one is the best?" Sam whispered to Marc as the pitch meeting got underway.

"Um, the meat loaf one."

Which is exactly what Sam had thought. Marc was talented.

"Who else has something?" Jane called.

Sam clapped a hand on Marc's shoulder. "Marc and I do. Everyone, this is Marc O'Moore." Because no one had bothered to introduce him. "You want to pitch it?"

Marc shook his head so sharply, it looked as if it might rip from his shoulders.

Not wanting to push him any further on his first day, Sam picked up his notebook. "Okay, so there's a new hit game show: *Is It Meat Loaf?* Except unlike *Is It Cake?*, it's very obvious what is meat loaf."

"Who's appearing?" Jane asked.

"A Paleo guy, a vegan, and then Meat Loaf, joining from the great beyond."

Sam finished the pitch. As he had expected, Jane approved it, and the meeting ground on.

When they were breaking up, Jane signaled to him. "I'd like to see you, Samuel."

He wanted to close his fingers in a folding chair. Damn it, he hadn't even yelled at anyone today. He'd been *nice*. Why was Jane calling him in?

Roxy chuckled. "What did you do now?"

"I swear to Whitney Houston, I don't know."

But when he marched into Jane's office, nothing could have prepared him for what she said: "Good job."

"I . . . there's some sort of problem in my brain, clearly. Because what I just heard was a compliment."

"That's because it was. Good job."

"With . . . ?" Honestly, Sam didn't like compliments, but he liked them even less when he didn't understand them. He hadn't done anything Jane should be complimenting him for. It made Sam want to vibrate out of his skin.

"Marc. He's talented, but I wasn't sure he'd be a good fit. I'm glad you're writing with him."

Which wasn't the point at all. Sam was doing his job—which was more than he could say for whoever hadn't bothered to tell Marc when to show up.

He wished for a rabbit's foot under his breath before launching into a tirade. "First of all, I can tell he's talented, but why didn't someone give him the information he needed to succeed, like an honest call time and an introduction? Second of all, why wasn't that someone Dennis?" Dennis Drummond was the head writer, and integrating Marc into the show was far more his job than it was Sam's.

Jane's eyes lit with mirth. She looked more amused now than she had at any point during the pitch meeting. "Are you giving me management advice?"

"No." Yes. "I would've thought you'd want Marc and any junior writers to stay far away from me." Really, he would have thought Jane would have wanted to keep everyone in the Western Hemisphere away from Sam.

"I don't think you know what you mean to these kids. They want to be you."

If that was true, it was because they only saw Sam's outward success. They'd never pondered what it would be like to have a horde of paparazzi outside your apartment or seemingly 10 percent of the people on earth debating your flaws, thanks to your ex. If Sam had known— well, he probably would have taken it anyway. But that was only because he came from complete crap and he fully expected to return to it someday. "God help them."

"My observation is that he doesn't often," Jane said, "but your encouragement is priceless."

"Or worthless. But that still doesn't answer why Dennis didn't tell the kid when to show or introduce him."

Jane's brows arched. "I told Dennis to knock that crap off. I'll make sure the message gets through."

"Well—good." Though honestly Jane's leadership wasn't very strong if a repeat lecture was necessary. Except, of course, that Sam always required repeat lectures.

"I didn't realize you noticed or cared, Sam."

"That is the most insulting thing you've ever said to me." Actually, he was going to have to flip through his mental index of insulting Jane comments, because she'd taken any number of shots at him . . . most of which had been well deserved.

"You're full of surprises. But that's not why I called you back. I had an interesting conversation with Videon this morning. I'm glad you worked it out."

Sam didn't know why she would care about that, but he guessed it was good for the show when the current cast members got outside publicity.

He shrugged. "They were dragging their feet."

"Because they thought you might take a pilot."

Hmm. Even Riaz hadn't known, or at least hadn't shared, that. "Sitcoms don't really appeal to me." That was a lie: sitcoms didn't appeal to him *at all*.

"You have to think about what you're going to do next."

"You trying to push me out the door?" If so, he felt a little miffed. Strike that, he felt a lot miffed.

"No, the opposite. You're either going to wreck your career because you have no discipline, or you're going to be the biggest comedian on earth."

Honestly, either outcome sounded awful, but Sam had no doubt which door he'd be going through.

He shifted in his seat. "I don't know what to say." Which was rare.

"You have to figure out what your goal is. I can tell you aren't sure where to go; maybe that's why you're flailing. But your agent ought to be having these conversations with you."

"Why are you?" he asked.

"It's good for the show."

"Bullshit." But he said it without any heat. "Just be careful, or else I'll think you care about what happens to me."

"We couldn't have that."

He snorted; then he considered what Jane was asking. He had no clue what he wanted to do next. It had always seemed impossible that he could plan his future, because he'd never expected to have one. He had expected to burn up like a meteorite in the atmosphere. No one ever asked a meteorite what it wanted to be when it grew up.

But he'd managed to make it work here for years, despite his antics and self-destructive episodes. He'd yelled at some fans in a coffee shop and become a national laughingstock, for crying out loud, and he still had a job. Maybe his flameout didn't have to be inevitable.

Which was enough to make him chuckle. He tried to turn it into a cough, but Jane didn't buy it. She gave him a look as if to say, *I'm serious.*

"I don't know," he told her.

"That's obvious." She turned back to her computer, ending the meeting. "But think about what I said. You need some firm plans."

Maybe for the first time, he did.

CHAPTER 13

Sam tugged at his collar. God, he hated this shit. The fancy clothes and the terrible food and the snotty, insincere people. He hated how they expected him to be funny on command—and he hated that he often didn't succeed because the entire situation stopped him up like an episode of constipation.

Bree, though—she looked nice. She insisted she was totally recovered from her cold. She'd pulled her hair into some kind of low bun thing that showed off her neck, and she had on a slinky black dress that clung to all the parts of her he wasn't supposed to be thinking about. He couldn't remember the last time he'd seen her outside of PJs and casual clothes, and it made him feel like an ass that he didn't take her to nice restaurants more.

"You're doing fine," Bree muttered as they walked away from an incredibly uncomfortable conversation with some socialite he didn't know who had kept telling him, *You'll get past it.*

Maybe I won't, he'd wanted to shout at the woman. She didn't know him. She didn't know what he was and wasn't capable of.

Besides, did anyone really get past global cultural humiliation? He should have Riaz reach out to some of those main characters on the internet who stepped in it and then got (deservedly) mocked and ask.

"There's no way for it to be fine until it's over," Sam said to Bree. "Can we leave now, or—"

"Not until you say hi to the people from Videon."

"Where are they?"

"No idea."

A guy in an expensive suit stepped into view, as if they had summoned him. "Samuel Leyland?"

Sam tried to decide what would happen if he pretended that wasn't him—oh, he was going to write that up as a sketch. "That's me," he admitted.

"It's great to meet you. I'm Larry Gomez. I'm a vice president at Videon." They were all vice presidents.

"Hi . . . Larry." This was why Sam tried to avoid these things. "This is my friend, Bryony Edwards."

"I like that name. Bryony," Larry said as he shook her hand.

"My mom heard it on *Lifestyles of the Rich and Famous*." Which was 100 percent true and not something Bree normally admitted to people. There weren't a lot of folks at events like these who'd grown up watching Robin Leach.

Larry seemed to have no idea how to respond and only said, "I'm glad you both could be here."

You basically strong-armed me into it, Sam almost said.

Next to him, he could feel Bree go tense. She'd realized he was about to blurt out something impolitic. She quickly interjected. "My pleasure. I wanted to see the new exhibit."

"I love de Stijl," Larry agreed.

Sam could only blink at the shocking revelation that this was a type of art and not just the name of a White Stripes album.

"So are there people you want me to meet, or—" Sam didn't say, *Can I get out of here*, but he implied it.

"We don't like to structure the evening," Larry explained. "We just like to put all the components in place and watch what happens."

"Much like your approach to programming."

Bree pinched the underside of Sam's arm. She wasn't gentle about it either. "I guess we'd better mingle, then," she said. "Thank you for inviting Sam."

"Anytime."

As they walked away, Sam muttered, "Yes, we better go mingle. The rest of those Videon execs won't kiss their own asses."

Bree grabbed his arm and whispered in his ear, "Don't bite the hand that feeds you."

Her breath on his cheek and her body pressed close to his reminded him a little too much of her sleeping on his chest. Somehow, they'd been friends for more than twenty-five years without him realizing Bree gave the best cuddle on earth. Just . . . perfect.

Which he needed to stop remembering in order to get things between them back to normal.

He pushed his thoughts to something cool and rational. "Let's get food."

"Must we?" Bree regarded the buffet skeptically.

It was pure fucking privilege to be able to turn your nose up at free food, but the food at these things tended to blow. He had a stark memory of the day when he'd given himself permission not to eat things he didn't like, and the ways he'd teased Bree into doing the same.

It had been terrifying to explore foods outside of pizza and burgers, to spend money on things you might not be able to stomach. But he also remembered the joy, sparkling like glitter in his veins, when he'd first taken Bree to the city's best dim sum restaurant, and she'd lit up like a Lite-Brite.

"We're totally picking up dumplings later," he assured her.

"This is why I love you." As soon as she said it, her eyes went wide, like a deer's right before you plowed into it on the highway.

Bree had said she loved him a million times, and he'd said it back as often. He did love her. What was the problem?

Before he could ask, she hurried away from him and grabbed a little plate. Still chewing on her stricken expression, he could only follow.

It was a good thing Bree might be moving across the country soon, because her ability to maintain a steely facade around Sam was cracking like an eggshell. The truth was about to leak out from between her fingers like a gooey, viscous egg white.

Even now, as they were finishing their inevitably disappointing snacks in a room completely filled with an exhibit of pastel-colored jars of various sizes, she'd nearly broken. When Sam asked casually, "Back there, what had you spooked?" she'd almost shouted back, *I said I love you, but that throwaway line seemed really fraught because it turns out that I really do love you.*

How she'd managed to keep this to herself for almost eighteen years was a mystery. She wasn't going to make it eighteen more minutes.

But in continuing to keep the secret, she got an assist from the strangest place of all: Salem walked by the doorway of the gallery, dressed in silver and shining like an angel tree topper.

In Bree's admittedly limited experience, famous people seemed to attract light more than normal people. Salem was glowing. It was the sparkles on her dress and her blonde hair and her jewelry, but it was also her warmth. Her beauty.

Bree felt so shabby, the Dollar Store knockoff brand.

She really didn't want to see Sam's first reunion with his ex-fiancée, which would be painful for him to experience and for her to witness. But she extra especially didn't want to give Videon the coup of the Sam Leyland and Salem reunion. While Bree was here to try to make that moment go more smoothly, it suddenly seemed imperative that it not occur at all.

"Salem," Bree hissed at Sam by way of explanation. She grabbed his sleeve and towed him past the frankly unnerving number of jars in the installation and out the door on the other side.

They shoved their plates at a passing waiter and hustled through one room that was heaped with white paper being churned out by printers attached to the ceiling, and through another gallery where the frames were sculpted and painted and adorned, but the space they surrounded was blank.

An impossibly well-dressed couple—seriously, those were the two best tailored suits Bree had ever seen—watched them fly through the gallery with evident amusement.

"No one told me there was a *Bande à part* remake tonight," the first man said.

"I've always been more of a Truffaut type," Sam called back, which made the guy's husband rock with laughter.

"What was that about?" Bree asked.

"Some arty French cinema shit."

"Of course." The thing about Sam was that he followed everything, had an opinion about everything. He might act as if he didn't understand art, but you couldn't write topical comedy every week for an audience of millions if you weren't smart and a voracious consumer of culture.

"What are we looking for?" Sam asked congenially as Bree tugged him through yet another gallery.

"This." It was a door marked EMPLOYEES ONLY. She wrenched it open, and they ducked inside what appeared to be a dark, dusty service hallway.

Sam leaned against the door with a chuckle. "I'm amazed an alarm didn't go off. That would've been the opposite of low profile."

"You don't sound annoyed at the possibility."

"I have to see her sometime."

Sure, but it should be on his own terms, which Bree started to say, except Sam interrupted her.

"Don't get me wrong, I appreciate the gesture, but what do you think I was gonna do, Smoosh? Yell at her?" A beat passed. "Okay, so that sounds like me. I wasn't, though. I swear."

"No, I—" Bree hadn't let go of his sleeve, and his wrist was warm against the backs of her fingers. She flexed, catching his hair against her nails. It felt explicit. Intimate.

It was so dark in the room. All there was in the world was Sam's mouth, amused and wine colored. And the pounding of her heart: there was also that. The insistent drumming reminded her she'd been carrying these feelings for so long, and she was too weak to keep up the effort much longer.

She tried to raise her eyes to his, to make some kind of joke, to—for God's sake—let go of his sleeve. But she couldn't.

She was trapped in this moment, trapped in the tractor beam of her attraction to him and the short amount of time she might have left to be near him. There was almost no sand left in the hourglass. Each grain that fell brought Bree closer to the moment when she would have to tell him.

"Bree," Sam whispered, and she finally managed to look up from his mouth. "Why were you upset earlier?"

Gently, so infinitesimally gently, he raised his hand and set it against her neck. Bree's hand fell, her fingertips tracing the length of his jacket.

Her dress—some practical black thing she'd bought for project openings—had a wide boatneck, and Sam's hand was against more of her skin than the fabric. The weight of him, the warmth of him, was like an anchor, pulling her down into this moment.

He had to feel how her pulse was going, and he had to know it wasn't from their dash across the museum. He had to know that it was him. He had to.

But the gap between what she thought Sam must know and what Sam acted like he knew was as wide as New York Harbor.

"I . . ." She licked her lips and resettled so she was facing him fully. Sam's fingertips dragged across her nape, and it took a substantial amount of self-control not to moan. "We've known each other awhile."

"Uh-huh."

"You're my closest friend in the world."

"Uh-huh." For once, he wasn't making a joke. He was watching her intently, as if he were going to imitate her for a sketch later. It was the kind of close scrutiny that made her think wild thoughts, as if maybe he wasn't going to bolt the second she told him the truth.

That was a delusion. She knew it was a delusion. But when she had all Sam's attention, when the world was still and dark, sometimes she almost convinced herself.

He shifted, bringing them closer. There was just him now. He took up her entire plane of vision, but then, he usually did.

"I'd fall apart without you," he whispered. "You know that."

"And so would I." *So will I, when I leave.* "I just—"

"Whatever it is, Smoosh, tell me. We'll figure it out."

Bree pressed her eyes closed. She couldn't meet the earnestness in his face any longer, not when she knew he believed what he was saying, but that it was impossible. They could get through anything except her loving him.

"What if we can't?" she asked, sounding about ten years old.

"We will." His fingers flexed, just once, against her neck, and all her soft places pulsed in response. He might not know it, but his sway over her body was total.

She managed to open her eyes, to face him, but it was a mistake. The way he was looking at her, it was as if he were seeing her for the first time. Something stole over Bree, something suspiciously like the feeling they were about to kiss. It had all the surprise and anticipation that moment always had, but this one had been aged in oak like bourbon from all the times Bree had wanted to believe it and it hadn't come true.

This time was five hundred times more intoxicating, and five hundred times more scary, than any moment like this Bree had ever been in.

They couldn't. They shouldn't. They were going to.

"Bree."

She was rocking up onto her toes, and his other hand was clutching her waist, and she was in his arms—

The door smacked into them.

"Oof." Bree bounced away from Sam, which was good. It was good. She was almost certain it was good.

A server pushing a cart, which sounded as if it was loaded with dishes, regarded them skeptically. "Were you making out in here?"

Nearly. No, not nearly.

"We're hiding from his ex," she explained.

"You're Sam Leyland?" the guy asked.

For the first time in maybe his entire life, Sam was speechless. His hand was over his mouth, and Bree couldn't judge his mood. What was he thinking? Had he felt that moment too?

Of course not.

She tried not to be deflated, but she couldn't manage anything beyond not sobbing. She was so stupid.

Bree pushed past the server. "Sorry about that." And without looking at Sam, she said, "I'm going to the restroom. Can you get my coat?" She shuffled in her purse and found the claim slip by touch. She shoved it at him, and his fingers didn't meet hers when he took it. "I'll meet you by the door."

She needed a minute.

"Bree."

Her name came from the seating area off the women's bathroom, because this museum was swanky enough to have a seating area off the bathroom.

Bree knew instantly who it was, because no one else on earth had that accent. Salem's voice carried the air of London, but it wasn't like the queen's. It had the vibe of some impossibly cool, cosmopolitan, but not-at-all-stuffy neighborhood that Bree would love and never fit into. Like her music, Salem was a fascinating blend of retro and cutting edge, and Bree hated herself for being jealous of Salem rather than being able to love her, like everyone else did.

Salem looked, in a word, amazing. Somehow her blonde bob was stylish and edgy, whereas the same cut would have made Bree resemble a second-grade teacher. It was probably the expertly applied makeup—what appeared to be a literal ton of winged jet-black eyeliner—and the skull and crossbones diamond earrings. She was wearing a silver sparkly minidress that hugged her generous curves perfectly, as if it had been made for her. It likely had been, because when you were the biggest pop star in the world, everything you wore was probably bespoke and cost more than Bree's rent.

Bree tried to smile, but she felt so stiff and awkward, she couldn't pull it off. Her cheek muscles might have perished from embarrassment. "Oh—oh, hi," she stammered. "I didn't see you there. How are you?" She nodded at the women with Salem. Whether they were friends or assistants, Bree had never known, but they were giving Bree the stink eye.

Which was probably fair. Bree had never, ever been rude to Salem, but she had been cold.

"Oh, grand." Salem had the number one single all over the world, everyone loved the video, and she had gotten in the last word on her failed engagement: What was there to not be grand about?

The part where all that hurt her ex, sure, but Bree certainly wouldn't blame Salem if that was part of the attraction. She'd never struck Bree as vindictive, but wanting to tell your ex what you really thought of them was human nature.

"Good." Good for Salem, at any rate. After a beat, Bree added, "It's a nice party." Maybe they could small talk themselves out of the awkwardness of this encounter.

But then Salem said, "Except for trying to avoid Sam."

Bree let go of a rush of breath. While it was almost certainly true, it was a lot to say aloud. Then again, the lyrics of "Lost Boy" showed that Salem had no problem saying, or singing, uncomfortable stuff.

It would've been doubly awkward if Salem knew Bree had almost kissed Sam. That five minutes earlier, she'd been in his arms.

Jesus. That had been a close call.

"I'm so sorry. I've been trying to keep him away from you"—oh God, talk about unintentionally blurting out the truth—"but it's not a huge place."

Salem genuinely seemed okay and unbothered. At Bree's stammering, she laughed warmly and asked, "How is he?" Which she actually seemed to mean. She was almost supernaturally cool.

How should Bree answer, though? *Actually, he's pissed and uncomfortable because you know him so well, but that can't surprise you because did I mention that you know him so well?*

Because Bree was *not* supernaturally cool, she said instead, "Um, as well as he can be."

"Was he mad about the song?"

"You should probably ask him."

"He wouldn't tell me the truth even if we were speaking."

Sam had put Salem on a pedestal. If anything, that had doomed their relationship. Sam treated romance as something outside of and apart from his life. For all that he had terrible luck in love, he did love *love*. Sam would throw a hissy fit big enough to put his pouting over Roxy's sketch to shame if anyone suggested it, but he was a romantic. Until he could treat his partners as people and share himself—his real self—with them, he was going to keep getting dumped, though.

Maybe he'd spawn an entire subgenre of pop breakup songs.

Bree had no idea how to answer Salem. She wanted to be honest, but she didn't want to betray Sam's trust. "He thought . . . it was annoyingly catchy. And it is. I mean, it's not annoying, but it is catchy."

Salem was watching Bree with a disconcerting closeness. "Were *you* mad about the song?"

"I . . . it's not my place to be mad about it."

"Isn't it?" While Bree gaped, Salem gave her friends—assistants, posse—a look. "Give us a second." When they crossed to the other side of the space, whispering to each other and looking daggers at Bree, Salem leaned forward. "I'm sorry we weren't friends."

When they had hung out, Bree knew she'd been distant because of pettiness, jealousy, and a million things Bree was ashamed she'd felt. "Me too."

"I really liked Sam."

"I know. When things didn't work out—" What was Bree going to say? That she had been sorry? That wasn't true. "He needs someone, more than he knows."

Even if it hadn't been Salem in the end, it would be someone. Bree was going to have to accept that. If Sam was going to be happy, it was going to be because he'd found someone to love. Someone he could channel his caretaking impulses—because he did have them—into, and someone who would take care of him in return.

This was why Bree needed to move to Michigan. She wanted that for him, she did, but it was going to hurt too much to see it happen every day, especially when, deep down, she wanted and needed the same thing.

"He has someone," Salem said. "You have to know he's in love with you."

Salem thought . . . she actually thought that Sam might have romantic feelings for Bree?

Bree almost yelped with laughter. When she'd wrestled that impulse inside, she could only blink and search for some way, any way, to respond. But there wasn't one. In the whole of the English language, there were no possible words for this situation, for the silliness and absurdness of Salem, Sam's ex-fiancée and the chronicler of twenty-first-century women's heartbreak and drama, thinking Sam might be in love with Bree.

After a long pause—a long, long pause—Bree said carefully, "He's really not." She almost succeeded in keeping her voice even. But what Salem had said had her trembling like the last dried-out leaf on an oak tree in October.

It wasn't possible.

Salem's eyes crinkled with generosity and kindness. "Bree, love, Sam could never have married me, he could never marry anyone, until he can face the truth. Anyone else he might try with, they'll never click because they aren't you."

Bree wanted to wipe her eyes, and she wanted to sit on the floor, and she wanted to slap her hands over her ears. It was just too much. Too damn much.

"I only wish that were true." Admitting it made Bree feel so, so exposed. She never said anything about how she felt about Sam to anyone. It was like shouting your bank account password out on the subway. Too risky. Stupid even.

But Salem only nodded, with so much understanding in her beautiful face. "Then it's good that it is."

Bree did rub her eyes then, because they were filling with all the feelings she'd kept inside for twenty years. They were rushing out into the world through her tear ducts because Bree had finally acknowledged them, had spoken them almost into being. They had been amorphous and abstract. Now, they were real.

The truth was so . . . watery.

Bree managed to wrestle herself into something like controlled, and she said to Salem, "Whatever Sam might feel, it would never, never work. There's some off-ramp to romance, and we missed it, like, decades ago. I can't risk backtracking. He's too important to me."

"This is why we have roundabouts." And that was why Salem was famous for her clever lyrics and songwriting.

"I have to say: I never tried to undermine you. I really wanted things to work out for you and Sam. I know that's probably hard to believe, but—"

"No, I know that too."

After a couple of deep breaths, digging through her purse for a tissue, and drying her eyes, Bree added, "I'm sorry." She wasn't even certain what she was apologizing for, but she definitely felt as if she'd messed up.

She couldn't believe what Salem was saying, but Bree wanted to, which made her feel like a snake in the grass. She hated it.

"I'm not." Salem shook her head matter-of-factly. "It was nice to pretend with him for a while, but that was all it was ever going to be."

This entire conversation was as if gravity itself had stopped working for an instant and then slammed back into place. Everything inside Bree had floated up for one amazing moment and then dropped back down.

Salem couldn't be right. She couldn't be. But even if she was . . . even if maybe at some level, Sam might have feelings for Bree that weren't strictly platonic, if maybe sometimes he wondered—like she did—whether their friendship might have additional dimensions, it would still be a terrible idea because Sam broke things. He broke jobs, and he broke people, and he broke relationships. The only thing he hadn't broken was their friendship.

If Bree told him how she felt, and if somehow, possibly, Sam felt the same way, what could the ending possibly look like except for heartbreak?

She could love him forever and be his friend. She'd been doing it for so long that the prospect, while it hurt, didn't scare her.

A life without Sam? That terrified her.

It was why she'd stayed quiet all these years.

Bree blotted her eyes one more time and then tossed the tissue into the nearest trash can. It swooped through the rim in a perfect arc.

The storm of emotion having passed, Bree was able to set her shoulders and look at Salem, who was watching her curiously. "I hope you're okay," Bree said, meaning it.

"Ah, me. Heartbreak is a thing I know well."

Wasn't that true for both of them?

"It's good for material, I guess," Bree said.

"That it is. But as long as I'm still hoping next time will be *the* time, you know, it's not all bad."

Yes, Bree understood that very well. That was why she needed to get to Michigan, where she could heal her heart and get back to some hoping of her own.

"It was good to see you." It had also been earth shattering, but she left that part out. "I should probably find Sam and get him out of here before he slaps a Videon bigwig with a glove or something."

Salem laughed. "You're very good to him."

But as Bree left the women's room, she wondered whether that was true.

CHAPTER 14

"We hope you'll strongly consider it."

Um, of course. But Bree managed to find a few more seconds of poised professionalism in herself, and she instead said, "I will. Can I take a few weeks to decide?"

Because while it was gratifying to be offered your dream job, while she knew she had to leave New York, Bree was still a cautious person. There were logistics to consider, plans to make, and disasters to catalog and guard against. Intellectually, she knew what she should do, but she needed to prepare her heart for the leap.

Sam, on the other hand, would've already jumped in with both feet, never pausing to digest the possibilities or to deal with the details or to make a backup plan to protect himself. Thinking about him hurt. Hurt even more than normal.

"Take all the time you need."

The people at Hutchinson-Baker certainly had approached everything about the interviews and offer with a single-minded determination that made Bree feel like the most competent person in the world, because they wanted her to join their firm so badly. She could get used to feeling like that.

"We'd like you to start after the first of the year."

That was seven weeks and a few days away. She could have one last Thanksgiving and Christmas in New York before moving halfway across the country.

"I'll get back to you soon." She hung up and set her phone on her desk.

It had been four days since the museum. Four days since Salem had suggested Sam might love Bree, and since that moment in the employees' hallway when it had seemed as if everything Bree had kept to herself for decades had been about to spill out.

Bree hadn't talked to Sam since then, though she was supposed to go to his mini Videon set in a few days. She ought to tell him about Michigan. She ought to tell him everything.

Or she ought to pull back totally. Begin the slow and likely painful process of ripping him out of her life.

"Hey, you're still around!" Megan was leaning out of her office with a set of architectural plans in one hand. "I thought you left hours ago."

Most of the rest of the office had. Bree and Megan were the only ones still there.

"I had to wrap up some things—and I had a call."

Megan stared hard at Bree for a second. "Did Hutchinson-Baker make you an offer?"

"Yes."

"Huzzah!" Megan thrust the plans into the air. In addition to *Severance*, she also loved *The Great*, and it wasn't only because she resembled Elle Fanning. She, too, would be good at planning a coup. "Congratulations! I'm not surprised, but I am delighted. Except, oh shit, we're going to need an army to replace you."

"Not an army." Bree had already made notes for a memo about her duties and begun drafting some job ads. It was good to think ahead, right?

Megan was going to need one senior person and one junior person to replace Bree. It should've been scary, knowing that Bree had essentially been doing the work of two people, but instead, it was validating. She hadn't been losing her mind: she truly was that busy all the time.

"I'm trying to compliment you." Megan's expression was wry and well practiced. This was a conversation they'd had many times.

"I don't trust compliments." Words could be empty and usually were—*thanks for that lesson, Mom.*

No, Bree only trusted actions. Megan had proved she adored Bree because she'd hired her, supported her, and cheerled while Bree had explored opportunities beyond Innovation X. That was how Bree knew Megan cared about her.

"Well, since you're going to be managing a big team in Michigan, you'll need to figure out how to motivate folks for whom that is the professional love language."

"If I do, I plan on investing in an industrial volume of finger traps."

Megan snorted. "You're going to take this job, right?"

"It'd be foolish not to."

"Which isn't yes."

Megan knew her well. Bree did have trouble making decisions. It was one thing to want things you couldn't have; it was entirely another to use whatever small measure of power you'd built up. What if you chose wrong? What if it all blew up in your face?

"How do you know if you're doing the right thing?" Bree asked.

Of everyone Bree knew, Megan had the best decision-making track record. At Innovation X, in her marriage, heck, with her wardrobe, Megan always seemed to make the right choice, and relatively painlessly. How did she manage it?

Megan held up a finger, set the plans in her office, and then returned. She sat down in Jeff's chair and fluffed her blonde hair. "You don't," she finally said in answer to Bree's question. "Not at the time. *Right* and *wrong* are labels you apply after the fact, and they're lies half the time anyway. You don't know what would've happened if you'd taken the other path, and you don't know if you've chosen wisely. That Robert Frost guy was a liar."

"I think that's the point of the poem. It's ironic." Or at least that was what Bree's literature professor had insisted.

"Whatever. My point is, as you live your life, you're making a map, but other than your path, the rest is all a blur. All you can do is say how the path you took made you *feel*. A wrong turn that teaches you something wasn't wrong, you know?"

Bree knew that on the one hand, she'd had incredible success. Getting to college, finishing college, moving to the big city—those were all triumphs. But since then, she'd stagnated, personally and professionally. Maybe she'd used up her store of risk. Or maybe she'd allowed her feelings for Sam to anchor her too long.

"My map would be . . . small. I've spent a lot of time standing still."

"You've already started working on a list for me, haven't you? Your projects, responsibilities, and all that jazz?"

"Yes." Bree was nothing if not predictable.

"Don't you think that says otherwise? Think about the people whose lives are better because of what you've done here."

"If I'd left years ago, you would've hired someone else. Those improvements would still have happened."

"It's as if you're determined to belittle yourself."

"No," Bree said quickly. "But I'm realistic. And . . . I guess I also mean my map is small for reasons beyond just the job. I mean, look at you! You're married. You have kids." Bree hadn't gotten anywhere close to those things, and she did want them.

"Can I interest you in one of them?" Megan asked. "I'll give you your pick. And I'm including Jack in that list."

Jack was cute, but still. "You know what I mean."

Megan's expression softened. "I do. Look, it's none of my business—"

"I'm pretty sure I'm making it your business."

"—but you have worked your ass off. You're always up for taking a meeting on the weekend, for picking up a project from your colleague on paternity leave, and for doing that extra research. You have two things in your life: this job and Sam."

All the way back at OSU, Megan had always made her skepticism of Sam clear in the kindest, firmest way. In some ways, she was Sam's mirror image. They were, the both of them, very defensive of Bree. It was like having two diametrically opposed guard dogs.

Bree could feel herself bristling in defense of him, but wasn't Megan's point something Bree agreed with? Why did Bree want to fight Megan for making *her own* point?

"Is it that obvious?" she asked instead.

Megan nodded emphatically, and Bree could feel herself turning stewed-tomato red. It was so embarrassing to know that everyone had been pitying her for years.

"Like I said, it's none of my business. But you going? It's good for the job, and it's good for the other thing."

Bree stuck out her lower lip. "He's not going to see it that way."

"Then fuck him. I'm serious. Look, he seems like . . . I was going to say a nice guy, but that's not true, is it? He's not that simple. I know you think I dislike him, but that's not it. I don't like how he tethers you. But I know—everyone knows—he cares about you. If he can't see that this is good for you . . ."

"I know."

He *would* see it eventually, but getting there was going to be awful. This news was going to take what she and Sam had, everything they had shared, and run it through a meat grinder. Who knew what would be left afterward?

A few seconds passed. Megan played with her wedding ring. "I never thought I was going to get married. No one was more surprised than I was."

This was true. Megan hadn't fallen in love so much as she had been ambushed by it. It had been amazing to watch—and nothing had ever made Bree so jealous in her entire life. She wasn't jealous of Jack but, instead, of watching someone find their equal and perfect match and having it be reciprocated. Goddamn, but she wanted that.

"I'm not going to say it's the fulfillment of my life or that I wouldn't be complete without it," Megan said, "because I was plenty complete before I met Jack. But where my map led me, it wasn't where I thought I was headed. And I was glad to be wrong."

When Bree looked at her colleagues, she saw that their ambition, their fearlessness, came out of their privilege. Out of the fact they had safety nets, from family and money, that Bree had never had. Maybe that was part of why she'd been satisfied for so long. But it was time to crawl forward this little bit.

"You know when you're on a badly designed freeway, and you can see where you want to go, but there's no obvious way to get there? That's been my life for the last decade."

"But, Bree, you recognize that, and so you have the power to change it. That's most of the struggle. You are very reasonably finding a new destination now."

"I'm trying to, anyhow."

"I think it's brave," Megan insisted.

Bree wanted so badly to believe that. But because she was her, she could put that label into reverse and see the opposite possibility as well. "Unless I'm running away."

"Just keep your eyes ahead of you," Megan said, "and you'll find something worth trying for."

Bree could only hope that would be true.

CHAPTER 15

Bree was late.

Sam had absolutely no idea why he cared, except if she didn't get there before he was supposed to go onstage, her absence would . . . distract him. Fucking ridiculous. He was trying to act nonchalant, to be nonchalant, but his drumming on the makeup counter in the greenroom of the comedy club was increasingly frantic. He was starting to annoy even himself.

"Was she taking the subway?" Roxy asked. "I can check for delays."

"I'm not sure. It's . . . fine." Except he was clearly about to climb out of his skin.

Roxy seemed to attribute this to nerves, not Bree's tardiness. "Hmm. When's the last time you did stand-up? You're looking a little green."

The answer was the weekend in Vegas when he and Salem had gotten engaged—and then, he'd been too infatuated to be nervous—not that he was nervous now. "It's been a while."

"Look, it's a bunch of rich people, the easiest audience in the world. They always want to believe whatever they've paid for is the best money can buy. You could do your set from fifteen years ago, and they'd be enraptured."

Sam wasn't actually worried about the set at all, but he didn't swallow what Roxy had just said. "This guy's supposed to be my biggest fan—"

"So he'd appreciate hearing the classics."

Sam had never met him, but Michal Blaese seemed to have a different edge to him than most billionaires, far more poisonous. Sam didn't like any bit of this, and he wanted to get it over with as soon as possible. As soon as Bree showed up, anyhow.

"Are you sure you're okay? You've been off all week. Did something happen at the museum?" Roxy asked.

Sam *had* been pretty damn twitchy since that stupid museum thing a week earlier. He couldn't seem to stop thinking about that moment with Bree, her waist under his hand, her eyes on his, the way the space had almost constricted around them—at least until the server had flung the door open.

For seven whole days, anytime his mind had quieted, all Sam could think about was what the fuck had been about to happen. Because it had felt monumental. And he wasn't a guy who looked at moments in his life and thought, *This is some monumental shit.*

He just needed to see Bree; that was all. He just needed to put his eyes on her, and then he would know . . . something. If they were okay. If she was still freaked out. If something important was brewing. She'd responded to his texts, but her messages had been short and delayed. It felt as if she was avoiding him.

"Did you see her?"

"Did I see who?"

"Did you see Salem?" Roxy clarified. "I assume not, because there wasn't a report of a nuclear war in Page Six."

Right. Of course. Why would Roxy be asking about Bree?

"Wow, unforced error, there," he said, shaking his head. "You just admitted you read Page Six."

"And you just admitted you know what Page Six is."

"Fuck."

He tried to enjoy the volley, but he couldn't. Something was barreling toward him—he could feel it. It had his hair on end and his boxers in a twist. It felt like his childhood, when he knew that his parents were about to brawl again and he hadn't been able to stop the onslaught.

Here, he could almost taste it, like pennies and salt, on the tip of his tongue. He had no idea what it was or if it was terrifying or exciting, but it was coming for him all the same.

"I saw Salem, yes. Talked to, no." He'd honestly forgotten all about the brief glimpse he'd captured of Salem before Bree had dragged him through the gallery. The only notable thing that had happened was whatever had *not* happened with Bree. But he wasn't about to get into all that with Roxy.

Just then, there was a knock on the door, and Bree poked her head in. "I take it this is the greenroom."

"Thank God you're here." Roxy stood up and hugged her. "Sam was panicking."

"I wasn't panicking." He *had* been, but now he was very calmly returning his heart rate to its normal range and forcing himself to sit back down since it would be weird for him to pull Bree into his arms.

That would be weird, right? He couldn't do it without seeming weird.

When Roxy released her, Bree gave him a half wave, but she didn't quite meet his eyes. She had on a stiff sweater and a tight pencil skirt. She looked . . . nice. Businesslike, professional. She had put on more makeup than normal, and something about it felt like a mask. He wished he had an excuse to camp out on her couch again so that he could see her ridiculous pajama collection, maybe have a movie night.

"When does this show get on the road?" Bree asked with false lightness.

"You in a rush?" he asked.

"No, I . . . no."

He sounded snippy, and she sounded defensive. Great.

Another knock sounded, but without waiting for a response, the door sprang open. It was the Videon exec from the art exhibit, and he was shepherding several other people. The men were all tall, all white, and all wearing different versions of what appeared to be the same suit. It could've been the opening for a Rich White sketch about the dangers of using the replicator at the country club.

"Sam!"

Sam couldn't remember the guy's name, so he just waved. "Hey."

"I don't want to keep you, but I had to introduce Michal Blaese."

He got to his feet and offered Blaese his hand. They had *not* negotiated glad-handing in the contract, but they'd probably thought that part was implied.

"I'm a big fan. Big, big fan." Blaese had an almost aggressive grip and was wearing the largest, shiniest wristwatch Sam had ever seen, and he'd met at least a baker's dozen of billionaires.

With regular-issue famous people, there were a few things that could be counted on: They were almost always better looking than you thought they were. They were almost always shorter than you thought they were. They almost always had the best hair and skin in the room because they invested big bucks in those aspects of appearance over which they had the most control.

Billionaires were different. They really weren't any better looking than your regular-issue corporate lawyer, but they were *shinier*. It was as if their money had installed some kind of filter over their appearance.

High-gloss assholes was how Sam thought of them.

"Glad we could set this up," Sam told Blaese, sounding not at all glad.

"And you've got moral support. Roxy Warren." Blaese offered his hand to Roxy, who took it with as much enthusiasm as she might a dead fish.

"Mr. Blaese."

Sam could tell that she was sizing him up, comparing the real thing to the version they often parodied on *Comedy Hour*.

"I liked the sketch you did about self-driving cars." Somehow, Blaese managed to make that sound like a threat.

The sketch had implied that Exocars, one of Blaese's companies, had accidentally switched the intended plans with a copy of Stephen King's *Christine* while developing its self-driving car. Since Exocars had recalled half the vehicles it had manufactured, it had seemed less like a sketch and more like reporting. It had been, and this was Sam's professional assessment, fucking hilarious.

"Oh, good. It was just for you."

Sam suspected Blaese picked up on Roxy's sarcasm, but regardless, it was scattered like LEGOs all over the room, waiting for unsuspecting victims.

Blaese smiled, and Sam would've sworn the place got three degrees colder. When he turned to Bree, it went arctic. "And this is . . . ?"

Bree was apparently unaffected. "Bryony Edwards."

He didn't shake her hand. He took it with the expression of a man who didn't give stuff back. "Sam's . . . date?"

"No, we're just good friends." Her smile wasn't real, but it was her words that had the back of Sam's head about to blow off.

Those words weren't wrong. But also, they weren't right.

Sam slid in between Bree and Blaese. "Now that we're *all* good friends, I better get ready."

"Sure, of course. Ladies, I'll see you out there."

Before they'd even left, Roxy made a gagging noise. When the door closed behind them, she said, "What a human shark."

"Hey, that's an insult to *Jaws*."

"I'm going to get a drink. You coming?" She directed that at Bree, but Sam wasn't ready to let her go yet. He wanted to check in.

"I need her for a minute." After Roxy left, he turned and said, "Hey."

For the first time that night, Bree met his gaze, and he felt—normal. That was what he needed to feel. Normal. She wasn't smiling, and her eyes were wary. But she was searching his face, and he could have stood for as long as it took until she found what she was looking for.

"How have you been?" he asked.

"Fine. You got snippy with the money."

"Just providing a novel experience for him. Thanks for coming to this. You just keep saving my bacon."

"That's my job."

He winced. "No, it's not. I'm going to try to stop getting in so much trouble." He could try, but he didn't have much hope that it would work out. But he knew he was taking advantage of Bree.

"I better get going. If I don't hold Roxy back, she might slug that guy." It was unfair that Bree saw that as her responsibility.

"Nah, she has more self-control than me." He grabbed a bottle of water from the makeup counter. "Walk with me?"

Somehow, he didn't want to have this conversation, wherever this conversation was going, here where it was bright and fake and Blaese's stench still hung in the air.

As they made it through the tangle of hallways, they fell into matching steps. "How was your day?"

Her shrug was stiff. "Fine. Sorry I was late."

"No need to apologize. I just . . . I hate every part of this."

She snorted. "You hate no part of this. You love the spotlights being on you, you love the crowd hanging on your every word, and you really love it when they laugh."

"But it's murder when they don't."

Bree was a normal person, so she would never be able to understand how Sam's favorite part was the gap between when he said the line and when the audience responded. That pregnant pause when he didn't know if it was going to fall flat or fly. That moment, the high of it, was what kept him doing comedy. It was why he knew he could never give up stand-up for movies or television without an audience. He lived for the exchange of energy. For the chance that he might fail.

It felt like playing high-stakes poker with the grim reaper. Every time Sam went onstage, he could destroy everything that he'd worked for—but he didn't. Or at least he hadn't so far, but he would someday. Those were the odds; the house always won.

But he could never explain that to Bree or anyone else who hadn't experienced it. Anyone normal.

"This is me." He gestured at the prompt desk, where the stage manager would appear soon. "Do me a favor and stay away from Blaese."

"Why?"

"I dunno. Just a vibe. Stick with Roxy." She was an actual, certified Muay Thai boxing instructor and would probably be happy to have a reason to kick Blaese's ass.

"Whatever. I'll see you afterward, you weirdo." Bree bumped Sam with her shoulder, and that gesture was the first thing she'd done or said all night that spoke to the affection that tended to flow between them. The affection that Sam needed like he needed oxygen and attention and another Videon special.

He kept his eyes riveted to the floor so as not to have another one of those strange moments, when he was watching her and she was watching him and there was some unspoken . . . expectation between them. He lived for the possibility his career might tank, but he couldn't face that possibility with Bree, if that was what those moments were about. What the fuck did he know?

But something was shifting, had shifted, between them. All Sam knew was that he didn't like it. He never would have thought of himself as someone who resisted change. He wasn't a conservative guy in any sense of the word. When it came to Bree, though, all he wanted was for things to stay the same. Now and forever. Of everything he needed in life, he needed her the most. He would do anything to maintain that, if only she could tell him what his marching orders were.

Instead of thinking any more about it, he shot the shit with the stage manager and tried to keep his focus on his job.

"You ready to go?" the stage manager asked.

"As I'll ever be." He went onstage to what passed for raucous applause when you had a handpicked crowd of rich people, none of whom were drunk.

"Well, hello, one-percenters," he opened.

That got a hearty laugh. The crowd seemed to think Sam was complimenting them, not indicting them.

Out in the room, he could see Roxy at the table with the Videon folks. It took a second for him to locate Bree.

She was at the bar, perched on a stool. He couldn't make out her expression—there was a halo of blue light around her—but the slant of her shoulders was tight. Probably because Blaese was on the stool next to her, chatting her up. In fact, his hand was planted on her forearm.

Adrenaline and rage washed over Sam. What an asshole, talking through Sam's set. He wasn't a fan; you wouldn't talk over your supposed favorite comedian. But knowing Blaese was awful was almost a relief. Sam had called that one right.

Sam ran his hand over his hair and tried to remember how he'd planned to start. He jumped into what he could remember from that last Vegas set, some bullshit observational humor Jerry Seinfeld would have thought was clichéd in the nineties, but it had been what sprung to the tip of his tongue, and so he went with it.

After a minute, Blaese took his hand off Bree, and Sam regained some of his composure. He riffed for about ten minutes about how disappointing famous people on the *Comedy Hour* set were. He didn't name names, but the audience ate it up like cheap Halloween candy.

Their laughter went a long way to assuaging Sam's feelings, and he was even considering doing an ad-lib about "Lost Boy." It was what everyone in the room really wanted, and Sam had trouble not giving an audience what it wanted in some form. But that was when the mine cart completely left the rails.

Blaese set his drink back on the bar, and then he put his hand on Bree's knee. Sam could see Bree react. She tried to swivel away from the contact, but Blaese wouldn't let her. Sam would've sworn he could see her flesh dimple where Blaese's fingers were pressing into her—and Sam quite simply snapped. It took everything in him not to jump off the stage, but when his own hand constricted on the mic, he remembered he had something far more powerful than a left hook.

"Enough about that," he said.

The audience groaned. Sure, they were laughing, but there was nothing Sam hated like tepid laughter—except possibly Blaese. He hated that guy the most.

"Have I ever told you why I invented Richard White? Good old Rich White. I've never actually talked about this publicly. This will be a first. A little Videon exclusive, just for you."

There was a round of applause, the kind that was enthusiastic but just a little bit tentative. As if the audience couldn't understand what kind of reaction he wanted them to have. Or maybe they could sense the venom in Sam's tone.

The power of that, of having everyone in the room—all of them except for Blaese, who was still gripping Bree's knee—willing to do and feel whatever Sam wanted them to was intoxicating. He was going to weaponize it.

"Most of the recurring *Comedy Hour* characters are wacky, right? Absurd. You take a caricature and put them in different situations— serious situations, silly situations—and you get to be iconic. Most of my castmates write characters who play to their strengths or their fantasies. You write yourself as the most interesting man in the world, or the pretty bimbo, or whatever you want to be. But with Rich White, I was writing the opposite: what inaccurate stuff people saw when they looked at me. He's not something I'm not. He's everything I don't want to be. Rich White is an exorcism."

No one was laughing, but they were hanging on his words, and that was close to the same thing.

"Like, take this guy." Sam pointed roughly where Blaese was sitting. In a bigger club, there would have been someone with a spotlight, but frankly, Sam didn't need it here.

He put a hand over his eyebrows to see more clearly. He skipped past the Videon execs—he didn't care how they felt or whether they knew what was coming. Roxy's eyes were wide in warning, but Sam kept scanning.

Ah yes, there he was, with his fingers still digging into Bree.

Bree was shaking her head. She was trying to tell him not to do this, but it was too late. Sam had already driven this car off the cliff. All that was left was the fall.

"What do you see when you look at Michal Blaese?" There: now no one was confused.

Someone in the audience gasped. Apparently insulting them as a group was expected, but doing it specifically and by name was not.

"I bet you see Rich White," Sam said, answering his own question. "An inexpressibly bad haircut, sure. And an expensive suit, sure. But you also think about how he's one of the ten richest people in the world. About how he won't take his hand off my friend. And you think about who or what else he feels entitled to. I mean, can you imagine being as rich as this guy and still not being able to keep your hands to yourself? All the murder cars are one thing, but that's some kindergarten shit you're failing there."

A couple of people in the audience chuckled, nervous and uncertain.

Sam didn't care about them. "I could see it up here, pal, clear as day. You were striking out, she was telling you no, but you wouldn't accept it. Why?"

At that, Blaese actually did take his hand off Bree's knee, except Sam was too far gone to stop. There was another strained, tepid wave of laughter, but for once, Sam didn't want to be the funny guy.

"I'll make a guess. You grew up rich, so you never had problems with girls. But you weren't really sure why they were with you."

Blaese hadn't changed his expression or his posture, but the air around him was humming.

Fair enough. Sam could generate a force field with his anger too. "You got older, you got richer. It's curious how that works, isn't it? No, it's not funny; don't laugh."

The audience stopped immediately.

"It actually isn't curious at all. It's our system, and it sucks. I'd bet that women kept falling at your feet, but your doubts grew, too, like a monster under the bed. Some nights, you throw the blankets off, daring it to get you. Your version of that is running over other people, isn't it? You have to assume everyone wants you. You can't give 'em a chance to say no, because if you admit you care about their feelings, you have to admit that you don't know how anyone feels about you anymore, not really. Maybe not ever."

Sam wiped his mouth with the back of his hand. He should stop. He'd said enough. But this felt as easy and as inevitable as a glass shattering on the floor when you dropped it. At least Sam was destroying his career for a good reason. He'd always assumed he'd do it through sheer petulance. But this, Bree, was worth it.

"See, that's the good part about being poor: everyone's honest with you. You have to be honest with yourself, too, about who you are. What you want. When I was a kid, I thought frozen cheesecake was the height of sophistication. Thanks, Salem, for sharing that with the world! And it's true. That's what I liked, what I still like. When I was a kid, if you'd told me I was going to be able to go to dinner and not have to worry about the prices, I wouldn't have believed you. And if I could order a drink *and* a dessert, I would've been shocked. But here's what growing up like that got me. When I set my hand on a woman's knee, and she tells me she doesn't want it there, I learned to listen, to take that no. Because why would I want anything other than a *hell yes*? That's your real problem, Blaese. You don't want people to be honest with you, because you can't take the no. But you also can't be happy, because you know you never get the *hell yes*."

Sam had gotten one thing out of tonight: he had absolutely proved looks couldn't kill. Sam had said all that to Michal Blaese's face, and he was still breathing.

You're welcome, science!

"So that's why I invented Rich White—to celebrate not being you and to try to get guys like you to stop being like that. You all thought I was hailing your avatar when I was really showing you how much you suck."

Nope, nobody was laughing now. Not even in pity. Not even in shock. A dry fart would have echoed in the room.

It was so ridiculous, Sam wanted to laugh. He honestly hadn't said anything thematically different in the last ninety seconds than he had in his first ten minutes onstage. The difference was how direct he had been. He wasn't giving them anywhere to hide. He'd burned down any potential cover, any way for them to say, *He didn't mean that.*

As soon as you killed the ironic potential and shouted, *No, I meant exactly what I said*, that was when you really made people uncomfortable.

Sam had always thought the subtext of his comedy had been clear as day, but people like Blaese, and even worse, the people who wanted to be just like Blaese, were absolutely determined to misunderstand Sam's work. It was probably because they envied his attitude or something. They didn't understand that you couldn't fake the attitude. You had to earn it, one hungry night at a time. These people hadn't earned shit.

"Anyhow, I know you're going to leave and say, 'Sam Leyland wasn't very funny.' Fair enough. But don't forget that you're the punch line. The joke was never for you."

With that, Sam put the mic back in the stand and left the stage. He didn't bother to say anything to the stage manager; he simply returned to the greenroom, where he hoped Roxy and Bree would meet him.

About a minute later, the door flew open.

"Dude," Roxy said. "I went to the running of the bulls once, and nothing I saw in Pamplona topped what you just did."

"Where's Bree?" That was all he cared about.

"Pacing in the hallway. She might disembowel you. Prepare yourself."

He pushed the door open. Bree's back was to him, and he had to smile. Good God, but he was dumb. "So that went well."

She turned on her heel, her hair swirling around her shoulders. "You fucking asshole."

"Bree, come on, I—"

"No." Her face was a thunderstorm: her eyes dark and stormy, and her mouth a lightning bolt. "I'm not talking about this here."

"I was—"

"I called a cab." She marched to the alley without giving him a chance to disagree.

"You gonna be able to get home?" he asked Roxy.

"Yup. You go face the music."

Outside, the cab was waiting. He followed Bree into the back seat, and she gave her address to the driver without once looking at Sam.

When the car jolted to a start, Sam said, "If you'll just—"

"I'm trying very hard not to kill you, Samuel. If you could manage to keep your mouth shut for a few minutes, maybe I'll let you live."

"Just tell me if you're okay."

"I'm *fine.*"

"Good. But I don't even—"

"Yes, you do. You do deserve it."

In the front, the driver shifted his eyes to the rearview mirror. "Sounds like you're in trouble, pal."

He didn't know the half of it.

CHAPTER 16

Bree couldn't remember the last time she'd been so angry. Not when she'd caught her mother's loan fraud, which had mostly been heartbreaking. Not when she'd had to appear in court to deal with a permitting dispute. No, this was another level of rage.

As she, Sam, and the cabbie crossed the city back to her apartment, she became more, not less, upset.

Sam did reckless shit. He was impulsive. But she'd never felt so responsible for it, or as if he had used her in order to justify torpedoing another piece of his reputation and integrity. It made her want to kick him in the shins.

For the rest of the cab ride, he stayed quiet, but his eyes kept darting over to her, and she could sense that he wanted to talk. She suspected he didn't regret telling Michal Blaese off. At all. Sam regretted that she was mad, even though he had no idea *why* she felt that way.

This was why she was bad at staying mad at him—because she could feel, palpably, how much he didn't like upsetting her.

After he'd paid the cabbie, they began tromping up the stairs of her building.

"Look," Sam began, "I can see that—"

"I don't want to talk about what you can see. I want to talk about how I *feel*." If they were going to have this out, they were going to do it on her terms. "What the actual fuck, Sam? I'm not the little girl trying to deal with the asshole on the bus anymore."

"I was standing up for you."

"Which I didn't ask you to do. I won't be some excuse for you to shove yourself back in the headlines or behave badly. I don't want that."

"That's not how you're supposed to feel."

"Really? How am I supposed to feel? Grateful that my best friend verbally assaulted someone on my behalf? What the hell?"

"This isn't how I thought this was going to go at all."

They got to her door, and after a few seconds of struggle—she was too mad for keys—she managed to get the door open. "Honestly, was *thinking* even involved? Because these last few weeks, you've felt like a loaded gun, searching for an excuse to go off."

"I'm sorry," he gritted out from between clenched teeth as he followed her. "I saw him hassling you, and I thought—"

"What? You thought *what*?"

They were standing almost nose to nose in the small entry space. With all her puffy winter coats hanging on the rack, they were filling up what little room there was with angry words and heated gestures.

Bree wanted to slam her fists into his chest, to wail and cry and scream. Because she just could not do this with him anymore. She couldn't take his protectiveness, his kindness, for a single more day, if that was all he could give her.

"I could see you were uncomfortable," he said. "And I wanted to . . . help. Bree, you're my best friend, and I—"

"There wasn't a less inflammatory way to do that?"

"I just saw red, and—"

"So it's not about me. It's about your unmanaged anger?" As if that made it better.

"No, but when I think about someone hurting you, I—I can't handle it."

"Why?" she demanded.

"Because, damn it, I'm in love with you!"

It was as if an air lock had snapped open in a space movie. There was no oxygen. No air. Bree gasped loudly, absurdly. Her vision blurred. She set a hand against the wall, needing to hold herself up. Her legs were unstable under her. Or the floor was.

Sam . . . loved . . . her?

No; no, he didn't. He was angry and vulnerable, and—he didn't.

She blinked up at him. His expression was bewildered, but after the reeling surprise faded from his eyes, something else came in. Focused, earnest.

It scared the ever-loving crap out of her.

"Say something," he whispered.

She couldn't. She literally couldn't.

Then he raised a hand. The gesture was slow, as if he were making it underwater. Soft. So uncertain. It landed, finally, on her shoulder, and the contact seemed to startle them both.

"Bree, say something."

"You love me?" she croaked.

His other hand drifted up, and he traced along her cheekbone with a finger. It was as if he were looking at her face for the first time. As if he were stunned by her. "That week, living here with you, changed something in me. I . . . I'm a fucking mess."

"Yup." There was no disputing that.

"The only place where I make any sense, the only thing that makes any sense, is when I'm with you." His fingers shifted into her hair. He shuffled through it gently, and Bree would have sworn that she could feel the contact radiating up into the nerves of her scalp. She was so hyperaware of him, she could have mapped the atoms he was touching.

"I . . ." *I have always, always loved you, and now that you've said it back, I can't think.* She didn't know what this was. Did he mean it? Or was he being impulsive? Would he regret it all in the morning? She wasn't sure, and absent that, she had no idea how to respond.

It froze her. He, this, froze her.

Sam misinterpreted her silence. "Oh, shit. You don't? Of course you don't. God, I'm—"

She couldn't say anything that would quiet his fears. *Her* fears. The almost pulsing vulnerability and insecurity of the moment.

So Bree did something: she sank her hands into his shirt, pulled herself up, and planted her mouth on his.

It wasn't suave or gentle. It wasn't the first kiss she'd imagined them sharing ten thousand times. It was a kiss to smother. To silence. To turn off their overactive brains.

For three endless seconds, all she could think was, *Holy shit, my lips are touching Sam's lips.* He was warm, so damn warm, though slightly in need of ChapStick. And he tasted like coffee, which he probably shouldn't be drinking so late at night.

He thought he was in love with her, which made her feel like someone had dropped the camera in a movie and she was looking at the world sideways. He couldn't. He didn't.

She wanted to believe he did.

With a shocked inhale, he caught up with the kiss. His hands dropped to her hips, and he boosted her up. After a moment of struggling with her skirt, she managed to wrap her legs around him almost automatically, as if they'd done it a thousand times, and then her back slammed into the wall and he laid siege to her mouth.

His tongue tangled with hers. Jesus, this was real now. There was no ambiguity in tongue kissing, especially when it made her moan. Made her melt. Damn near made her come.

Sam ground himself against her in response. He was hard—holy wow, he was hard. She didn't mind the freezing plaster against her back, not when she could feel how badly he wanted her.

He was massaging her hips, her ass, and it was so filthy and perfect. Spit and tongues and lips and teeth, combining and recombining, and all of it tugged on every nerve of her body. She'd never been so alight.

No one had. All the anger she'd felt had just transformed into horniness. A lifetime of it. Two lifetimes. All the lifetimes.

She liked kissing. She liked sex. But someone's tongue in her mouth and hands on her back had never connected so directly, so strongly, to her lust valve before. She was like Three Mile Island here, melting down, all because Sam was finally touching her.

This was going to hurt. This was probably going to hurt so bad. Because all her worries from before, none of them had evaporated. She still had a job offer in Michigan. Sam was still a human disaster. But he wanted her, and she couldn't stop herself.

Sam's mouth was on her neck now, which was good, because she needed to catch up on some oxygen. The entryway echoed with the sound of their bodies, fighting through fabric and physics and more than two decades of telling themselves that this couldn't happen. Discarding that truth, it remade the world. It remade everything.

He pulled back the slightest bit and very carefully said, "Baby." A pause. His hair was ruffled and his expression befuddled, but something dawned in his eyes. A smitten, gentle clarity. "Is this what you—"

"Less talking." She didn't want to have to think about what they were doing or not doing or why. God, especially not why. She'd spent what felt like a lifetime thinking about Sam. Now, she just really wanted to do Sam.

Her hands were in his hair, and she'd been wrong—so wrong— about everything. His hair was surprisingly soft. She explored his shoulders (broader than she'd let herself notice) and his arms (how was he so strong?) and his chest.

"Damn, you're so cut," she managed to gasp between kisses.

"Good thing too."

"Stop talking."

He stumbled across the living room—thank God for tiny New York apartments—and into her bedroom with her still wrapped around him. They fell onto the bed, and it was cold, but he was over her. He was heat and wetness and the center of the goddamn universe.

Sam's hands were on the hem of her sweater, his fingernails trembling against her stomach. "Is this okay?"

She couldn't answer with words. She was past speech. Past thought. She didn't want to talk, because she might talk them out of this. Sam had made a lifetime of bad decisions. She didn't want to contemplate being one of them. She couldn't.

So instead, she tugged her own sweater off and flopped down on the bed. She hadn't planned for this. Hadn't expected it. She was wearing a totally normal, totally not sexy mesh-and-cotton bra. She'd left the strand of Christmas lights plugged in in the living room, and she was grateful there wasn't more light. She wasn't a waifish pop princess or an actress or a model or any of the kinds of women he normally took to bed.

But if his exes were here now, it was because Bree was bringing them. Looking up into Sam's face, she had to believe he wanted to be here. That there was nowhere else he'd want to be, and no one else he'd prefer to be with.

Sam ran a finger over her cleavage slowly. "You're fucking stunning."

She beckoned him to her, needing to do and not think, and when he kissed her now, it was sloppy. Horny. Not from surprised lust, but with purpose. She was shaking with questions—*Is this a good idea? What if we're bad at it? What if we ruin everything?*—but the way he touched her seemed like the answer. Reverence turned into certainty.

She slid her hand beneath the hem of his sweater. His stomach was taut; he was working so hard to hold himself in check. She tugged the knitted fabric up, and when his stomach touched hers, they both gasped.

It was so bracingly intimate.

"Off," she said, ridiculously, pulling at his shirt.

Sam rolled himself back onto his feet and removed his sweater and undershirt. They hit her floor with a soft thud. There was just enough light for her to make out the scoring of the muscles of his stomach, his chest, and his arms.

"Holy moly." It felt ridiculous, but his physique was equally ridiculous.

"That's my line." He lowered his weight on her, and she arched her spine, trying to bring more of their skin into contact. For the first and perhaps only time in his life, Sam was the one slowing things down while Bree wanted to gallop toward the finish.

She pushed at Sam's shoulder, and he flopped onto his back. She slid over him, struggling behind her back with the clasp of her bra. Her breasts dropped when it finally opened, and she shucked it to the floor.

Sam rose onto his elbows, nudging one of her nipples with his mouth. "To sip on?" he murmured.

"Don't push it."

He didn't. He kissed and nipped and licked until she couldn't take it anymore. Until she had to move against him. God, wanting him, wanting to come, exposing all that—it made her feel so ridiculous and vulnerable. She'd forgotten how terrifying sex could be, especially, particularly, with someone you cared about.

And she'd never had sex with someone she cared about as much as Sam.

When she bucked against him again, he asked with wonder in his voice, "Could you come like this?"

"Probably." She'd never managed to before, but Sam set her on fire in a way her previous partners hadn't managed. "But I need . . ." She hid her face in his shoulder. This was silly. She was thirty-two. She could say, *I need you to touch my clit.*

"What?"

She took his hand and guided it to the waist of her skirt. She undid the clasp and inched the zipper down with her free hand. Then together, they slid their fingers past the band and into her panties. They parted her folds, and his fingertip skidded over her clit. She could feel a tremor go through him; then he did it again. Firmer. More certain. The breath caught in her throat, and her hips rose to meet the contact.

"Fuck," he breathed. "Got it." His mouth returned to her breast, and his fingers began to work over her body.

Bree couldn't keep her eyes open. She couldn't watch him reduce her to ashes with his mouth and hands after a lifetime of wanting. It was too much to feel it, to think about it, to hear it. She couldn't watch it too. Her brain would overload, like a circuit during a power surge.

"Sam, please, pleasepleaseplease."

He didn't relent, didn't slow down, didn't let her catch her breath. And then she was coming, extravagantly, loudly, as if she would keep shaking from the pleasure of it forever.

He rolled her onto her back with so much tenderness, she almost couldn't believe it was him. "Bree, this is . . . God, is this too much?"

She finally got the zipper on her skirt all the way down, and then she rolled it and her panties off. "I want you. I can't . . . I don't want to wait, I don't want to talk, I just want you."

What seemed like suddenly, he was naked. This was it, the final threshold that lay between them and sex.

She'd pictured his cock a gazillion times. Maybe she'd thought by laying out every possible option—long, compact, thick, gaunt—she could compensate for the fact that she'd never know. But now she did know, and he didn't lack for inches or girth. More importantly, when she saw him, saw all of him, her entire body said, *Yes.*

She touched him, soft and exploratory, and he pulsed in her hand.

"I don't have a condom. I didn't think—" He meant he didn't think he needed one, and he hadn't expected to need one.

"I have an IUD." Which, frankly, he knew, because he knew everything about her. "But there are condoms in the nightstand."

It would be hard to grow up like Bree had and be comfortable with risk. Frankly, every choice she'd made had been about avoiding risk. She'd never had sex without deploying at least two forms of birth control. She'd never bought a plane ticket without also buying the travel insurance. She was a supremely cautious person.

Sam wasn't. But for her, with her, he would be careful.

Also in the nightstand was her vibrator, but Sam only chuckled when he opened the drawer. "Next time."

Which meant he thought there would be a next time. *Ack!*

Then he was sliding the condom on, and he was between her legs, and he was finally—finally—pushing into her, his mouth on her shoulder, her collarbone, her ear. "Bree, baby, *fuck.*"

She couldn't handle that any more than she could have handled him repeating what he'd said in the entryway.

He was moving into her, and it was perfect. He was perfect. The way he touched her, right where she needed him to, the noises he made, as if this was battering his heart like it was hers, the shuddering of his muscles where she clung to him.

But afterward, when he was disposing of the condom, she could only think, *So how badly has Sam broken his career, and how badly is he going to break my heart?*

He thought he loved her—she believed that without reservation. But that he could stay in love with her and forgive her for considering moving to Michigan, that they could find something like forever happiness together? She only hoped that was possible.

Sam slid back into the covers and crossed his hands over his stomach. He smiled pleasantly, as if they were talking about gardening or baseball or something else extremely boring. "Are we going to talk about this?" he asked.

"We can't just fall asleep?" she countered.

"No."

Of course they couldn't. They needed to have oh-so-many conversations, but she would prefer to avoid this one. "Should we begin with how you just torched your career because an asshole put his hand on my leg?"

"You're right," Sam said, surprising her. "I really should have hit that guy."

And there it was. "You really shouldn't have. Should you check in with Riaz?"

"I should most definitely *not*. He can wait until morning."

Bree doubted Riaz would agree, but she also didn't trust Sam not to blurt out that he was calling from Bree's bed, and so Bree could support putting that conversation on ice until tomorrow.

"Instead," Sam said, "I'd like to know when you decided you wanted to kiss me. Because I suspect that wasn't a game-time decision."

She pressed her eyes closed. "Hmm."

"Bryony."

Oh, things were serious then. She was going to have to be brave.

Without opening her eyes, she said, "I've known for a long time how I felt about you."

"How long?"

She cracked one eyelid. "You need some bucking up?"

"Always."

Which was true. He could seem like the personification of confidence, but she knew how much of that was faked. Sam basically had a PhD in fronting.

She'd let him inside her body. She could tell him the truth. Part of the truth. "I'm not going to feed your ego. But . . . since Leanver. Since we were virgins."

"Why didn't you tell me?"

"I knew where I was coming from, what I wanted, but you were not in that place." He started to argue with her, and she shook her head. "You weren't."

"Yes, I was," he insisted. "There were moments, once I figured out what I wanted to do with girls . . . and I saw you that way. Sometimes I'd look at you, and I'd feel—dizzy."

She sat up, suddenly angry. "Okay, why didn't *you* ever say anything, then? It's not as if you had any problem going after everyone else." Even now, thinking about all the women he'd chased around her made her eyes sting.

His response was blunt. "I'm shit at relationships. I burn through them like a pack of sparklers. The cheap ones."

The only sparklers Bree had any experience with were the cheap ones.

But his larger point had also been why she hadn't confided this particular secret in him before—and the reason why them together was a terrible idea. She couldn't be mad at him for saying out loud what she'd been thinking.

"You can get better at it." She wasn't certain if she was talking to herself or to him.

"It's fine to say, 'You don't have to be like your dad.' I know that." A pause, as if he were trying to decide whether he did in fact know that. "But."

Wasn't that just an elegant summation of all the crap they were both stewing in?

"This is a classic example of what therapy is for," she said.

"Can you imagine me in therapy? I'd argue every step of the way. No, that wouldn't work."

She wished he hadn't dismissed seeing a counselor out of hand, but they could only have one fight at a time. "So you thought, 'Whoa, I like Bree, but—'"

He pushed himself up so that they were almost nose to nose. "I thought you were too important for me to fuck up with like I always do. I could break everything else in the world, but not you. Never you."

"So why now?" Because that was what Bree really cared about. Why, when she was on the cusp of deciding to move on, did he have to pick that moment to tell her how he felt?

He softened. "Because you wouldn't let it go tonight. You were just so insistent. And your eyes . . ." He followed the arc of her brows with a fingertip, and his tenderness with her made her turn to powdered sugar inside. "You dragged it out of me." A pause. Then, "Why did you kiss me?"

She almost guffawed. "Can you honestly tell me you didn't know?"

"Know what?"

Oh, Sam could be dense.

"Why do you think none of my relationships work out?" she asked.

"I mean . . . bad luck?"

"It's you. I can't let myself fall for someone else, because I'm in love with you, Sam. I always have been."

Bree couldn't count how many times she'd imagined saying that any more than she could count the stars in the sky. Now, she'd given Sam those words, and the world was continuing around them. No large objects had fallen from the sky to crush them. But how long could that possibly stay true?

"And you didn't think you should share this?" Sam asked.

"I guess I lack the 'shooting my shot' gene. Besides, I'm not the one who's dated models and pop stars and actresses and everyone else under the sun. It felt pretty clear that my feelings were not reciprocated." At least not in any proportionate way—and not with any true potential for them to have a future as lovers.

There was a long pause in which Bree could almost watch Sam want to argue with that but convince himself not to.

She interrupted his struggle with a question. "What do you want this to mean? Like, this has all been very heavy, and we've shared some truths, but tomorrow, what are you going to want?"

He didn't even pause. "You." He kissed her forehead. "You." Her nose. "You." And he took her mouth with his.

Which was an answer . . . and it wasn't. But when his body moved over hers and his hands touched her with such certainty, Bree couldn't bring herself to care.

CHAPTER 17

Sam had never understood that guy dancing around in the rain in the old movie. You know the one: jumping gleefully into puddles, giving away his umbrella, and singing about how he was in love with love. Or maybe that other guy, the one who needed five hundred days to know Summer wasn't into him, dancing through the park to Hall and Oates.

What a load of crap—or at least so Sam had thought until the morning after he spent the night in Bree's arms.

He only just managed to keep himself on the decent side of crowing on the subway, but he did pose for several selfies with fans without even whining in his head about it, so bring on the rain, basically.

What Sam did know was the crowd of paparazzi would be back and bigger than ever outside *Comedy Hour*. They were like gremlins he'd fed after midnight or something. But he couldn't bring himself to care. He waved at them, knowing he was probably still wearing the shit-eating grin he'd had on since he woke up. The journos could enjoy speculating about *why* he was so damn happy the day after he'd torched his career. Holy shit but he was happy.

Inside, Derek started to apologize, but Sam shook his head to stop him. "At this point, we all need to accept I must like the attention, or else I'd behave differently." Jane wasn't going to buy that, though.

Upstairs, just off the elevator, Roxy grabbed Sam and towed him to a vacant office. "I tried to call you about fifty times. Is Bree okay?"

"She's fine. Listen, we're sort of—I think we're together." He hadn't asked Bree if it would be okay if he told people, but, well, he needed to tell someone. He couldn't keep it inside any longer.

"You and Bree?" Roxy clarified. "Together?"

"Yes."

"Fucking finally!"

"Wait, you knew?"

"Sam, *everyone* knew. No one who has ever spent time with the two of you didn't know she was in love with you and you were in love with her."

"I spent time with us, and I did not know."

"That's because you can be very thick."

"I'm actually exceptionally observant about the human condition. A critic said that once." And Sam had memorized it because it was such an odd comment. What did it even mean? If he actually was that observant, wouldn't he need to be aware of it?

"But you're very thick about yourself. You've probably been in love with her your entire life."

That made a lot of sense. "Maybe that's why I didn't notice. Loving Bree is my natural state. Like breathing. Who notices their own breathing?"

"Asthmatics."

"Point taken. But no one else."

Roxy was watching him like a scientist looking through a microscope, as if she was trying to figure out how he worked. Roxy's own relationship history was nearly as messy and convoluted as his own, so it was possible she was trying to wrap her head around something that was as alien to her as it was to him.

"Are you afraid?" she finally asked.

"Because my average relationship is three weeks long?" He pondered this. "I mean, I know I should be, but I'm not. She's just . . . perfect. She already knows every bad thing about me. The stuff I try to hide? She knows it all. I don't try to impress her, but she must be impressed." The joy and the novelty had his blood feeling like grape soda in his veins: sweet and acidic and bubbly.

After he'd almost had a panic attack last night while Bree had dozed next to him, this position was what he'd talked himself around to. The cost of losing her would be too high to contemplate paying. So he'd have to make sure that he didn't pay it.

"I care about her too much to fuck it up."

"I hope that's right," Roxy said, slowly.

"You sound skeptical."

"I know you."

He had to laugh. "I should be pissed, but . . . I'm not saying it right. I dunno—I just feel confident about her. About *us*." His chest lifted because Bree was his.

"I'm glad. You deserve it. You both do." A pause. "How's Videon?"

"Them I do not feel confident about." But he was trying not to think about his career. That was a mood-killer if there ever was one. "I haven't talked to Riaz." Besides noting the sheer number of texts and emails on his phone, Sam had focused instead on how buoyant his heart was. A balloon straining on a string.

Bree loved him.

She fucking loved him.

At some level, Roxy was right, and Sam probably should've been scared. But he also knew that he had been telling Bree the truth the night before: while he'd never sat down and told himself, *Don't pursue Bree*, it was almost as if he'd done it reflexively. Maybe he'd been afraid that if any thoughts about how he wanted her had become real, he wouldn't have been able to resist them. Repression had been the only logical course.

Because the night before, while he'd stood in Bree's doorway, he'd gone from thinking she hated him to needing to kiss her—to having that be the greatest and only directive in his life—in the length of a heartbeat.

There wasn't anyone else who was as important to him as she was. Now she was just important to him in a different way.

Last night, the fear had been there, sharp like a knife under his skin. He had been so stupid with so many women. He'd been selfish and dense, absorbed by his work, emotionally closed off, too blunt, too withholding, too obsessed with sex, not obsessed enough with his partners' pleasure—he could keep listing his mistakes for a while.

He had been a fuckup. He knew it.

But with Bree? He wouldn't fuck up because he couldn't. Once he'd realized that, any anxiety about changing the nature of their relationship had lifted.

He was grinning again, he knew it, remembering how gently, so gently, he'd moved the hair back from Bree's face to behind her ear. Her expression as she slept, the deliberate way her eyelids were buttoned shut and the dare of her nose. He'd traced it with his fingertip, and she'd wriggled against his touch.

"Don't you tell me I'm cute," Bree had muttered.

"Okay, I won't." He'd just think it. "I have to get going pretty soon." He'd heard his phone beeping all night. "I probably made a big mess."

Bree's eyes had popped open then, and she'd started to argue, but he'd insisted he didn't care, and he'd meant it.

Roxy shattered the memory: "So, now that that's out of the way, your agent is in with Jane."

There was the proverbial wet fucking blanket.

"Can we keep hiding?" Sam looked around. "Maybe we could get a new lamp, a fridge, and just—live here." It was nicer than Sam's first apartment in New York, anyhow.

"You put a quarter in the machine. Now you have to face the music."

"Do I?"

Roxy walked him to Jane's door and then gave him a sisterly pat on the arm. "Go get 'em, champ."

He knocked on the door and was instructed to enter, and then he found Riaz and Jane glaring at each other across her gleaming desk.

Oh, good. Maybe he could keep baiting the two of them to yell at each other, and then they'd forget to yell at him.

"Greetings and salutations," he began.

But Riaz had other plans. His head pivoted toward Sam like he was some kind of murderous marionette. "I gave you two instructions, and you disregarded both of them. I told you not to muck that set up."

Before Sam could respond—his plan had been to explode Pompeii-style—Jane interjected. "Is Bree okay?"

"Yes, thanks for asking."

It was quite possibly the only time he'd ever thanked Jane, including when she'd called to ask him if he wanted to join the cast of *Comedy Hour*. But it was sincerely nice that she hadn't begun by assuming he'd lashed out for no reason at all.

Sam turned to Riaz. "I won't apologize, because I'm not sorry. If someone in the audience is manhandling a woman like that—"

"Then it's none of your damn business."

Sam pinched the bridge of his nose to stop himself from punching the chair in front of him. "I'm only going to tell you this once: don't ever say anything like that to me again. I didn't lash out at someone who was heckling me. I wasn't drunk, I wasn't actually violent, and I didn't say anything offensive. I shouldn't have done it, but I don't regret it."

There was a long pause. "*Fine*," Riaz said, "but Videon is considering canceling your contract. They're livid."

Sam nodded. "Fair enough. I'm not expecting you to save things. I knew they'd be pissed while I was doing it."

"There's another issue," Jane said.

Which Sam had been assuming since he'd found out Riaz was in here with Jane.

She cut right to it. "We're losing some sponsors. Specifically Exocars."

"Their founder didn't appreciate being verbally flayed," Riaz spat out.

If the show's advertising was on the line, this was bigger than Sam's career. It wasn't only Sam's mortgage and his ability to feed himself and to decide where he was and what he did with his time.

But Sam did what he always did when he got scared. He made a joke: "Hey, you said that I was his favorite comic. He should've known what I was like. He talked through my set, too, at least before I suggested he's never known if anyone actually loved him. That got his attention. I strongly suspect he lied to us."

"I'm certain explaining that will change his mind," Jane deadpanned.

Okay, Sam was being a wee bit of an ass here. While he'd acted out of noble motives, he had publicly ridiculed someone. "Sorry, I'm being glib. Do you want me to sit this week's show out?" It would be a financial loss to him, but that was fine. He'd made this mess. He ought to live with the consequences.

Jane ran her hands over her face. "I thought I was done with this shit, you know? I used to have these fights in the 1970s, but I am too old for this."

"I don't think you're too old for this."

"Don't try to kiss my ass."

"I'm not, honestly. You have more fight than anyone I know. Including me. Which doesn't mean you have to fight for me. Bench me if it'll help that sentient case of athlete's foot heal his bruised ego. You can even fire me—"

"*No!*" Riaz interjected.

"I'm just saying, I'd understand." Sam had lashed out fully cognizant that getting fired was a possible outcome. He'd almost expected it.

Jane had watched all this carefully, levelly. "You really care about this woman?"

He knew she meant Bree. "More than anything."

Jane chewed on the inside of her cheek, then said, "Get back to the writers' room, Sam. I'm going to call the network and tell them that from my point of view, Monsieur Exocars can kiss my ass. I don't want his skeevy sponsorship anyhow. Those are murder vehicles. We'll see what the suits say."

"You're a goddess among mortals," Sam said.

"Get out of here."

Sam let the high of the day carry him over whatever minuscule doubts might be lingering in the bottom of his stomach.

He and Bree were perfect. He knew it.

"Why don't I ever get to be the bad cop?" Bree asked Jeff.

They were about to go into a meeting with Sebastian Matthews, who sat on the Central Brooklyn Economic Development Corporation and who had just a "few little ideas" he wanted their input on. This was going to be tedious and mind numbing, which suited Bree fine, because her brain was on overdrive.

She'd slept with Sam. She'd been yelling at him, he'd decided he wanted her, and they'd fallen into bed together.

Tumbled? Rushed? Plunged? What did waterfalls do?

It had been terrifying and wonderful, and every cell of her was aching and throbbing and *singing* with it. She could use a few boring meetings to process everything she was and had been feeling: the good, the bad, and the orgasmic.

"You were the bad cop that one time with Oscar Hawkins," Jeff said. "It was a disaster."

"Harrumph." It *had* been a disaster, but it was sort of rude for Jeff to point it out. Besides, Bree had dealt with Hawkins by siccing a neighborhood letter campaign on him. It had been poetic justice, in the end.

Jeff was tapping away on his phone. "You seen who's trending on social media?"

"The president?" That was always a solid bet, though she assumed that wasn't what Jeff was referring to.

"Care to add any context?" Jeff held up his phone. It was an article about Sam's set, but the picture wasn't from last night. It was from Sam's previous, and likely last, Videon special. The headline screamed, LEYLAND'S LATEST VICTIM? EXOCARS CEO MICHAL BLAESE.

"Victim?" she scoffed. "Is he Jack the Ripper?"

"Bree."

She suspected she was about to get this question a lot. "Hm. I'd guess when you strip the exaggeration away, the basic story is right. Sam was . . . Sam."

Explosive, righteous, protective. But enough about what he'd been like in the sack.

"And he was mad because Michal Blaese bothered you?"

"Is that what the story says?" She wanted to call Sam and hide away from the world with him. But Sam needed publicity like pigeons needed stale pizza crust. "I mean, basically."

Jeff released a breath. "I wondered if you told him about the job in Michigan, and if that's what set him off."

"No." But she was going to have to soon. Oof, that was a fraught thought. She'd almost forgotten about Hutchinson-Baker during the rush of everything else, but she'd jerked awake at midnight remembering that she might leave New York—should leave New York, if she knew what was good for her—to take her dream job.

Holy sneakers, she had some decisions to make.

"This week's show is going to be amazing. Again. Jane Feeley must *love* him."

Which was probably what everyone on earth was thinking. "I doubt it. I'd guess Jane wants people to tune in because they love the show, not because Sam threw a public fit." Bree hated Sam's antics so much, it had never occurred to her anyone might see them as anything other than a liability.

"One thread I saw this morning suggested it was staged, to stay relevant and change the conversation from 'Lost Boy.'"

"I was there, and I assure you it was *not* staged. Honestly, no one who's ever met Sam could believe that. He doesn't take direction." Except in bed, where he'd been very, very good at taking direction.

Oops. She needed to get her mind out of the covers.

But all this was a reminder that with Sam, there was no privacy. People were going to connect Sam and her publicly, if they hadn't already. Whatever they were doing together, whatever it meant, it was going to get the same scrutiny as all his relationships did, as if it were the Zapruder film and not Sam's and her lives. And when it did, the stakes weren't just their hearts—which was a scary enough prospect—but also his career.

When she looked at him, she saw the kid she'd known forever. It wasn't that she didn't see Sam as being famous, but that wasn't her first frame of reference. But she shouldn't, couldn't, forget what else was at play here. Both their jobs and futures.

A secretary waved to get Bree's and Jeff's attention. "He's ready for you."

Bree stood and shouldered her bag. "You're sure I can't be the bad cop?"

"I'm positive. You're about as intimidating as a strawberry shortcake."

She felt about as vulnerable as one too.

CHAPTER 18

After she and Jeff met with the absurd economic development commissioner, Bree was listening to the second of three X-rated messages Sam had left on her voice mail when he texted, asking if she wanted to come over to his place for dinner. PS, Bring an overnight bag, he included.

It set off another swarm of fireflies in her stomach, a swirl of fear and uncertainty that she couldn't quite seem to tamp down. When you spent decades trying to convince yourself that you couldn't tell your best friend you were in love with him because it wouldn't work, those concerns didn't go away instantly.

Bree wanted to believe in them as fiercely, as uncomplicatedly, as the messages showed Sam did, but she couldn't. He fell in love at the same speed he wrote and discarded jokes. There wasn't any magic wand that she could wave to vaporize her very reasonable fears.

But she also couldn't tell him no, not when he was offering her everything she'd ever dared to want.

When she got to Sam's building, bag in hand and ridiculousness most firmly lodged in her stomach, the doorman, Frank, immediately recognized her. "Miss Edwards!"

She'd been here countless times, but she'd always come in with Sam. She tried not to think about how many other women the doorman must have seen with Sam and what he must think about them all. New York City doormen must have legendary stories.

"Um, hi," she stammered awkwardly.

"You can go up." Then Frank winked.

Did it count as being together when you apparently told the door-man about your relationship? The thought only made her more nervous.

After an elevator ride, she knocked on Sam's door, but it opened as soon as her fist connected with it. He'd left it open for her; now *that* felt like a metaphor.

"Sam?" she called, feeling foolish about just walking in.

"Back here." Because his apartment was a large enough place that you couldn't see the entire inside from the front door. It was basically an unheard-of luxury for New York, and no one else she knew had it.

Sam's apartment was *nice*, but it felt staged. It was all gleaming wood and veiny marble and funky vases—and he'd lived there for years.

"You could do more to personalize the place, you know," she said as she walked into the kitchen. "Isn't that supposed to be the best part of buying a condo?"

He was busy transferring what appeared to be Vietnamese food from take-out containers to two plates. When he saw her, he smiled so big and so open and so goofy that her heart swelled and shattered in her chest. He shouldn't do that to her, display his emotions—*those* emotions—without any hesitation. Didn't he know this was probably a bad idea? That she or he or both of them were going to mess up, and then where would they be?

But he didn't know, apparently. His hands were in her hair and his mouth was on hers, and he tasted so good. And then she was kissing him back, shutting her eyes against her fear, trying to ignore the silly tear that leaked out and tracked down her cheek.

Kissing him, experiencing his joy at seeing her: that had to be enough. She needed to file that feeling away, keep it forever. Use it for comfort when all this went pear shaped in a not-so-distant future.

"I missed you," he whispered between kisses.

"I always miss you." And it was true. Every moment they weren't together was a burden, and the only thing that helped was she could tell him so now.

"Stay tonight?"

"I'll stay as long as you want."

That was the truth, wasn't it? As afraid as she was, she didn't have it in her to resist, not if he was asking.

"So how bad was today?" she asked, when he finally released her and went back to arranging dinner. After what Jeff had said, she hadn't been able to stop herself from reading the coverage, and it had been brutal. The press could never seem to contain their glee when Sam melted down, and he was all too willing to accommodate them.

"Riaz is pissed. Jane was annoyed, but she also asked about you."

Bree hadn't been expecting that. "She asked about me?"

"I got the sense she thought I did the right thing, and, I mean, I did. But Blaese threatened to pull his ads from the show. I told Jane she could bench me. I even offered to quit—"

"You what?" Okay, so Bree shrieked that.

Sam didn't even blink. "I knew she wasn't going to agree. I'm still not sure if Riaz will be able to salvage my Videon contract, but I don't care."

He did, though. That was infatuation talking, and it scared the shit out of Bree.

She knew Sam cared about her. Sam would always protect her. But Sam also cared about his career. Whatever he might think he felt right now, he wouldn't be happy if his outburst cost him that.

"Sam, I gotta ask: Why did you do it?"

"He was touching you, and you didn't like it."

"Sure, but as soon as you drew attention to him, he stopped. I mean why did you go overboard? Why did you humiliate him?"

Sam smiled, enjoying the memory, but that flash of joy disappeared, and Sam appeared . . . troubled. His eyes flicked up, over Bree's face, then to the floor. He went over to the drawer and grabbed some silverware. Over his shoulder he said, "You know me pretty well."

That sounded like the prelude to something heavy.

For one moment, Bree almost guffawed at the possibility they were both harboring massive secrets from each other, but she knew that wasn't right and it wouldn't be at all funny.

"I know you better than I know myself," she said wryly. "What have you been keeping from me?"

He turned, and his expression was stricken. She'd almost never seen him looking so serious. "I'm not supposed to be who I am. It's some kind of cosmic joke—this apartment, the show, my career. The wires got crossed someplace, and someone like Blaese is struggling because I got his luck."

Oh. Well, she understood impostor syndrome in the abstract, but she had the sense Sam meant all this literally.

"No one like Blaese could ever be as funny as you are. Would never work as hard."

"Be that as it may, it's a mistake." He said it in a way that made it clear he was bone-deep certain about this. "It won't last. It can't. I've known that for a long time."

"Can't last as in . . . ?"

"I'll fuck it up eventually and move back to . . . well, not Leanver." No, he'd long ago vowed he'd never go back there again, and as far as she knew, he never had. He never even did shows in Ohio; that was how badly he hated the place. Well, it wasn't the place, but it was what it represented: the kind of future they'd been condemned to and which they'd somehow both managed to dodge.

"You'll never move back to Leanver," she assured him.

He shook his head. "Someplace like it, then. I've always known my time doing this wouldn't last. So maybe I've enjoyed inching close to the edge, yelling down into the cavern, you know?"

"No, I don't. I like staying behind the barrier for a reason."

"I love that about you." He didn't even seem to realize the significance of what he'd said. That less than twenty-four hours after he'd first said "I love you" to her in a romantic way, he could repeat it with so much certainty and nonchalance. As if they hadn't shifted the earth on its axis in less than a day together. "But I like the risk. It makes me feel alive."

Suddenly, a lot of things about Sam made more sense.

"If you think you're going to fail, why tempt it?" she asked. "Why not enjoy the ride for as long as you can?"

"It seems like a cop-out."

Of course. You *had* to tempt fate, because otherwise, you were a coward. Sam Leyland, folks: comic and fatalist.

"When you do fall—in this formulation you've got going on— what then?" she asked.

"Once you've failed, you've failed. You're a failure. It's the end." He would have to be black and white about it.

She shook her head. "I don't believe that."

"I know you don't." He gave her a fond smile. "You're an optimist. You think there are second chances."

Bree wasn't an optimist. She was a pragmatist. "It comes from being a designer."

"It comes from being a better person than I am. Last night, I watched that guy being an ass, and I realized it was only a matter of time before I burned down my career—and there would never be a better reason than to do it for you."

Bree could see how Sam was thinking about this, and how, to him, what he'd done was romantic. That verbally flaying Michal Blaese had been the ultimate act of devotion, rather than something unnecessary,

177

aggressive, and self-destructive. The main thing she wanted Sam to understand, though, was that he could never, ever do that again. "That is the most ridiculous thing I have ever heard."

"No, the most ridiculous thing is that it didn't work."

"Because you still have a career?"

He nodded.

"Doesn't that show you're wrong?"

"Nope. It just means I didn't muck it up *right now*. Speaking of which, this weekend: you, me, and a walking tour about Jacob Riis."

Bree was still busy processing his fatalism, and so it took a second for his digression to land. "Excuse me?"

"I had some downtime today, and I found one you hadn't dragged me on yet." His eyes were sparkling. He was really proud of himself.

Bree wanted to cry. "But you hate walking tours."

"True, but I love being with you. Let's eat."

Stunned—numb, overwhelmed—Bree picked up a plate and followed him to the table. As she munched on her spring roll, she tried not to think about what he'd said, and the ferocity that was baked into it, and so she again took in the space. The kitchen was all dark cabinets without hardware and gleaming white marble, probably Carrara, and there was glass everywhere. Bree had worked on multifamily units that didn't have as many windows as Sam had in his living room. But despite how gorgeous it was, it was more akin to a really nice Airbnb than a home.

"Why haven't you done more with this place?" she asked. He had the money and the space, which were most people's first and second problems.

"I don't have good taste."

"You could hire someone to do it for you." He did have an assistant, after all. In fact, his assistant probably should have just taken matters into their own hands.

"But then it wouldn't be personal. When I think about what I thought nice places were when I was a kid, it was like . . . side tables that matched and lamps that had shades."

"Whereas I grew up in Versailles." Actually, though, Bree's mom's apartment had been a touch nicer than Sam's. Her mom hadn't been able to hang on to money for any length of time, and those explosions of spending sometimes went in the direction of home goods—at least until she'd decided her daughter might also be her meal ticket and had tried to profit off it.

"See, you can pronounce Versailles." But of course Sam said it correctly too. "No, when I think about houses that I like, I think about your apartment."

"You enjoy being able to see the kitchen when you're in bed? Being able to hear the toilet flush from the hallway?"

"Yup, that's my favorite. No, I'm serious. It just feels . . . good."

Telling her that her space made him feel comfortable was better than any compliment he'd uttered about her body.

"Is it the decorating, or is it me?" Oh God, Bree shouldn't have asked that. Whatever he might have said after they slept together the first time, being with him still felt like the kind of muscle ache you got when you overdid it exercising after too long away.

She didn't, shouldn't, demand too much from him, or else her foolish heart was going to decide that this meant more than it probably did.

But he reached around the table and then gently tugged her into his lap. "It's five hundred percent you," he said against her neck.

After a few minutes, she wound the kiss down and went back to her seat. "When I was yelling at you last night, were you listening to me?"

"A little, but I was busy having one of the biggest revelations of my life."

"I mean, setting aside your belief that you have an expiration date—"

"We all have an expiration date; it comes with being human."

"Whatever you do, it can't be because of me. That's not what I want from you."

"What do you want from me?"

The answer she couldn't give him, and which she knew was unfair to even long for, was she wanted for him to have realized they were perfect for each other when they were kids. She wanted a do-over for the last twenty years. Barring that, she wanted him to be reasonable when she told him that she was considering leaving New York, maybe in a matter of weeks. She'd been sitting on the job offer from Hutchinson-Baker, and she was rapidly approaching the limit of how long she could expect them to wait.

Instead, what she said was, "I love you, Sam. I want to be with you. But, like, in a normal way. Not in the way where you have to save me. Or where you leverage your celebrity in any way—"

"Leverage my celebrity? Oh my God, what kind of influencer Ponzi scheme videos have you been watching?"

"Shut up, I'm serious. If we're going to make it work—"

"Baby." He picked up her hand, and he pressed his lips to her knuckles. "Honey." He flipped her hand over and kissed the inside of her wrist. "Smoosh. There's no *if*. I can't live without you. Now that we've slept together, I can't live without that either. So we'll make it work."

He believed that. It was in his eyes, in his body. There wasn't a thread of doubt for him.

But how many other women had he said that to? Believed that about? He had insisted that he'd been playing with Salem, but Bree had seen them together.

Bree knew that this was different. But how different? Did she want to roll the dice of the entire rest of her life on this actually, literally being different?

"It's as if you didn't listen to anything I said last night." Even worse, he wasn't in any place to listen to the things she hadn't said.

She couldn't tell him about Michigan, not right now. Not only did she want a few more precious days of the fantasy, but she wanted to wait until he was in a more practical mood, until he was seeing what was true and what was false, until he was being more realistic about his own wants and needs. Now, he was in dreamland, and it would be just so, so easy to let him entice her to go there too.

She'd spent what felt like a lifetime imagining what it would be like if Sam could love her. Was it so wrong to enjoy a few more days of the uncomplicated version of that?

He stood and carried their plates into the kitchen. Then he returned and dropped a very soft kiss onto her mouth like it was the most natural thing in the world. He couldn't seem to touch her enough, and it was convenient, because she couldn't seem to get enough of him touching her.

"I was listening. I particularly liked it when you panted my name."

"*Sam.*"

Then he dragged the sound from her several more times.

CHAPTER 19

A mutiny broke out at *Comedy Hour* Monday morning, and for once, Sam wasn't leading it. It had started the day after Sam's meltdown, when several of his "favorite" cast members had directed a few spiteful jokes about Exocars at Sam. Sam had mostly been confused. Wasn't it always open season on assholes in comedy?

So when Roxy slid into her seat next to Sam and muttered, "There's blood in the water," he was already on alert.

He scanned the room. Gibson was glaring at him as if he'd plowed over a few grandmothers on the way to the studio.

Sam had never liked Gibson, but he'd also never taken him seriously. The guy hadn't seemed worth it. While he'd occasionally been snarky to Sam, he also hadn't challenged him directly. Frankly, Sam thought it was clear that he and Gibson weren't on the same level. They weren't direct competitors for anything.

"What did I do?" Sam asked Roxy. He could think of any number of answers to that question, but none of them involved Gibson. This was like a hummingbird dive-bombing a rhinoceros.

"You were the golden boy," Roxy replied.

"I ain't no one's golden boy."

Sam wasn't going to pretend he hadn't had some successes that he took pride in. But he had pissed off anyone and everyone along the way.

He'd made a career in spite of himself, not because anyone had loved or boosted him. Jane treated him like a child she couldn't wait to stop babysitting, and last week, Sam had tanked the career goal he'd been working toward for the better part of a year.

What was there to envy?

"Look at it from Gibson's point of view."

"No, thank you."

Gibson ruffled the feathers of the writers, bullied the prop mistress, hit on the servers at the after-party. He punched *down*, and Sam couldn't stand that. That, among other things, was why Sam tried to avoid him. Even if it was unsettling, he didn't really care why Gibson was glaring at him.

Roxy gave Sam a pointed look, but before he could try to squeeze more answers out of her, Jane called things to order. "Okay, everyone, let's hear some comedy."

Gibson jumped in, something about unionization at the first Starbucks on the moon. It was so bad, it felt like a trap.

"Is he trying to bait me?" Sam hissed to Roxy.

"Reactions?" Jane asked, and while she wasn't looking at Sam when she said it, Sam definitely felt as if she was saying it to him.

Sam was the killer of bad ideas. Okay, so it was a self-appointed title, but since Sam wasn't invested in the cast politics—his only objective was writing a good show—he was good at it.

Everyone got smacked down some of the time. Hell, most of the pitches Sam had made over the years had been rejected. No one succeeded all the time. If you had a reasonably healthy ego and learned from the notes, you did fine.

Neither of those things were true of Gibson.

After a pause, Sam said, "The target is wrong." He was going to fetch the ball Jane had sent out in front of him if no one else would. "Why are you attacking the baristas and not, you know, Starbucks?"

"I'm not *attacking* anyone," Gibson shot back. "I'm writing comedy."

Are you sure *that's what you're doing?* But something else was going on here, so Sam kept that to himself. "You can't pretend a sketch on an overtly political topic could ever be neutral."

"It's supposed to be absurd."

"Then why does it reference a real thing?"

"That's rich coming from—"

"I'm going to stop this right here." Jane didn't even shout, because she could somehow project her voice right into a fray and still get everyone's attention. "I'm going to say no this week, because I don't think it's very funny yet. But keep working on it, and we'll revisit next week. Think about Sam's question, though."

Gibson rolled his eyes in a ludicrously exaggerated way. "Sure thing."

It wasn't that Sam expected everyone to kiss his ass, but Gibson tended to defer to the more successful members of the cast, or at least to Jane. A few weeks ago, Gibson might've wanted to shoot off a snarky retort, but he wouldn't have actually said it.

"Interesting," Sam muttered under his breath.

Roxy nodded.

Then Marc pitched a sketch about spring training for the Puppy Bowl, and while it wasn't a masterpiece, Gibson attacked, calling it manipulative, clichéd, and unfunny. Sam could practically see Marc wilting under the criticism, which was over the top and not accurate.

Jane shook her head. "I disagree, Gibson. But it isn't focused enough yet, Marc. Let's keep it in the mix, and you keep rewriting. I'll make a call on it tomorrow, because we'd need time to round up some puppies if I green-light it."

When the conversation moved on, Sam signaled to Marc and whispered, "That wasn't about you. That was about me. Don't sweat it."

If Gibson had complaints about Sam, the very least the guy could do was to direct them at their intended target. Gibson was smart enough not to attack Roxy—she had claws—but he'd clearly decided Marc was relatively defenseless and under Sam's protection.

Sam immediately wanted to pound him into the ground, but then he remembered what Bree had said. He needed to rein in those impulses if he was going to be good enough for her.

When Jane called a break, Sam stomped across the room to Gibson. "Can we have a word?"

"We can have two."

Sam suspected they were *fuck* and *you*.

They walked out into the hallway together, and the handful of people meandering around began, not at all covertly, to eavesdrop.

"Why are you attacking me and anyone you see as my ally? Because I have to warn you, Roxy can and will kick your ass."

Gibson pursed his mouth. "You've got a lot of nerve."

"Obviously. But what did I do to you?"

"It's what you're doing to this show. You're a crabby toddler who's being cosseted to protect him from the consequences of his actions."

Sam scrubbed a hand over his face. "Care to put that in words a simpleton like me can understand?"

"You have no business being here after what you pulled."

"Telling off Michal Blaese? *That's* what you object to?"

"He's a great businessman, but what mostly pisses me off is that if anyone else here did what you did, we'd be on probation or fired. But for some reason, Jane can't seem to get enough of you. You're the teacher's pet. And yeah, that pisses me off."

Sam almost laughed. "You're jealous," he said, clarifying.

"No!" Gibson couldn't admit what was patently obvious to the half dozen or so people who were now nakedly watching this conversation.

"You are. And look, there are times when . . ." Okay, Sam had never really been jealous, in part because he was the kind of asshole who thought he was better than everyone else, but he could imagine what it would be like to be Gibson and feel as if you were overlooked. Sam would've probably taken that as a cue to be *better at his job*. But sure, this worked too. "I've been—"

"No, you haven't," Gibson interrupted. "Because you never pay any penalties."

"That's not true. I've lost gigs before. Videon's probably going to cancel my contract, and I offered to quit the show."

"But Jane kept you around!"

"Because I'm good at what I do."

In the version of this in Gibson's head, Sam probably bellowed that. But in real life, Sam didn't need to raise his voice. He wasn't even that annoyed. Hell, on his best day, Sam spent at least an hour wondering how good he actually was. He could promise his own self-inflicted anxieties were far darker than whatever inferiority complex Gibson was trying to infect Sam with.

For a second, Sam thought Gibson might self-destruct. Instead, he spluttered before throwing his hands up in the air and shouting, "Gah!" and storming around the corner.

"Well, that was delightful," Roxy deadpanned. At some point, she'd joined the crowd. Pretty much the entire cast had witnessed the end of Sam and Gibson's conversation. Jane hadn't been there, but her assistant was, and Sam was certain Jane would be getting a full report soon.

But the thing was, deep down, Sam couldn't be mad, because he knew what Gibson was saying: Sam kept dancing on the edge of that cliff. As he'd said to Bree, he knew one day, perhaps very soon, the fall would come. He could handle it if it came at work. But losing Bree was too much to contemplate.

"Let's get back in there. We'll be starting again soon."

Roxy scoffed. "Like you care."

The thing was, while it lasted, Sam did.

That morning, Bree dug out the contract she'd been offered by Hutchinson-Baker and contemplated something irrational: not signing it. Sure, it was everything she had ever wanted at work, but for the first time, she was beginning to suspect work wasn't everything.

She couldn't bring herself to talk to Jeff or Megan about it, because they'd be aghast, which left her contemplating it on her own, since she normally hashed this kind of thing through with Sam.

Why hadn't she invested in a wider circle of friends?

A few hours later, she met Sam at the Morton Williams near her apartment to pick up stuff for dinner. He dropped a kiss on her cheek—and she pulled back. They hadn't gone out since getting together, but Bree had spent enough time in public with Sam to know where this was going. She wanted no part of the tabloids, thank you very much.

Sam gave her a knowing look. He grasped her elbows and towed her back into him, where he kissed her thoroughly. That short-circuited any and all objections. Her body couldn't resist his.

Against the base of his throat a minute later, she whispered, "We haven't been in public yet."

"Now we have." And he kissed her temple. "We've got to rip the Band-Aid off someday, Smoosh. There's no avoiding it."

She wanted to stomp her foot and stick out her lower lip and whine. He made her regress to the emotional age of sixteen, but . . . well, this was something they should have talked about. It wasn't a nothing issue, not when everyone was going to call her his rebound girl while tipping Bree's life upside down and riffling through the contents.

"You know what being with me entails. You having second thoughts?" He said it lightly, but she knew it wasn't a light question to him.

Sam had been rejected often enough, humiliatingly enough, as a kid. He was basically a walking bruise. That mix of vulnerability and bluster, the truth-or-dare of him, it left her defenseless. She couldn't, she wouldn't, withhold from him emotionally.

"No," she told him with utmost sincerity. "But I'm nervous." She had every other emotion under the sun, including guilt that she couldn't be as honest with him as he was with her and distrust of his faith in them. *Nervous* was accurate but too basic for all of what she was feeling.

"Me too," he agreed. "But I'm not going to hide how I feel about you." He held out a hand.

From a lifetime of observing him, she knew that at the surface level, it was that simple for him. Underneath, he was crawling with fears and emotions and wounds, but since he wasn't willing to face those, he'd moon over her publicly instead. It was like watching someone do a magic trick and fool himself. She, however, was too sensible to let herself fall for his sleight of hand.

She linked her fingers through his, but there was a twinge in her chest. Sam picked up a basket, and they began to peruse the shelves.

"How was your day?" she asked, considering the spinach. One of the rare food things Sam was picky about was spinach. He hated it cooked or even wilted, but he also hated tough, big leaves in a salad.

"There was some . . . drama at work," he said.

"Drama behind the scenes at *Comedy Hour*? Ooh, tell me more."

He tweaked her nose. "You know, it boils down to some of my coworkers thinking I'm a spoiled baby who's insulated from the consequences of his decisions."

Bree halted. "Seriously? Well, I hope you told them you haven't been insulated a day in your life."

"Why, Bryony Edwards, I think you'd fight someone for my honor." He slapped a hand dramatically to his brow and affected a southern accent. "I do declare, I might swoon."

"Shut up." A pause. "But sure, I'd fight people for your honor." Someone needed to fight for Sam sometimes, rather than him always throwing down for others.

Sam began towing her down the aisle. "Here's the thing, though, Smoosh. He might not be wrong."

"What do you mean?"

"I mean, I should've torched my career the other night, but somehow I . . . didn't."

Bree stepped in front of him. "Sam, I'm serious. Look at me: your career withstood that because you're good at what you do and you've worked hard."

For a second, Bree wasn't certain if Sam had heard her, but then it occurred to her: price-checking chickpeas wasn't that interesting. He was trying *not* to absorb what she was saying. He needed compliments, but he couldn't believe them.

"You really think highly of me," he said after a second. Disbelief. Wonder. *Longing.*

The way she felt about him, in all its colors and textures, and his need of those things fitted together like bricks in *Tetris*. She might have real, legitimate concerns, but all he had to do was flash his insecurities at her, and they seemed secondary.

She gave him the words again. "I love you."

When Sam looked at her then, he didn't smile. He illuminated like a Halloween glow stick. "I love you so much." He didn't have to touch her. He didn't have to kiss her. Bree felt branded by his naked adoration. He splayed her open more thoroughly than anyone or anything else could.

She moved to grab some tomatoes. "I was thinking pasta with sausage, but—damn." Bree stopped herself. They were out of the brand that was marked down. "Maybe something else. Maybe black bean tacos. Or—"

"Just get this kind." Sam grabbed the expensive San Marzano tomatoes that were actually from Italy. He set them in the basket.

"Sam," she hissed.

"What?"

"Put those back."

His eyes sparkled—because he knew exactly what she was thinking. "No, it's time for both of us to rip off this Band-Aid too. We're buying the organic imported tomatoes. This is basically our second virginity. It's more momentous, even. Who cares about hymens? Expensive tomatoes are where it's at. We should have a commemorative plaque made."

"The other tomatoes are just as good." So what if the budget tomatoes weren't available? There were intermediate tomatoes. They didn't have to jump to the Ferrari of tomatoes.

"We can't know that," he said. "Not until we try them."

"Sam."

She dove for the can to put it back on the shelf, but Sam got there first. He hefted the twenty-eight ounce can over his head—and he was absurdly tall. Even when Bree popped up onto her toes and reached as high as she could, he could still easily hoist it out of reach.

"This isn't going to work, Smoosh, but it's fun to watch you try." He inched backward, and she tumbled into his chest. His free arm came around her waist. "I like this better."

She grunted with the effort to reach the entirely too expensive tomatoes, but it was no good. "You're obnoxious."

"No one has ever mentioned that to me before."

"You're not going to let this go?"

"Not a chance. By the way, if your goal was for this to be a low-key shopping trip, you are single-handedly landing us on social media right now."

Damn. He was right. Two people in the aisle had their phones raised.

Bree dropped her heels to the floor and took a few steps back.

"I'm putting these in the basket right now," he warned. "Don't make any sudden moves."

"Bastard."

But even as Bree relented, even when she let him get the kind of sausage that you have to ask the butcher for, the kind wrapped in brown paper, even when she let him pay, she was aware of the eyeballs and couldn't quite let go of the fears. The monetary ones and the emotional ones.

CHAPTER 20

Sam had no idea why he and Bree hadn't gotten together ages ago. Kissing her, sleeping with her, eating dinner with her every night: these things were so simple and so perfect, they put the lie in every other moment of his life. He loved Bree. He truly loved her.

After taping Saturday's show and making a brief appearance at the after-party, he'd convinced her to head home early. But even when they were settled into her couch and flipping through her movies, she was still skeptical.

"You'd rather watch a bad movie and be snarky with me than hang out with an Oscar-winning actor?"

"That's even a question? Though, honestly, Smoosh, he was sort of a dweeb."

"Don't take away from my triumph: you're saying I'm better than an Oscar winner." She offered this in a singsong tone, but there was something under it, something Sam could feel, but couldn't quite understand.

"Way better." He tried to pull Bree into his lap so that he could show her how much better, but she wouldn't budge. Apparently she'd thought he wanted to go home and watch a movie *literally*. He could work with that. "So are you in a Jean-Claude Van Damme mood?"

Among the eighties and nineties action stars, no one else committed to the entire ridiculousness of his persona in quite the same way Van Damme did. Bree found it hysterical and endearing, much as Sam hoped she found him.

"Nah."

"Oh my God, you're ready to finally give Nic Cage another go. I knew it!"

"Ha! Never." She beamed, but the smile fell from her face in an instant. "You pick."

"See, there, *that*. What's that? You never pass up a chance to argue with me."

"I didn't do anything," Bree insisted.

"Yes, you did. I can see you smiling, being real, and then you just—stop yourself."

He normally had a good run with a relationship before things went bad. He and Bree shouldn't have been anywhere near that expiration date—no, he and Bree should never be anywhere near that. Sam was going to do everything in his power to make sure he and Bree never expired.

Bree wouldn't meet his eyes. She was playing with the fringe on one of her throw pillows. "I've wanted to be with you for so long. And now that I am—it's hard to believe," she finally said.

He released a long breath, watching the hair around her face stir and willing the panic that had been rising in his chest to relax. She needed reassurance. He got that. He needed reassurance about fifty times a day.

"This will last," he said to both of them.

"No, I . . . I think, I hope we will." He liked hearing her say it. "But that's not exactly what I mean. It's more—love in the books, in the movies, solves everything."

"Yes, Romeo and Juliet were famously problem-free."

She laughed and finally looked at him. "No, but it's supposed to be the answer for everything. I think about my mom and how my dad was really not the answer for her."

Sam tried not to think about his parents, but the only lesson he could take away was *never be that*. That wasn't exactly a game plan.

"When I thought about the future, I wanted something real, something permanent. Not like the house in the suburbs with the picket fence, but stability. Someone to build a life with. I'm thirty-two. I thought I'd be in that relationship by now."

"Smoosh—"

"No." She held up a hand to him. "Don't even respond to that. You have impetuousness in your eyes, and I'm not fishing for anything we're not ready for. But honestly? I thought I'd be further along with all that by now. I thought I'd own a place. I thought I'd be with someone to think about kids with. I thought I'd have a fancier title. Instead, I'm basically where I was eight years ago. That's the pandemic, it's this expensive-ass city, but it's also . . ." She trailed off, and that look came into her eyes, the one where she realized she'd gone too far.

The other issue was him; the way she'd felt about him.

"Me?" he offered. He tossed it off like a beanbag, but inside, it landed like a wrecking ball. Damn it, he'd really hurt her.

"Maybe. Yes. Partially." Which were contradictions. "I couldn't move on."

In the last week and a half, as they'd fallen into this thing, he'd wondered more times than he could count which deity he needed to make a sacrifice to. How was it possible that she'd been there, still single, still the greatest fucking thing on earth, while he grew enough to deserve her?

She cared about him. He knew that. But he still had no idea why she'd waited for him. That had been a bad bet, and he could only spend the rest of his life trying to make it pay out for her.

"You probably should've." Which was honest, but it hurt—oh God, it hurt—to say.

"I probably should've." The smile she gave him said she was glad she hadn't. "But now that we're sort of together—"

"We're together." He wouldn't hear any debate on *that* topic.

"—I guess I sort of assumed that if we were together, all the rest of it would seem unimportant. And in some ways, it is. But some of it isn't."

She'd said it matter-of-factly, but he could feel himself bristling. And cringing. And wanting to fight.

He was nothing if not predictable.

But the look on her face at the grocery store when she'd realized people were taking pictures of them, the way she occasionally didn't respond to his texts for a few hours, the distance in her eyes sometimes: they lost their mystery.

"You're right," he said, "I haven't solved all your problems in ten days."

"Sam." She interrupted him with infinite patience. "You aren't listening to me. I never expected you to. But you're asking why I stop myself from being fully in the moment, and that's it."

He twisted so that he could face her head-on, trying to let go of the emotional churn in his gut. "If you had a lot of dreams about your future, I had no dreams about mine. I think what we need here is for me to transfer half of my 'there is only today' attitude to you, and half of your 'let's make a spreadsheet about the future' attitude to me."

She considered this and then asked, "Other than the Videon special, what is it that you want?"

Jane had asked him the same thing the other day, and he still didn't have a good answer. "Not to end up like my parents."

"Oh, hard same. But what do you *want*?"

"You." That was the only thing he was certain of, but for her . . . he tried to stretch to give her a fuller answer. "I want to feel like if I stop running for a second, I won't die. I want to stop trying to burn down the world because I think it's going to burn down no matter what."

He'd said to Roxy that he couldn't mess up with Bree, and he wanted to believe that maybe Bree was the one pillar he could salvage when the flood came. But despite all his fronting, in the deepest vault of his heart, he still carried the ice-cold fear of losing her.

"Yeah, I want you to stop being self-destructive too," she said wryly.

Okay, that was clearly enough about him. "And what do *you* want?"

"Hmm." Her eyes moved over his face for several seconds, weighing something. Then, she said, "I don't know if my goals are different now than before. A life with someone . . . and to do work that matters."

He couldn't believe she'd missed that she had those things right now. "You're already doing amazing things with Megan. I mean, I saw you up close when I was staying here. You're making the world better at Innovation X."

"Am I?" Her tone made it clear that Bree didn't totally believe him.

Well, they were going to have to work on that. Sam pushed his fists into the couch and began crawling toward her. "Yes. And now, you have a life with someone."

Then he got down to what he'd been wanting to do this entire time: kissing her until nothing else mattered.

Bree should've told him about Michigan. That had been the moment to tell him. But Sam wasn't hearing her, and she needed him to understand when she told him the entire story. Her reasoning wasn't going to make his anger go away, but it would put his feelings and her decision into context.

That context *wasn't* her bed, where they'd relocated after a few minutes of making out on the couch.

Sam was kissing down her stomach. He'd stripped her of most of her clothing, and now his fingers pushed under the elastic of her panties, and his breath wafted over her belly button in a way that made his intentions pretty clear.

"I don't normally . . . come from that," Bree whispered, feeling self-conscious. "So, I mean, don't feel like you need to." His hand, her vibrator, her hand: those things would get her there before oral sex.

Sam pushed up, and his muscles, scored and bulging, were far more arousing than the thought of his mouth on her pussy. "That a hard no, or you just telling me I don't have to?"

"The—the second one," she stammered. "I mean . . . I don't have an objection to it, but it makes me feel—I just can't let myself go enough to come."

He watched her levelly. "I really want to."

"You do?"

"Yeah, the last time I took a shower, I was imagining how your pussy was going to taste. I jerked off."

At that confession, Bree felt herself get wetter. She would've rubbed her thighs together if Sam weren't in between them. She didn't need him to taste her, but she did need him to fuck her brains out.

She pushed her hands down her torso, needing some skin-to-skin contact. She was breaking out in goose bumps, and she almost moaned at the sensation. "What did you . . . imagine?" she asked.

"Me licking you until you were screaming."

The words were so much hotter than the act would be; that was the problem. "I just . . . it won't be like that."

"Because it never has been before?"

"Yeah."

"But this time, it'll be different." He was dead sure. "It'll be with me."

"Sam." She sounded so needy and breathless.

"What about this?" He pushed himself all the way up until he was standing. He stripped off his shirt and let it fall to the floor, where it was quickly joined by his pants and boxers. Within seconds, he'd devested Bree of her underwear. He fisted his cock, blowing out a long breath at the contact. Then he climbed back onto the bed, but not how she thought he was going to. Now, his face was next to her hip, and his cock was at her shoulder. "I'll put my mouth on you," he said, "and you put your mouth on me."

"I . . ." Bree licked her lips. His cock was pretty mouthwatering. "I mean, sure. But we could also just get to the main event. I'm ready." She was beyond ready.

Sam chuckled. "If we start, and you're not into it, you tell me, and I'll do that. But I think you'll be into it."

"I just, in the past—"

"The past doesn't matter." He dug his fingers into her hip and tilted her toward him. "That a yes, Smoosh?"

She squeezed her thighs together, needing the friction, needing— well, just needing. If anyone was going to be able to turn off her thoughts, it would be Sam. And if he wanted to try, they could try. "Yes."

"Good." Gently, so gently, he bent one of her knees, making room for himself, before he dropped a sloppy kiss next to her mound with a satisfied growl.

Bree couldn't help it: she shivered. She was still worried about how she might smell, how she might taste, but he seemed into this. Very into this.

As he continued to drop sloppy kisses on her, she began running her fingertips over the tip of his cock. Nothing about Sam was soft or vulnerable, except for this. He almost pushed his hips toward her, and then he stopped himself.

"Greedy," she whispered.

"Yup." And then he buried his face in her.

She gave a little yelp. It had just gone from nothing to full contact so fast, and she was so wet, so ready, so exposed. But the sound he made—good gravy, the sound Sam made. Like he'd never tasted anything so good. Like there was no place he would rather be than face-first in her.

It gave Bree the courage to push across the last few inches between them, lips parted, and slip his cock into her mouth. She had no objection to giving blow jobs, but they'd never done much for her. But this *was* somehow different.

It was with Sam, of course. Everything hit harder because it was him, because of how well he knew her and how well she knew him. Because of the full force of what she felt for him. But it wasn't only that: it was the shared trust of giving and receiving at the same time.

She was absolutely awash in feelings. Just drowning in them, while her mouth slipped up and down his hardness, while he sucked on her clit, while his fingers pushed into her, while she could hear him moving against her wetness, while her hips couldn't help but shift and buck while she searched for what he was trying to give her.

Feeling dizzy, almost seeing stars, Bree let his cock fall from her mouth and pressed her face against the coarse hair on his thigh. She made some inarticulate noise of pleasure.

He lifted his mouth from her for a second, though his hand didn't stop working. "Good?"

"Please."

"'Cause we can stop," he teased.

She was practically riding his fingers. Later, she might feel ridiculous—but she wouldn't. She wouldn't let herself be embarrassed by what she was showing him, how exposed she was with him, because he wanted to see this. Wanted to coax it from her. He was seeking her abandon, and it would be the worst thing in the world to withhold that from him.

"Please don't stop," she breathed. "I . . . it's never been like this."

"Can I get you there?"

"Yes. Please, just, please."

Then he was groaning, and he was where she needed him again, and suddenly, the expression *face-fucking* wasn't abstract. His cock was in her mouth, and she was giving him everything she had, everything she wanted, because with him, it all seemed possible.

When she came, because of course she did, she screamed, which felt inevitable. It felt incredible. Her orgasm made her back throb and the soles of her feet tingle and her eyes water. And when he pushed up from the bed and he licked his fingers clean, it didn't feel like a performance. She believed that he thought she was delicious. She believed that going down on her had turned him on because she'd felt the evidence of his response against her lips.

"I won't say I told you so."

All she could manage was a little laugh. She didn't have any energy left.

When he climbed over her and his erection brushed her belly—she hadn't been as successful with him as he had been with her—he looked deep into her eyes, and she knew that he saw her. Saw everything. Even what she might rather keep from him.

His cock dragged through her pubic hair. "I've never not used a condom. Ever," he said.

It took her a minute to figure out what he meant.

He was suggesting they have sex without a condom. She had an IUD; she'd been tested at her last doctor's visit. But she'd never dropped her need for multiple levels of protection. She'd never let herself take this particular risk.

"Have you been tested?" she asked.

"Yes." He wouldn't lie to her about that. Not about anything. "If you want me to use one, I will. I would never not, if that's what you wanted."

She trusted him implicitly. But the idea of Sam inside her without a barrier, as bare and real as they'd just been together—she wanted that. Nothing hidden. Nothing shielded.

She let both her knees drop to the bed so that she was more open than she had ever been before. More open than open.

"I haven't either," she said. "Not used one."

Sam rubbed the tip of his cock through her folds. Her body had been so sensitized by his mouth and his fingers and his tongue, she could feel his progress millimeter by millimeter. She moaned.

"We probably should talk about this when we're clearheaded." He moved over her again, and she tilted her body to chase him, to prolong the contact.

Fuck fuck fuck fuck.

She already knew what was going to happen. This felt like a memory. An incredibly hot memory.

"Probably," she breathed back. "But—I need you."

"Like this?" He moved over her again, and she could feel the question there.

"Yes. Yes. God, please, yes."

He thrust into her, deep and true and certain. And she knew Sam wasn't just moving into her body. For twenty years, she'd thought she'd loved him as much as it was possible to love someone. She'd never imagined that telling him, having him reciprocate, letting him into her in every possible way, might somehow amplify her feelings. Make her love him more.

As she came again and felt him find his own release, she knew there were depths of emotion she hadn't plumbed, hadn't even known about. Together, they could find them.

When he wrapped himself around her, she said softly against his chest, "How did we not become them?"

"Not become who?"

"How did you become a person who could never hit a woman?"

He stiffened under her, then relaxed. "I don't know," he whispered back.

"How did I become a person who could never embezzle money from her kid?"

There was another long silence. Then he said, "We found each other."

Bree had grown up thinking the most romantic declarations would be flowery and over the top, probably involving champagne and iambic pentameter or, at the very least, diamonds.

But with those four words, Sam destroyed those notions. He'd given her the truth. Simple. Unvarnished. And it was the most romantic thing anyone had ever or could ever say to her.

But as she fell asleep tucked against him, one thought floated back to her from the darkness of his bedroom: they had nothing shielded from each other—except that she might leave New York.

CHAPTER 21

In the weeks since they'd started sleeping together, Sam had basically moved into Bree's apartment, and they'd stopped talking about when he might leave. They'd gone on the Jacob Riis walking tour. They'd watched movies. They'd done crossword puzzles. They'd had a private Thanksgiving, just the two of them, the day before. It was everything Bree had thought being with him could be, and it felt awful because she still hadn't told him the truth.

"I'm sorry, but I'm not smart enough for this," Jeff said when Sam finished his explanation of how to play Settlers of Catan.

Roxy had invited herself over because she and Bree hadn't hung out in forever, and then Bree had invited Jeff because the game worked best with four players.

Jeff's expression conveyed that he regretted saying yes.

It could have been high school, it could have been in college, it could have been when Sam was struggling to make it—except for the moments where Sam had touched Bree's knee under the table and caught her eye, and she'd known he was thinking about last night.

"Everyone is smart enough for this." Sam was something of a table-top-game evangelist, with all the subtle condescension and bullying that implied.

"Just watch out for Sam," Bree warned Roxy and Jeff from the kitchen where she was making cocktails and mocktails and pouring wine. "He's vicious."

"Hey, all I do is refuse to make most trades."

"This is what I mean," Bree explained. "Vicious."

"It's not my fault if I don't want to make a deal that might come back and bite me in the ass."

Bree carried the tray of drinks over to the table and set it next to the charcuterie board that she'd assembled on the fly once she'd realized they really were throwing a party here.

She and Sam. Hosting a party. Together. It felt like a significant first.

"Not everything is a trick or a shank, Samuel."

"Just most things."

Bree and Roxy exchanged a look. Roxy seemed to be judging whether Sam really believed it, and Bree—who knew he did—was curious whether Roxy understood he was being serious.

"Hey, no nonverbal communication," Jeff warned, wagging a finger at them. "That's not fair to the rest of us."

"We're only concerned for Sam's obviously very wounded soul," Bree deadpanned. It was only 10 percent a joke. She, at least, was concerned for his soul.

"Is this Settlers of Catan, or Freud the Game?" Sam asked.

"Ooh, I didn't realize that was an option. I vote for Freud," Roxy said. "And I call dibs on that idea for *Comedy Hour* next week." She directed that to Sam.

"There can be a phallus-or-cigar draw pile," Bree suggested.

"No, it's too highfalutin for the show. But less talking, more playing." Sam tapped the table in front of Jeff's pieces. "It's time to place your first settlement. You want to have access to a range of resources, especially if they have numbers on them that get rolled a lot."

Jeff's eyes were wide as he surveyed the array of hexagonal biomes. "Which numbers get rolled a lot?"

"The ones in the middle. Like not two or three and not twelve."

Sam was nervous, twitchy. He didn't like the setup part of the game. He liked the part where he beat the pants off everyone, which pretty much happened all the time. Part of it was his ruthlessness—because whatever Sam might say, he *was* ruthless—but he also had the most incredible luck when it came to rolling dice and drawing the cards he needed. Someone somewhere in the world was never getting the twelve they needed because Sam was soaking up more than his share.

Bree wouldn't have believed it if she hadn't seen it happen over and over again. Sam seemed able to bend the world to his needs through sheer force of will.

Look at her, for example. She knew that she ought to tell him she had an amazing job offer in Michigan, but he had her vacillating. They'd just gotten together. She couldn't move halfway across the country and give up her only shot with the man she'd loved forever, could she?

Sam set his hand over Bree's on the table, scrolling patterns on the back of her hand. The last two weeks had been like that: small gestures of affection. Inside jokes.

Pictures of them at the grocery store had in fact dropped on social media, and that, plus her attendance at the Videon museum party and disastrous stand-up set, were taken as evidence that she and Sam were together. That Bree was his latest flavor of the month. So far, it had been more buzz than roar of annoyance, but Bree knew it couldn't last. The next time Sam melted down, the next time he burst into the news, the attention was going to bury her.

Unless it didn't. Unless, somehow, he managed to turn over a new leaf.

It was like when you stored up your laundry for weeks and sorting out all the pairs of socks took forever. Bree was still trying to get her feelings laid out and in the right order. But she and Sam felt so effortless—so inevitable—that maybe it could work. Maybe they brought out the best in each other, and maybe they were meant to be.

"How about here?" Jeff tentatively placed the small wooden settlement.

"Sure." The second Jeff released the piece, Sam gleefully slammed his piece down on another junction. "It leaves this one for me."

Bree groaned.

"We're off to a bad start?" Jeff asked.

Since Sam had claimed the most advantageous location, she said, "We're off to a totally normal start." She toasted Jeff with her wine. "Gird your loins."

Everyone placed their settlements and roads, and the play began. The early part of the game was always tedious until everyone got the numbers in their heads and built up some resources to be able to do things.

Bree had seen Sam play so many times, she knew his tricks. For every game in his repertoire, he had about three strategies, and he'd rotate through them, much like a playboy through his Rolodex. This game, he was going for the longest road, and he was happily ruining everyone else's expansion strategies in the bargain. But he did it so charmingly and with so much glee, she only wanted to laugh.

"What? Why can't I build there?" Jeff demanded.

"Because of Sam's road," Bree explained.

"Well, unbuild your road, sir."

Sam gave Jeff his most appealing smile—and it was a *very* appealing smile. "You can't."

"I'm an urban planner, and I'm telling you, you can. Take Boston and the Big Dig." After managing to place his road elsewhere, Jeff turned to Bree. "There isn't enough wine for this."

"I just opened another bottle."

"Do you want some more?" he asked as he got to his feet, grumbling.

"Nah. I'm set." Bree rolled and collected a lumber card. "So which of you lovely, lovely people are going to trade me some clay for some stone?" She addressed this question to Roxy and Jeff, despite the fact that Sam had two clay cards, because she wasn't in the habit of pursuing dead ends.

"I will." Sam offered her one of his cards. "Give me that stone."

"Hey, no fair! I asked for the same deal three turns ago," Roxy whined. "Why are you making it with her?"

"Because I like Bree more."

"Ooh," Roxy and Jeff chanted simultaneously, and Bree felt her cheeks burn. She really didn't need any more wine. She was buzzed enough to be flushed. She placed another settlement before sinking back in her chair.

And that turned out to be her final good play of the game. Sam might have been willing to be generous to her for one play—he did love her—but that was his one and only moment of magnanimity. He basically annihilated all of them.

When Sam declared he had ten victory points, he literally pounded on his chest, declaring, "Good game!"

"Has he always been so low key?" Roxy asked, glaring at him over the rim of her glass.

"Believe it or not, this is the mellow version."

Sam began putting the game away and whistling "We Are the Champions."

"I do make him clean up, though," Bree explained. "He has to tell you that you played well, which he doesn't mean, but he says anyhow."

"I have the highest standards for organization," Sam said. "And I clean up the best."

When you did enough puzzles from the Salvation Army that were always missing seven pieces, this was how you ended up. A lot of Bree's and Sam's childhood game experience had come at a store called Trivial Pursuits, which had games and tables in the back. You could play them, but only if you could prove you were responsible and wouldn't lose the pieces. Getting the owner's okay to play there had been one of Sam's chief accomplishments as a kid.

Christ but she loved him for it.

Bree almost said, *Do you remember*, before she shut her mouth. She knew Sam remembered. But while Sam and Roxy were close, and he and Jeff were friendly, Sam wouldn't like it if Bree spilled that kernel from their past to Roxy and Jeff. It was private.

"That was educational," Jeff said, downing the rest of his wine. "Thanks for having me." He carried his glass and plate to the sink. "I'm going to miss this when you move—"

Oh, shit.

Jeff caught himself, but the look of abject apology he gave Bree sealed the deal.

It was that moment when your subway train crunches to a halt and the lights flicker out and you realize you're in for a *long* night.

"Move . . . where?" Sam had paused with a baggie of yellow settlement, city, and road pieces in one hand.

Roxy's eyes darted back and forth between Sam and Bree; then she jumped to her feet. "Well, I think that's our cue." She dropped her dishes in the sink, shoved her feet into her booties, and grabbed her coat. "Let's go, Jeff."

"You said it."

Bree stood up stiffly and closed the door behind them. She briefly considered thumping her head into it.

At the table, Sam had continued to clean the game up, but he could do things quietly with the same force as a jackhammer. Bree could feel each of his movements, as if they were sending shock waves through the air. When he set the top on the box, it might as well have been a timpani sounding.

She knew whatever measure of grace she'd experienced was done. She had to tell him. She had to tell him everything.

"Move where?" he repeated.

Let him be reasonable. Let him listen to me. But Bree wasn't certain who she was sending that prayer up to. There wasn't any deity who could help her.

She turned and leaned against the door. "I have to tell you something."

His eyebrows were arched and his body tight. "Clearly."

"When you and Salem got engaged, I applied for jobs in other places."

"Uh-huh." So calm. So, so calm.

"I got some offers. But I didn't take any. I dunno why. It felt like there was unfinished business here. Then about a month ago, I heard from a firm asking if I was interested in interviewing for a primary consultant gig."

Sam's expression didn't change. Not a skosh. "And?"

"You'd just come to stay with me, and I was . . . Sam, I was in such pain. I knew how I felt, and I was certain you didn't—and you couldn't—reciprocate. Like I said to you the other day, I felt as if I was in the same place where I'd been for so long, wanting my life to change."

She forced herself to stand up straight, push her shoulders back. She wasn't ashamed. She was telling him the *truth*. She knew why she'd done it. But it was easy to imagine how all this sounded—and more importantly felt—to Sam.

"So?" he finally asked.

"So I did the interview."

"And?"

"Then I did a second interview. And three weeks ago, they offered me the job."

She always wondered why Sam never broke character on *Comedy Hour*. Everyone else did. Roxy's "break face" was famous because she was such an unmitigated badass that when she got the giggles, people loved it even more than when she stayed in character.

Sam never did.

Bree had always wondered what it would be like to stare down his set expression. Now she knew. Being the prey object of a peregrine falcon in a full dive must be a similar experience, qualitatively. Her spine threatened to bow and her knees to collapse, but Bree stayed tall.

"It's a great job," she said quickly. "It's in Ann Arbor, Michigan. It's a lot more money, but it's also more variety. I could work on projects all over the country. Even the world! Sustainability, accessibility: it's everything I care about."

Except for you.

"I'm actually excited about it." And, if she didn't look at it from the Sam angle, she was. "They want me to start just after New Year's."

"You're leaving New York." It was a statement, not a question. It wasn't mad. It was whatever mad turns into when it burns itself out.

Bree would've preferred mad. She would've known what to do with mad. "Maybe."

"It didn't sound like a maybe when Jeff said it."

"I haven't accepted the job. I told them I needed some time." She probably needed to give them an answer by Monday, but she omitted that part.

"Why? It sounds *perfect.*" There, Sam had cracked there. Just for a millisecond. But under this mask, what he was feeling had hurricane-force winds.

Bree had known him since the age of five, and she could predict his moods like the weather or a tsunami. As a result, she knew he felt abandoned. He thought she didn't love him. He assumed she was rejecting him.

None of that was true. *None of it.* Bree had loved him for almost her entire lifetime. She'd been more devoted, more constant, than anyone else had ever been for him. But because she'd tried to take care of herself once, none of that mattered.

Sam got to his feet. With his back to her, he walked to the living room. He'd taken off his shoes because he knew she hated to vacuum, and one of his socks had a hole in the heel. Sam Leyland, one of the most famous and successful comedians in the country, was wearing holey socks, because he still thought they had some wear or because no one was around to make him throw them out, to prod him to get new ones.

The little bit of his exposed skin made her chest constrict, cracking her heart. The pieces of it were jagged against her sternum. Scratch-scratch-scratching, threatening to poke out into the room.

"I don't know what I'm going to tell them," she said.

He turned, his eyes dark. "Okay, but when were you going to tell *me*?"

That response was fair. God, his anger was so fair. She couldn't be defensive. He was right to feel this way. That didn't mean she'd been wrong; though, okay, it was wrong not to have told him. But he was right too.

"I'm sorry, Sam, but I have loved you for—" Her voice cracked. "Just so long. And I didn't think you did or could love me back. I thought if I didn't put some distance between us, I was going to ruin my life."

"How could love ruin your life? Or was it just loving *me* that might ruin your life?"

Bree blinked. If there was ever a moment to cry, this was it. She let the tears stream down her face. She didn't wipe them away. Didn't try to hide them. She wasn't trying to manipulate or soften him—there was no way to soften him—but it was how she felt. "No, it was that you couldn't possibly love me back."

"Which you decided on your own."

"Was that unreasonable? It wasn't as if you ever suggested you might be attracted to me."

"I'm oblivious, and I repress everything I feel. I have that on good authority." There was "Lost Boy," screaming into this argument as if on cue.

Even now, as stirred up as Bree was, she wanted to argue with Sam, to point out that Salem hadn't gotten that bit quite right. He obviously wasn't repressing very much right now, for example.

Instead, she argued for herself. "You don't get to blame me for this."

"For lying to me?" he demanded. "I sure as shit do."

"I tried to tell you. I did." Except if Jeff hadn't forced her hand, Bree didn't know when the truth would have spilled out. For her sake and for Sam's, she wished she could say. "Before we got together, if I had told you I had a job offer in Michigan, you'd have wanted to know *why* I wanted to leave, and I would've had to confess I was in love with you. And it would have been awful. Everything between us would have been weird and strained. I would've lost you."

I am losing you. It was absolutely clear, and it hurt so bad. Everything hurt.

"That's not fair. You're making assumptions."

"Sam, the last few weeks have been wonderful." For one moment, she remembered his smile against her palm, the gentleness of his mouth on her shoulder, the joy of him choosing her. They'd been so happy, but it felt distant, unreal. Like a movie they'd watched, not something they'd lived. "But they were great partially because they were so damn surprising."

"Because I always break everything." That wasn't even a question. It was what he believed about himself. As she told him the truth, her truth, she couldn't help but bolster his own worst nightmares about himself.

But if she was going to tell him everything, she had to actually tell him everything. Even the ugly parts. "No. You aren't some chaos agent. That's not how I see you. But I always thought I had to know we were soulmates before I could tell you how I felt. There was no point risking it unless I was sure, because it would be better to have you in my life as my best friend than to not have you at all. While I wanted you as my partner"—she almost stumbled on the word—"our friendship never felt like settling. No one else understands me, Sam. I could never explain all the things that you just *know* about me. If I had told you how I felt, and you had rejected me? I don't know how I could've gotten past that."

Sam was breathing hard, his chest straining against the fabric of his T-shirt. "You thought we might be soulmates?"

"Yes." In those moments when he'd moved inside her, she'd known it. "I hoped we were meant to be. That we could beat the odds, together."

He didn't respond, but she could see the war inside him. He was still so, *so* angry, but he also needed the promise of forever with her—which she understood. She also knew that he was comfortable with the promise, while she needed a firmer guarantee. He could take that leap, and she . . . couldn't.

"I know I should've told you sooner," she said. "How I felt, but also that I was considering moving."

"Yes, you should have," he agreed.

"When we got together, I wanted to tell you. Basically every conversation we've had, I've been trying to figure out how to say it. But those first few days were like a dream, and if I'd been like, 'Hey, I have this great opportunity, but it's in Michigan,' it would've shattered. I just . . . wasn't sure what to do. I've been a *mess*. That's not an excuse, though. And I'm sorry."

For a long, long moment, they stood there watching each other. There were so many emotions zinging around them, they might as well have been in a batting cage. She was sorry, but she knew why she'd acted like she did. She knew why she'd hesitated. For his part, Sam was livid, but he also wanted the future they'd been building together. And she knew that wanting made him vulnerable, which he detested.

Then he asked the question that she should've known was coming: "Are you still considering taking this job and leaving New York? Leaving me?"

Bree blew out a long breath. There was no way for this conversation to go that didn't include that question, and she had no idea how to respond. "I don't know. I've thought about telling them no." Even though giving up the job—that would hurt. A smaller hurt than leaving Sam, but a hurt all the same.

Which wasn't an answer, and so, of course, he pressed. "But?"

"This is so *new*, Sam. I had a lifetime to get used to loving you and thinking you could never love me. I hated it, but that was normal. This thing where you kiss me at the grocery store"—*and blow my mind in bed*—"it's like new shoes that have rubbed me raw. I want to believe in it."

"But you can't?" he asked.

"You love falling in love," she almost shouted. "You're good at the beginning of relationships; you're not good at keeping them going. So maybe I didn't want to tell you because I didn't think, at some level, it could last. If I wanted you in my life, it had to be as friends. Leaving would be . . . saving myself."

"From me?"

"For myself. A few weeks ago, I went to coffee with a guy Megan knows, and as soon as he found out I knew you, it just fizzled. It became the Sam show."

"Imagine how much worse it is when you're me." The acid in his voice burned her, but it must've corroded him.

"But I'm not you! I need my own oxygen, sometimes." Rather than always being his.

"I see."

"I had good reasons to be worried about telling you the truth. Can't you admit that?"

He scoffed, but he didn't disagree. Probably because he knew she was right too.

"I needed some space for myself. And maybe you needed some space from me." It wasn't that he took advantage of her, but there were ways that she had held him back too.

"We're friends," he insisted. "We're *lovers*."

"I know. Except . . ." Bree paused and almost kept the rest inside. But if they were going to have this out, they had to have it out. She couldn't lie to him, not anymore. "Sometimes maybe you need to stop dancing on the edge of the cliff. I will always try to save you. Always. But your recklessness, your need to push the envelope, it's not good. The way that makes you feel alive. The way it satisfies some self-destructive streak you have. It's hurting us both."

"So you're just going to run away?" he demanded.

The more he didn't listen to what she was saying, the more he refused to see how all this had looked and felt to her, the more his pissed-off response became contagious. "Sam, you have to realize how rich this is. All you've ever done is run away. You left home, insisting you'd never go back there ever again. You left college." *Left me back in Columbus.* "You fight with managers, and you walk out of gigs. You push away your exes before they can leave you. You're always running."

"But who's running now? You say you love me, you say that you think we might belong together—not for a year or a moment, but for forever—and then you tell me that you can't even decide if you're staying."

"Yes."

That brought him up short.

Bree would've given anything for the ability to exit this and come back to it after a nap. After they'd cooled down. After she'd been able to process.

Sam might be used to improv, to thinking on his feet, to shooting from the hip, but she wasn't. She made plans, she shared them, she revised. She was a slow digester. A consensus builder. If she and Sam could just have time, they could work this out.

But she knew Sam wasn't going to give her time. So she had to take care of herself.

"This fight that we're having now, you pushing me away after the two weeks we've just shared? This is exactly why I didn't want to tell you I was in love with you, it's exactly why I looked for jobs other places, and it's exactly why I didn't tell you about Michigan. I know why you're pissed, and I really am sorry. But you aren't making your point. You're making *mine*." She would've given anything for that not to be what she had to say. But it was.

For a long, terrible moment, she wasn't certain how Sam was going to respond.

But he surprised her when he reached out across her table, and with infinite gentleness, he cupped her face. The storm in his eyes had abated. "I love you, Bryony Edwards." Then he drew in a long breath and delivered his verdict: "I wish you believed in me, in us, the way I do."

Once, just once, his fingertips bit into her cheek. Then he was gone.

Bree folded in a chair and pushed her hands into her hair. In the course of fifteen minutes, the truth had finally screamed out into the open, spraying Sam and Bree with shrapnel. Old hurts and new ones, all throbbing alike.

The truth was supposed to be shimmering and golden, like Wonder Woman's lasso. But for her and Sam, it was a land mine. She didn't even have his friendship to help her pick up the pieces.

CHAPTER 22

The news that Videon was officially canceling Sam's contract came on Monday morning, and it was the least fucking surprising thing in the world.

Sam hadn't left his apartment all weekend, and he'd barely slept. The last night, he hadn't even managed to close his eyes. He'd lain in bed, watching the lights from his phone and his clock mix with shadows and streak across the ceiling. All he'd managed to think about was how Bree was leaving him to move to Michigan.

Freaking Michigan.

Okay, so he didn't actually have any distinct impressions of Michigan. It bordered Ohio, and he hated that place. But Michigan had melded with Wisconsin and Minnesota in his brain, and he'd filed them away under "green and leafy in summer, but unbelievably bleak and snowy the rest of the year." Leaves made him twitchy; who could trust anything so delicate and green that depended on the sun? And snow made him cold, though he'd never managed to live anywhere that didn't get a lot of it, and wasn't *that* a goddamn metaphor for his life.

He couldn't believe Bree had signed up for Michigan voluntarily. She must be *really* tired of saving his ass, which was convenient because he was also tired of saving his ass.

Sam was just so monumentally pissed. At Bree. At himself. At the world and at everyone in it. It was a cycle of rage and guilt and exhaustion, and it hurt: his joints, his veins, even his hair was sore.

While his initial anger had cooled, he still hadn't cycled through his feelings. He'd spin her news through another angle, look at it another way, and he'd be off again.

His phone rang, and he didn't answer it.

It made the text alert noise, but he'd been ignoring that all night too.

It made the email alert noise, and he pulled a pillow over his head.

There wasn't anyone on earth he wanted to talk to except Bree, and he wasn't ready to do that yet. He couldn't untangle the pieces of their conversation. It was like that picture with all the different stairways twisting around a building, leading everywhere and nowhere.

His feelings, and the things she'd kept from him. Her feelings, and his talent for slamming his fingers and career in various doorways. His bruised pride, and her legitimate concerns. His feelings.

It all came back to his feelings again.

He was pissed, but mostly he was hurt. Hurt that she hadn't told him, and hurt that she was leaving, and hurt that he couldn't blame her. It would've been easy if she'd been totally wrong. But Bree wasn't totally wrong, not even in this.

Sam had pushed his good luck and asked too much from her since the day they'd met. She should've called him on it years prior, and maybe he would have managed to rein himself in more. Been . . . better.

But Sam didn't have a mode for better. He'd checked himself all over for some switch he could flip to be the man she needed, but he could only manage to be himself, and himself wasn't enough. That was what had his eyes crusty from the sleep he couldn't get. Sam wasn't good enough for her.

His phone rang again, and Sam flung the pillow across the room. He tapped around on the nightstand and found his phone. When he saw it was Riaz, he answered, "Yeah."

His agent voiced the exact thought floating through Sam's head: "It's over."

"Like . . . planet Earth?" Sam wouldn't be surprised. If the world had ended last night, Sam wouldn't have noticed. He'd had the shit kicked out of him a time or a thousand, but this was next level. Every muscle in his body was burning. His head was like a pinball machine, all jolts and bumps and rattles.

"The Videon deal." Riaz sighed. He wasn't even pissed, just sad. "They're done with you."

"Oh." Sam had spent years wanting another special, and a year pretty openly lobbying for it. It should've been crushing that not only was he not going to get it, a nonzero percentage of the entertainment reporters in the country were going to write pieces about how and why the deal had fallen through.

Sam had alienated so many people. Everyone he knew—except possibly Bree—was probably going to give them juicy quotes speculating about everything Sam had done wrong.

It would be a long list, too, like Santa's naughty list, but every item would be about Sam.

But all he could think about was that he'd lost Bree.

"I'm sorry," Sam finally said. "I know you worked really hard for this."

"Damn right, I did! I was like the bird. The early one. With the worm." The Videon news had broken Riaz. He couldn't even get the clichés out, let alone use them wrongly.

"Am I the worm in this scenario?" Sam was probably lower than a worm.

"Argg."

"Look, I deserve that. You can fire me if you want. I bet the *Times-Ledger* would write a very sympathetic portrait of you about how hard I am to work with."

Someone was going to write that story; Riaz might as well get something out of the deal. And maybe if it started from the professional angle, they could avoid rehashing the Salem disaster and the Bree stuff—God, he hated that he'd made Bree go public with their relationship. Now she was going to get sucked into this too. That was another thing he'd messed up.

"Why are you trying to pitch a story about how you're the worst?" Riaz asked.

"I suspect I might be the worst." He knew it, actually.

"What happened?"

"Bree dumped me." Well, maybe he'd dumped her. He wasn't certain about the order of events, but he was certain that their relationship had been obliterated.

Riaz made a choking sound. "I don't do relationship advice!" Because there was no way he could collect 15 percent on that.

"I'm not asking you to. Just answering your question."

"It seems kinda shitty that she dumped you after you scuttled the Videon deal for her."

"That's . . . that's not how it went down. She didn't, well—no." He took a second, and decided that no, he wasn't comfortable blaming her. "It's not her fault." She should've told him what was going on, but he was the one who'd overreacted. Or maybe just reacted. His *normal* was everyone else's *over*. "I'm still not quite sure what happened, but it was bad."

"I'm sorry." Riaz genuinely seemed to mean that. There might be a selfish angle for him; certainly it made his job easier if Sam was happy, but it was also kind. "I do have advice. Not about that, but for you."

Advice hadn't ever really helped Sam much, but at this point, when he was at rock bottom, what did he have to lose? "Hit me."

"You should go to therapy."

Sam released a long breath. That hadn't been what he expected. "Damn."

"No one's more shocked than me. But you need to stop blowing yourself up. You're like a profane Inspector Gadget. It's getting hard to watch."

Sam wanted to argue, because of course he did, but wasn't that what Riaz was saying? "I want to make a joke about how I can skip the couch and just jump right to the part where I tell you I hate my mom—but that's cliché, and besides, haven't I already told everyone that?"

"Yup. So just think about it."

Sam rubbed his eyes. "I've treated my comedy as therapy. I go onstage and rip my heart out of my chest. If I could make everyone laugh while talking about my pain, it seemed worth it, you know? I felt . . . lighter."

"That's pretty sick."

"Yeah." Sam agreed. But for years, it was how he had coped.

"I'm just saying, I think a therapist might do that for you, but, like, in private."

Sam lifted his phone from his ear and checked the time. He probably needed to get up if he was going to go to work, and he never missed work. "You're sure you don't want to fire me instead?"

Sam was certain Riaz was considering it—he'd be stupid not to.

"Yup. I'm going to make you get some help first."

"Then you'll fire me?"

"Maybe."

Sam scoffed. "You sound like Bree." Damn, saying her name was like getting punched in the chest. His breakups tended to be embarrassing, and they left him feeling lonely. But they didn't tend to be inherently painful, probably because he didn't allow himself to feel. His feelings often hadn't been engaged below the skin level.

He would've sworn his DNA hurt.

"Did you love her?" Riaz asked.

"I still do. Always will. This one . . . it's not going to go away."

"Well, then, get yourself some help, and then go get her."

Sam wished it were that easy, but, well, it was him. Nothing was easy.

CHAPTER 23

"This should feel more celebratory," Megan said. "Why isn't it festive?" Bree had accepted the Hutchinson-Baker job at the end of the Thanksgiving weekend, and now she was at work, sharing the news with Megan.

"Well, Sam and I broke up," Bree explained. She didn't flinch, but she wanted to. Saying the words to someone else made it real, when she'd spent the entire day before trying to pretend it had been some horrible nightmare.

Megan had been lightly teasing, but her expression immediately went serious. "Damn, I'm sorry."

"You don't want to say, 'I told you so'?"

"Nope." Megan wasn't one to gloat, at any rate. "It's a shame things didn't work out with him. I *am* glad they worked out with this job."

Okay, maybe she wasn't one to gloat *that* much.

Since Bree wasn't certain how to respond, she just gave a sad shrug and went to her desk, where she worked in fits punctuated by staring into space. She felt like a sentient contusion.

When Jeff showed up a half hour later, he had a face full of contrition and a white cardboard box stuffed with bagels and two types of cream cheese. "I'm *so* sorry."

"You thought carbs would get you absolution?" Bree couldn't decide where precisely in the history of groveling this gesture might rank, but it was probably pretty low. Her brain was stuck in a loop between Sam's smile immediately before learning she might move and his look of anguish when he'd left her apartment, and it couldn't adjudicate bagel-related groveling.

Jeff shifted his attention between Bree and the box, the fruitlessness of the bagels just hitting him. "Is it working?"

Working had no meaning. Bree hadn't felt this bad when she'd had COVID, and that had been bad.

"Did you get everything bagels?" she asked Jeff.

"Yes."

"Then yes."

They had sat across from each other for five years, so Jeff knew her preferred bagel flavor. Losing Jeff would be sad. But losing Sam was personality annihilation on a cellular level. The extravagant moments of his kindness and generosity. The crinkles of his eyes when he smiled. The fierceness with which he'd always protected her. The expert judgments he made of her mood and how he tried to give her exactly what she needed. The way her stomach ached from laughing with him. The sweet sting when he'd leave at the end of the night.

Twenty years of memories and moments were just—poisoned. Everything reminded her of Sam: food items, songs on the radio, places where he'd worked, movies they'd watched together. This morning she'd biked by a coffee shop where he'd worked for two weeks, and she'd almost crumbled. Every benign reference to him gave her emotional whiplash. Losing their relationship was losing some part of herself forever, and it couldn't be replaced.

The only way she'd been able to get out of bed to write Hutchinson-Baker and come in this morning was that Ann Arbor was gloriously Sam-free. It wasn't stained with memories of him the way New York was.

She had to keep breathing in and out, focusing on the details. Getting dressed in the morning had felt like a cowboy she'd seen in an old western once, binding his chest tight to keep a broken rib together. Bree knew if she unbent for a second, her broken heart would come oozing out of her chest, and she'd never be able to gather it all up again.

After Bree covered her bagel with a double-thick layer of cream cheese, Jeff arranged himself at his desk and asked the obvious: "So how bad was it?"

"Well, you were right about that one. He was pissed." It hadn't just been Sam's anger, though; it was how hurt he was. He needed her to be as all-in as he was. Any hesitation from her was too much for him. "He left, and I didn't get the sense he'll be coming back."

It was cold, cold comfort, but it did prove that Bree had always been right. Trying to have something romantic with Sam had destroyed their friendship. She shouldn't have told him. She should've taken her love to her grave.

"He just needs a minute to process it." Jeff didn't sound convinced, but he was a good enough friend to lie.

"It might look worse the more he thinks about it," she said.

Sam hadn't used the word *betrayal*. He hadn't needed to. The problem with knowing him so well, with understanding his feelings as well as her own, was that she could read between the lines. It had been like having an argument with your mirror image.

She blinked against the emotion building in her eyes, trying to find the calm center again. But it was gone. She had nothing calm or centered left.

"So Ann Arbor?" Jeff asked.

"Yup, I accepted the job and gave Megan my notice." Next would be Bree's landlord and a moving company. She'd have lots of paperwork and logistics to distract her. While her excitement for the new job would come back, she was running away. Sam had been right about that.

"What are you going to do now?" Jeff asked.

"I have to finish the response to the Central Brooklyn Economic Development Corporation." After that, she was going to throw herself into the hundreds of details and tasks and bits of paperwork that moving was going to entail so she wouldn't have to think about how she'd fucked up the one chance she was going to get with the person she loved and needed more than anyone on earth. Because if she actually processed what she was feeling, she would never get going again, like an overheating engine that seized the second it stopped.

So she was going to wrap up everything here at Innovation X, find a great temporary apartment in Michigan, and master all the little tasks of packing and moving and cleaning. She was going to think about the best way to wrap stemware and the merits of different kinds of cardboard boxes. And maybe in a week or month or a year, she wouldn't have to remind herself not to cry at her desk.

"Well, before you leave, we could revisit some of our favorite projects."

"Um." Bree scrubbed her hands over her face. Favorite projects . . . favorite projects. Well, the ones about books, she supposed. "You remember that library on Saint Nicholas Avenue?" They'd been adding an atrium to make the building more accessible and to offer better space for programs and community organizing. They'd come in on time and under budget.

And Sam had showed up at the opening, which had meant media attention. He'd hated it, but he'd done it for her.

Nope. Bree shoved the thought away.

Jeff, who wasn't living in broken heart hell, was still beaming. "You kicked so much ass on that project. You were on fire during that neighborhood council meeting."

They had been worried that the design was trying to change the "neighborhood character," and Bree had given a speech about the history of architectural styles and access. She'd been so nervous beforehand, she had almost passed out. It was one of the first projects where Bree had taken the lead on the public side.

Sam had helped her write and practice the speech, of course. He hadn't been able to come to the meeting itself because of *Comedy Hour*'s schedule, but Jeff had held up his phone so Sam could listen to the whole thing.

Damn it. There was something in her eye. Bree wiped at it.

Don't cry. Don't cry. Don't cry. It won't always sting this bad. It couldn't, right?

"My finest hour," she managed to say to Jeff, though her voice was shaky. After a minute, she wrestled herself under control. She'd spent two decades keeping her most significant emotional truth under wraps. She could cinch herself back together. She could.

"There's a Thai place near there that I like." Jeff started writing an email to someone. "I'll add it to the list for your going-away party."

"There's a list?"

"Megan wants it to be an occasion. She's already sent a planning email."

Of course she had.

"I don't want it to be a big deal. Just let me slink off into the sunset." In shame. Like Bree deserved. She'd been the one to wreck things, in the end. Sam, who she'd never been able to imagine might want her, had been all-in. But she had been the one to keep things from him and blow things up.

Sam might be self-destructive, but she was the one who'd planted a poison pill in their nascent relationship. She had no one to blame but herself: that was the most terrible part.

"I don't think you get what your work has meant to people around here."

Bree thought she had a fairly healthy sense of herself. All her strengths—and all her weaknesses. At her job, she'd done solid, dependable work. She hadn't changed the world. She'd done what she'd been asked to, and she'd been diligent, capable, and kind. The people she'd met had felt listened to. And several neighborhoods looked and worked better because she'd been involved.

But on the other hand, there was the absolute wreckage that she had made of her heart, of Sam's heart, and of her personal life. She'd never thought she was a reckless or destructive person. It had been her goal to be the exact opposite. And she'd failed. Just full-stop, no-second-chance failed.

She took another bite of her bagel.

There was no way to make things not hurt. Not in the short term. So her new goal had to be *moving on*. Literally, but also from Sam. It sucked; it hurt; she would always miss him. But she couldn't hold herself back anymore. She had to think about her own roots, her own growth, and nothing else.

"I hope that's true," Bree told Jeff. "I just hope the next stage will be different."

"Particularly the end?"

"Especially the end."

CHAPTER 24

A week passed. Sam sleepwalked through work, writing almost nothing. Staying quiet during Wednesday's slug fest. He did what he was told in terms of performing, and Jane and Roxy rammed him into some secondary roles in bland sketches.

Gibson was delighted. He had made it very clear to everyone in the cast that he fully supported benching Sam. Sam should've found some way to fight back, to stand up for himself, but he couldn't manage to care about cast politics. He couldn't bring himself to care about anything except his own stupid broken heart.

Being pitied and managed by his friends should've been mortifying, but Sam was too numb to care. The immediate pain had gone all diffuse, as if he were watching his life from the bottom of a pool. Light and sound penetrated, but it was a big, indistinguishable mass. *He* was a big, indistinguishable mass. He wanted Bree back, but he was too much of an oozing blob to know how to achieve that.

In the meantime, Roxy and Jane and Riaz were trying to protect him. The press had written about Videon canceling the deal, and thanks to Sam's public outburst at Michal Blaese, Bree's name was all over it. He hoped it wasn't causing too much drama for her, but he wasn't certain how to reach out. He didn't think she'd want to talk to him, and honestly, the idea of talking to her again while the wound was still so fresh didn't thrill him. But he would talk to her at some point; he would lose his mind if he never did again. He just couldn't figure out how.

He didn't have a good go-between. Bree's urban planner friends all thought he wasn't good enough for her and was holding her back—and, ha, hilarious story, Bree thought so too! Unbearably, Sam didn't disagree with them. But even if Bree had wanted to break up with him, he wished there were some way for them to still be friends. Goddamn, but he missed his best friend.

A week and a half after the breakup, Jane opened Monday's meeting by pointing out that it was the final show before the Christmas break. "I'm not saying it's the third most important show of the year, but it's the third most important show of the year."

She meant after the season opener and closer—but that was fucking bullshit. The shows that were important often came because of current events and pop culture explosions (à la "Lost Boy"). But Sam didn't want to be pedantic and point that out, especially not when he was currently the least valuable player on the cast, so he let it go.

"It can be a hard time of year for people, and a nostalgic time," Jane went on, "so we want to get it right. What does everyone have?"

Joya proposed a sketch about a reality dating show with the North Pole's elves ("Santa's helpers are finding love"). Marc had one about how horrifying trees found wrapping paper ("That's my uncle Ted!"). During these pitches, Sam sat stone-faced and contemplated the ugly carpeting in the room.

Just before they would normally take a break, Gibson called out, "You're quiet, Leyland. That's two weeks in a row. Nursing another broken heart? Does that make it three this year?"

Two, but who was counting. Oh yeah, clearly Gibson.

Sam just gave him a bored look. "Trying to make sure there's some openings for you. Merry Christmas."

Gibson's smarmy grin fell off his face. He recovered quickly, though: "I'm polishing one about all your exes. What was the latest girl's name? Is it *Bree* with two *e*'s, or with an *ie*?"

Roxy's hand was on Sam's arm before he could leap to his feet. Sam could guarantee he'd been in more fights than Gibson had. That dude had clearly never thrown a punch in anger. It would've been an instructive situation.

Jane quickly intervened. "Gibson, can it. Let's take fifteen."

Roxy towed Sam out of the room and into her office.

There wasn't enough space for Sam to pace, which was annoying, because aggravation was thumping in his veins like bass in a Europop song. "That bastard," Sam hissed. "That absolute piece of shit."

"Everyone was horrified. Even Joya and Alan."

"They should be." But—and this was annoying—Gibson wasn't wrong. Sam was moping. "Do you think I need to get up off the dirt?"

Roxy gave him a look of sisterly indulgence. "It makes sense to lie low for a few weeks. You said she was supposed to start the Michigan job when?"

"The first of the year, I think."

"You can stay in bed the entire break, and when it's done, she'll have left New York." Roxy said that as if Bree's physical proximity were the problem.

"I doubt that's going to help much. It's not as if I'm going to run into her in a city of twelve million people." Which was a crying shame.

But the idea of seeing her again—it took his breath away. He'd probably fall to his knees and beg her to take him back.

"You've gotten over broken hearts before."

"*Bruised* hearts. Breakups. Nothing like this." This was the big one, the kind of event that happened in your life and you measured every event as either before or after. Before he'd kissed Bree, after he'd kissed Bree: those were the hemispheres of Sam's life.

"You'll feel better someday."

"I don't want to." If he couldn't have Bree, then he didn't want to feel better. Feeling bad was the final souvenir of her. He wasn't going to give it up that easily.

"Okay." Roxy made a firm nod. "Then get her back."

Riaz had suggested the same thing. In the moments when Sam wasn't totally despondent, he'd thought the same thing. But like world peace or Sam and Gibson becoming besties, it seemed impossible.

"How?" Sam asked.

"Apologize."

"I don't think she'll listen to me." He should've called or texted right away. The more time that had gone by, the more impossible it had seemed.

Bree and Sam hadn't talked every day for the last twenty-seven years, but they'd talked most days. Without her, he might as well have been drifting behind the moon. On his best days, Sam felt isolated, alone. Without Bree to ground him, he almost felt theoretical.

"I haven't tried calling. I wouldn't blame her if she blocked me."

"Oh, jeez, how sad that you don't have a massive platform," Roxy said.

That sat between them for a minute.

"Use the show?" Sam finally asked.

"Why not? And bonus, think how mad Gibson would be."

Sam snorted, but laughing at that butthead would have to wait. "What if she won't take me back?"

"Then at least you know. At least you tried."

Sam's brain was like a lawn mower, trying to turn over for the first time in the spring but finding it hard. "What did Gibson just say? He was working on a sketch about all my exes?"

Roxy's eyes were dancing. "Yup."

"But why stop with my exes? I have an entire lifetime of being a shit that I can mine for content. I've hurt, like, a lot of people." Sam was going to have to make a list, flip some coins, get a Magic 8 Ball, *prioritize*.

"That's the spirit," Roxy said.

"The Christmas spirit." Sam tapped his pockets. In his anger, he'd left his phone and notebook back in the writers' room. "I need some paper."

Half an hour later—*Comedy Hour* wasn't known for its fidelity to Jane's "fifteen minutes" proclamations—Jane called things back to order. "Who's next?"

Sam's hand shot into the air. She hadn't finished calling on him before he launched into his pitch: "The title card reads, 'A Jerk's Carol: A Ghost Story of Christmas.'"

Gibson groaned, which he did pretty much every time Sam pitched anything. Normally, he did this low, only for the benefit of his friends. Now he was feeling emboldened, and he didn't care who else could hear him.

Jane ignored Gibson but asked Sam skeptically, "This is autobiographical?"

"Yup. So it's a Victorian bedroom at night: the four-poster bed with the curtains around it. A candle. I'm wearing a nightgown and one of those sleep hats with the tassel. You get the picture. It's the night before Christmas, and I'm in bed when the Ghost of Christmas Past appears. He tells me I'll never be happy until I deal with my issues. My past."

Sam had considered Riaz's suggestion that Sam get therapy, and it wasn't misplaced. But it also wouldn't work fast enough for him to get Bree back.

"So he takes me to an elementary school. Finger paintings on the wall, a blackboard, the ABCs, and there's Mrs. Ortiz. She singled me out to give me a present because she knows I won't get anything at home, and I yelled at her. So now . . . I apologize."

For a long minute, Sam seemed to have forgotten the mechanics of breathing. He only just managed not to gasp when he remembered no one knew this story—no one except for Bree. He hadn't told his parents or Salem or anyone. As soon as Bree saw the classroom set, she was going to realize what he was up to.

God, he hoped she would realize what he was up to.

Sam managed to focus himself. Jane was watching him steadily, and he had the uncomfortable feeling that she knew exactly what he'd just thought.

"Anyhow, it doesn't sound funny, but trust me, it'll be funny."

Sam ran through several more scenarios, several more people whom—some because of kindness, some because of misunderstanding, and some because of spite—Sam had hurt and he owed apologies to.

"And then he shows me Salem, who's performing 'Lost Boy,' and I apologize for proposing when I knew we didn't love each other." He could tell her what he needed to: that the song was annoyingly good and that he hoped he hadn't hurt her. "And finally, I apologize to Bree for—well, everything."

He was going to have to write it carefully, to say what he needed to her but not share all their shit with the world—because after this, Sam was going to be done sharing his shit with the world. He'd given it entirely too much of himself.

"At the end, I wake up alone. But I run to the window, and I shout down to Gibson, 'You there, boy! What day is it?'"

"Hey," Gibson snarled, unhappy to have been sucked in to this, especially in such a humiliating fashion.

He could join the club. This was going to be infinitely humiliating for Sam.

Under the table, Sam could see Roxy's hands shaking with suppressed laughter.

"And that's the basic idea," Sam finished.

Jane made a face. "Don't get me wrong, you probably should apologize to these people, but is *Comedy Hour* the venue for that?"

Which was a pretty reasonable point. Sam hadn't had enough time to think through the entire thing; he was still hashing through the concept. "Since my screwups were public, I think my apologies need to be too."

"And you can't hold a press conference?"

"You don't think the people want me on a platter, baring my soul, for the holidays?"

"Oh, they probably do," Jane agreed. "But . . . will it actually be funny?"

That was the number one question for everything they did on *Comedy Hour*. It had been, in many ways, the number one question in Sam's life. And he knew himself well enough to know that there was only one answer.

"Dictator perpetuo, it'll be hilarious."

Jane tapped her pen against her chin. "I'm not saying yes, but you can write it. We'll see on Wednesday."

Sam would take it. He certainly didn't think Jane owed him the platform of the show unless he could write something that might have some value for viewers: making them laugh and maybe convincing them to give some sorrys of their own for the holidays.

It was the least he could do after being an ass so publicly for so long.

"And another toast to Bree, the queen of the spreadsheet." Megan raised her glass.

The cry that went up was more diffuse than it had been to the first toast, one hour and several bottles of wine ago.

"And the queen of the passive-aggressive email!" Jeff added.

"Hey, some of those emails were just aggressive," Bree said.

But Bree couldn't complain. Not about her friends and coworkers who were being so deeply kind. About the persistent and self-inflicted sadness that was following her like a rain cloud? Well, she wouldn't complain about that out loud.

Despite the smile on her face and the delicious Thai food in her stomach, Bree still didn't feel a single, solitary ounce of joy. While she wasn't starting the job until the new year, she didn't see the point of staying in New York. It was just too painful. So she'd spent a week and a half dutifully packing her apartment, loading a storage cube, and cleaning. She had two days in a hotel room in front of her before she'd be driving a rented car filled with the bare essentials to start a new job—and a new life.

She'd worked hard enough, steadily enough, that the ache in her chest had quieted to a dull buzz. Tonight, though, it had revved up again. Sam's absence was so conspicuous. He'd never missed a night like this of hers, ever.

But Jeff and Megan had probably put the word out that no one was supposed to mention him or *Comedy Hour*, and so far, at least, it had been a perfectly Sam-free zone . . . except for Bree's head. That was never a Sam-free zone.

"God, do you remember that playground project on Ninety-Sixth Street?" Rachel asked. "I've never seen such patience."

Bree tried to demur. "I didn't, I mean—"

"You made that happen. Just like the library." She gestured with a crispy egg roll in the direction of the library, which was certainly the most architecturally beautiful building Bree had ever worked on.

"I don't think—"

"I don't think; I *know*. In fact, I ran into Siwoo Jang at a Brooklyn Beautification meeting the other day, and I mentioned you were moving. She sent a card." Rachel pulled it out of her purse.

Ms. Jang was deeply lovely and deeply opinionated, and she'd taught Bree most of what she knew about building community consensus for a project.

"And the girls from the Ida Straus school sent one too," Megan said, adding another card to the pile.

"But it's not just cards—think about that development on William Street," Jeff reminded her. "How hard you fought to get those low-income units."

"You're not going to convince us, Bree," Megan said, throwing an arm around her. "We're all the founding members of your fan club."

Not the founding members. That had been Sam, at least until Bree had driven him away.

Don't think about Sam.

Bree tried to make her answer light: "It's a big city, and the work I did, while fine, was drops in the ocean."

"All we ever are is drops, Bree. The best you can hope for is to be a really good drop."

"Are you high?" she teased Jeff.

He snorted. "No." But he was flushed and buzzed, and everyone was trying so hard to make her happy.

Bree knew she was a mess. For years, she'd told herself that if she could just have Sam, then she'd be happy. But when she'd had him, had she been happy?

Well, yes. She'd been happy when they'd been laughing together and he'd dropped a smacking kiss on her mouth and she'd thought, *Maybe it can be this simple.* She'd been happy in the moments where she'd shared her doubts with him and he'd validated them. She'd been especially happy when he reciprocated, and when she felt like she was the only one who saw him. She'd been really happy when they'd been in bed together.

Sure, their relationship hadn't erased *all* her doubts. It hadn't fixed everything in her life.

What relationship could? What had she thought, that Sam was magical?

No, she'd messed it up. Her lies and his temper. And now she was leaving, without even feeling like she could reach out and say goodbye.

It was the worst of all possible outcomes. She'd gotten to see how good they could be together, but it was too late. She'd been correct: they were only going to get one shot.

"Our point," Megan said, dragging Bree back to the party, "is for a little raindrop, you made a big splash."

"On the Big Apple?"

"Don't mock. You did great work, and we're very excited to see you fly the coop."

Bree thought she'd been stuck, but her coworkers were telling her that while she might've spent eight years in one place, she wasn't leaving the *same* place where she'd arrived. The difference had been her.

In his own messy, flamboyant way, Sam had tried to say that to her, too, and she hadn't listened.

More than anything, Bree wanted to see him one more time and tell him that she understood now. But he wouldn't want to hear it. Usually, Sam's anger passed, leaving things cool and sweet like after a rainstorm. But this time? She'd hurt him too deep.

Which was why Bree's voice cracked when she said, "I'm going to miss you all."

Because even though she knew now, knew it deep, that she had to leave New York, it was scary to leave the last group of people on earth who knew her well. She'd already lost Sam. Without Megan and Jeff and Rachel and everyone else, Bree was a blank slate, clean and empty.

She needed to get to where she could see the potential in that and not just the loss.

CHAPTER 25

"Leave your cravat alone," Roxy said.

"It's droopy." Sam poked it. He was pretty sure the thing tied around his neck was twice as large and three times as deflated as it had been during the dress rehearsal. Prop-based humor was so lazy, but in this case, he'd take whatever help he could get. He'd promised Jane that if she let him use the show for what was clearly a selfish purpose, he'd give her something funny. The cravat was part of his attempt to keep his end of the bargain.

Roxy swatted his hand away from his costume. "It's funnier that way."

Jane's needs aside, Sam had a more important goal than mere humor. He had things he wanted—needed—to say, and his future was riding on whether Bree saw and understood his apology. Not his career—his actual future.

"The only part of this that's funny is Gibson's Victorian-street-urchin outfit," Sam said to Roxy.

"That was a stroke of genius, my friend. The sketch justifies its existence through that alone."

Across backstage, Alan and Joya were trying to get Gibson to say, *Please, sir, I want some more.*

"Like, if Alan shared a spoonful of good ice cream with you, what would you say?" Joya prompted.

Gibson glared at her.

"If you were up for a production of *Oliver!*, what line would you read?" Alan—who was in costume as the Ghost of Christmas Present—asked.

Gibson could only roll his lower lip crabbily. Trying to pretend he was being a good sport but refusing to go along with the joke had him about to lose it.

"Hilarious as Gibson's pain is, it's not my measuring stick for whether this works."

Roxy propped herself next to him against the wall. "You realize Bree might not take you back."

"I am aware of that possibility, yes."

"The main thing you have going for you is she must have forgiven you before."

Sam racked his memory. He'd certainly been *annoying* more times than he could count, but he and Bree hadn't had a real fight before. At least not that he could remember. They'd had differences of opinion. Moments where he'd pushed even her endurance. But he'd always avoided having the kinds of spats he regularly got into with other people with Bree. He'd just valued her too much.

"Not for something like that," he finally said. "And I don't think I've ever needed someone's forgiveness as much as I do here." Certainly he'd never wanted someone to tell him, *It's okay, we're okay,* the way he wanted to hear Bree say it.

"Well, it's showtime."

The set designers and prop people had never worked such magic for Sam's sketches before. The bedroom they'd put together really did look appropriate for a serious adaptation of Dickens, with minisets arranged around it for an elementary school classroom, a threadbare living room in the early two thousands, a glittery pop concert, and then Bree's apartment. Since they weren't using her name, it was crucial for the details to be right. He wanted her to know this was for her. That he was trying to say to her through the show what he should've said when they'd fought.

Sam held a hand out to Leonard, the head designer who'd been with *Comedy Hour* since the beginning. "It looks amazing, man. Thank you."

"Eh, I hope you get the girl back."

"So do I."

Then the director was counting down, and they were on. The audience for the dress rehearsal had had a muted reaction because, Sam assumed, the sketch had surprised them. But he had to remind himself this piece had an audience of one. It didn't matter how the people in front of him responded. It only mattered how *Bree* responded.

Sam pretended to be asleep. When Alan burst into the room, Sam discovered that the props people had also doubled the length of his beard and added twinkle lights to his crown. He looked even more like the Muppet version of the character that way.

"Ebenezer Leyland, come in and know me better, man!" he bellowed.

Sam feigned astonishment, and then Alan described the setup.

"Aren't there usually three ghosts?" Sam asked.

"Layoffs," Alan explained.

That, at least, got an audience reaction. Sam's heart was going in a way that it normally didn't during the show, but if the audience liked it, maybe this would work.

They ran through the bit with Mrs. Ortiz. Sam felt as if he were having an out of body experience. He knew that he was pulling himself out of reality because it was easier that way than dealing with everything he was feeling, but it was still uncanny to almost watch himself do a fictional version of something he'd almost watched himself do the first time.

Uncanny, but probably easier.

Then they moved on to Sam's mother—and Christ if this one wasn't just as hard. Sam had certainly written this to be as difficult as possible for himself. He wasn't sparing himself anything here.

"You were trying your best, Mom," he said. The only thing that was keeping him from totally losing it was that Joya in no way resembled his mother. He should have insisted they deviate even further from reality so he could keep it together. "I see that now. You tried to protect me from the worst of Dad. And when I used our home life for material—well, I know now how hard that is to hear."

"You gonna stop?" Joya demanded.

"No." Sam had to pause for a big laugh at that, because this was working, at least for the studio audience. "But it isn't to hurt you." These things had happened to him, and he had a right to talk about them. But he had to find a way to do it that telescoped in on *his* perspective and limited how much damage sprayed over bystanders.

And maybe he'd said enough about his childhood anyhow. Maybe he could stop talking about that, at least in public. Maybe he needed to.

The ghost then conveyed Sam to the stage where Lauren, a newer cast member Sam didn't know well, was singing "Lost Boy." They'd nailed the wig and dress, but no one but Salem had the right impish smile. Lauren was a good mimic, but she wasn't going to win a decent bar-costume contest as his ex.

"I thought these were past Christmases," Sam said to Alan.

"Just be glad I'm not showing you your future screwups too."

Well, wasn't that the truth?

Lauren stopped dancing—they had the "Lost Boy" choreography down—and demanded to know what Sam was doing there. If her accent was a little *My Fair Lady*, it didn't matter: the audience was in stitches.

"Salem, I honestly thought we were both playing. But 'Lost Boy' . . . well, it's clear I hurt you, and I'm sorry. You deserve better than me."

He'd been so focused on getting Bree back that he hadn't really thought about who else he might be helping move on. He owed that to Salem, his mom, Mrs. Ortiz, and anyone else he'd trampled all over. Maybe he needed to do an entire apology tour when this was over.

The ghost then revealed a facsimile of the couple from the coffee shop that Sam had yelled at.

"Nope, that one's a lost cause," Sam said, turning on his heel.

"Fair enough," the ghost replied. "But—"

And who should appear but Jane Feeley—playing herself, something she'd done only a handful of times in the show's history. Sam had never thought Jane cared about him one way or the other, but her willingness to do this demonstrated he'd been wrong.

"Oh no, ghost, not this," Sam whined. "Anyone but this."

"You said you wanted to repent."

Sam faced Jane and said what he should have for years: "I don't know why you gave me a shot. And I don't know why I have to be such a dweeb about it. I have a problem with authority."

"Clearly," Jane replied, the eye roll obvious in her voice.

But Sam wasn't fooled. She appreciated this and knew it wasn't purely an act. Sam had spent his adult life saying shit in public, but he was discovering the power of words only now. He really was thick.

"I'm sorry for going too far sometimes," he told Jane.

She gave Sam a look of pity before turning to the ghost. "How many more of these do we have this year?"

"The entire cast from 1983 to 1984 is at the stage door."

"Damn it, it's the same thing every year." And she stormed off to raucous applause.

"There's one more," the ghost told him.

"How many people did I hurt?" Sam demanded.

"How much time you got?"

Then Roxy came onstage. She was too tall and too assertive to pass for Bree, but she wore a wig that bore an uncanny resemblance to Bree's hair. Sam couldn't make eye contact with her, because he would have completely lost his composure, and he couldn't risk it because he needed this performance to be sincere enough for Bree to listen to what he had to say. It was his only shot to get her back.

"Oh no, it's a dream girl who is in no way inspired by my best friend. I hurt her the worst of all."

The audience *aww*ed. Sam assumed they'd been prompted by a cue card he hadn't approved, but he couldn't care less about that, not right now.

He turned to face the camera and tried to make it clear that he wasn't acting. That this was real—maybe the realest thing he had ever said. "I never meant to hurt you. I know why you didn't tell me about the job offer. I overreacted and made it about me, and I didn't listen. You were right. You're always right. I can lose anything else, but I can't lose you. So if you can see a way to let me camp on your couch, I'll come to you anywhere. We'll fix this."

At last, he shifted his eyes to Roxy's. Her expression was pure kindness and belief. They'd decided she shouldn't say anything; Sam didn't want to put words into Bree's mouth. He didn't want to feel as if he'd scripted her into forgiving him, assuming that she did forgive him.

Sam had given it his best shot, and everyone at *Comedy Hour* had helped. There was nothing else anyone could do.

Then, like all the others, Roxy whirled away.

"Wow," Alan-as-ghost deadpanned. "Those are some pretty specific and not-at-all-hypothetical apologies."

"It turns out, ghost, I'm an ass. But hear me! I am not the man I was."

"You're no longer funny?"

"Was I ever?"

"I dunno. Let me go ask Michal Blaese."

Then Alan, too, whirled away, and a clock chimed, and Sam ran to the window of the Victorian bedroom set. He wrenched it open and shouted down at a petulant Gibson.

"You there, boy! What day is it?"

"Why, it's Festivus, sir," Gibson hollered back.

"Let us keep it and air our grievances—and apologies—all year," Sam said, as the lights cut to black.

The audience was clapping, and Sam was changing into his costume for the next sketch, but all he could think was, *God, I hope that worked.*

Sam flat-out skipped the cast party. He had absolutely no desire to be photographed by the press, not after everything he'd just revealed. Frankly, he didn't have the patience for anyone who wasn't Bree, and he wasn't going to pretend he did. He stripped off his work clothes and rode his exercise bike for an hour. He scrubbed himself in the shower, ate a piece of toast, and paced around his apartment.

Finally, *Comedy Hour* started.

He almost never watched it. It was too weird when he knew everyone involved, and he'd never quite gotten used to the sound of his own voice, recorded. Someone had told him it had to do with how the sound resonated differently inside your own skull than outside it, but he'd never really believed it. His voice was weird. He couldn't believe anyone would want to listen to it.

His sketch aired in the middle of the show, just before the musical guest. Sam could barely watch because he kept checking his phone.

If Bree were watching—*if*—she'd know immediately what he was up to.

He almost shot through the roof when he got a text alert, but it was from Riaz. This is dark.

Even I can't be funny all the time, Sam responded.

The hell you say. Which, given how many problems Sam had caused for him, was actually sort of generous.

The sketch ended, and Gibson's forlorn expression actually sort of worked.

Sam received several more texts: Roxy wished him luck. Jane said that, speaking only for herself, she was considering forgiving Sam.

Then one popped up from Jeff: Hey, you know Bree is driving to Michigan, right?

Nope. Sam had not had that information. She must have decided to get out of town early because of him.

Sam quickly replied, I didn't. Where is she?

Leanver, OH. She's supposed to get to Ann Arbor tomorrow. She's been keeping me updated.

Ohio was roughly halfway between NYC and Michigan, so that made sense. Sam had always sworn he'd never go back to the town where he'd been born and had spent so many shitty years, but that vow, like everything that wasn't Bree, couldn't have mattered less.

Thanks, he texted Jeff.

He was off the couch the next instant, calling Roxy. "I need to borrow your car."

CHAPTER 26

Bree set the remote down on the nightstand of her crappy hotel room in her crappy hometown. Sam had apologized. Not only to her but to a not-insignificant percentage of the people he'd hurt.

She hadn't been planning to watch *Comedy Hour*, but she'd put it on out of reflex. No, that was a lie—and she was done with lying. She'd put it on out of desperation. She'd been desperate to see Sam, to know if he was still a column of fiery rage. She was confident that even in character, she'd be able to read his posture, his expression, his voice. To know if he'd cooled down enough for her to reach out and . . . apologize? Check in? Just hear his damn voice again.

And there it had been, saying that not only was he beyond his anger, but he wanted her back.

Her heart knew exactly how it felt about this: *yes!*

Her mind, though, was a mess.

For eighteen years, she hadn't thought Sam could possibly love her, but he had. The funny/not-funny thing about it was that she didn't doubt Sam believed he loved her. From the moment he'd said the words, standing in the doorway of her apartment, she'd known he felt them. Sam's emotions were like balloons in the Macy's Thanksgiving Day Parade: gigantic, requiring many people to handle, and potentially crushing.

But despite the power of what he self-evidently felt for her, Bree hadn't been able to believe he'd keep on loving her for forever. The balloon doesn't stay inflated every day of the year.

What Bree could see now was that her fears had come from the future, not the present. Was she really going to let concern about some potential change someday ruin her chance of happiness today? Was she really going to reject how Sam felt because she thought she knew better? Because she was *afraid* she knew better?

What she knew, absolutely, was that life without him sucked.

She crossed to the window and pushed the curtains aside. This strip of development, with a hotel, several chain restaurants, and the biggest gas station she'd ever seen, hadn't existed when she and Sam had been kids. This side of the highway had been all weeds and hopelessness.

Despite the meager growth, the town was pretty much the same. She didn't know why she'd felt like she ought to come back. She hadn't convinced herself that closure was possible; she hadn't called her mother. But when she'd been trying to figure out where to break her drive, Leanver had seemed the only possible choice. Maybe because it was eternal, never changing.

But *she* wasn't. And whatever he might bluster about, Sam wasn't either.

Salem had told the world Sam was a lost boy—but Bree knew that when they were together, Sam didn't feel lost. She didn't either. Together, and maybe only together, Bree and Sam were found.

Bree found her phone next to the remote control. As the kids would say, it was blowing up. She had texts from Megan, from Jeff, from Roxy. The only person she hadn't heard from was the person she most needed to talk to: Sam.

He was probably raw from having put himself out there, having paid out some of his deepest secrets to show her that he meant it, that he was trying to grow.

Ignoring everyone else's messages, Bree opened their message chain. The last one was from him a few hours before game night with Jeff and Roxy. Can't stop thinking about last night. They'd been sitting next to each other on her couch when he'd sent it.

Sam had been wrong about many things, but he'd been right that she needed to trust him—and that she needed to trust herself. If she could be just a little braver, there was a chance, a good one, that she could have everything she'd ever wanted.

That risk seemed like a small price to pay.

Bree almost texted Sam then, but he'd always said he'd never come back here, and, honestly, now that she had, she didn't blame him. She was never going to make this mistake again.

She was filthy in the way you can be only from spending ten hours in a car. She was exhausted, from the move, from the drive, from the heartbreak. So Bree decided to go to sleep and to call him the next night once she was in a new place, literally and figuratively.

Bree sat down gingerly on the merry-go-round. It had been here for at least thirty years; she'd played on it with Sam. She wasn't an expert in playground design by any means, but you didn't see a lot of these anymore. It was almost vintage. Give it a few years, and ritzy suburbs would probably be including them in their "playful learning landscapes" for the sake of millennial parents.

The metal was ice cold under her butt, but she didn't intend to stay long. Dawn had just broken, and she'd be back on the road to Michigan before the sun was much higher in the sky.

She blew into the to-go cup of coffee she'd made herself in the hotel lobby and took in the space. Like Leanver, the playground had changed, and it hadn't. Gone was the timber tower and the old slide. She couldn't calculate how many slivers she'd gotten on that thing or how many times the slide, heated to boiling under an August sky, had fried her thighs. It had been replaced—recently, too—by a modern high-density poly structure, including a climbing wall. The neighborhood was the same, down to the fading plastic flowers in the window boxes of the nearest mobile home.

But Bree could see the care here too. The attempts to create something fun in a place that didn't have enough of that. She ought to find out who the designer was and send them a note. They were clearly kindred spirits.

She took a sip of her coffee—still too hot—and tipped her face up to the anemic December sunlight. Not much was making it through the buffer of clouds. Sam was right about this place feeling oppressive.

A car flew down the street and parked behind Bree's rental. She'd gotten a big sedan: practical, decent gas mileage, but with enough space for the essentials she'd need until her moving cubes arrived. But this car was anything but practical. The lines of the cherry-red sports car screamed it didn't belong here.

Wait . . . Bree knew that car. Before her mind could connect it to its owner, Sam emerged from the driver's side door.

"Sam!" Bree didn't mean to shout it. It felt ridiculous. Absurd. But she couldn't keep her shock inside.

Sam was back in Leanver. He was less than a block away from her. All the things she wanted to say to him, she could say them. Just as soon as she recovered from her shock enough to remember what they were.

He moved across the playground at a brisk, steady, relentless pace. Was anyone else so *hot*—so intentional—when just walking? It wasn't fair.

He stopped in front of her. "Thank God I found you."

Bree didn't let herself fidget with her hat as she said, "Hi." It came out a little strangled, but she was too busy trying to count exactly how many days had passed since Sam had stormed out of her apartment.

She was too tired to complete the calculation and too grateful he was five feet from her to care.

"I wanted to know . . . if you saw the sketch," Sam asked.

"You drove to Ohio, to this place, to ask if I watched your show?" It was almost funny, and she could tell Sam almost laughed.

But the things they had to say to each other? The hurts they had to heal? None of that was funny.

"Yes," he said.

Because she knew what it had taken for him to come back here, she gave him the truth: "Yes, I saw it."

Her eyes were swimming with moisture. She set her coffee down on the merry-go-round and patted in the pocket of her puffy jacket for a tissue with which to wipe her nose and eyes.

"*Smoosh*," Sam said, and that broke her.

Bree sobbed, and Sam hauled her up and into his chest. She threw her arms around him, which was precisely where she'd wanted to be from the moment he'd stormed out of her life.

Thankfully, Sam kissed the top of her hat and then pushed it from her head and kept pressing his mouth into her hair. The scent of his detergent and deodorant filled some hole in her heart. She'd missed this, needed this, so badly, she wasn't even embarrassed she was sup-supping against the triangle of his T-shirt exposed by his unzipped jacket.

Once she'd gotten ahold of herself, she finally pushed back so that she could see him. "You're a dork."

That clearly hadn't been what he'd been expecting, but she loved the way he smiled in surprise.

"Yes?"

"That sketch? Sharing about Mrs. Ortiz—why did you do that?"

"Obviously, I needed to tell you I was sorry." He said it as if he'd done this in the standard and accepted way of apologizing, instead of doing it in a way that was going to show up on lists of the most shock-ing *Comedy Hour* moments for the rest of time.

"And you couldn't just . . . do that? *I* have to tell *you* I'm sorry. I have no intention of going on national TV to do it." No, she was going to do it here, in the place where they'd met. In the place where they'd saved each other.

And from that point of view, this playground suddenly seemed perfect.

The cocky was clearly inching back into Sam's spine when he asked, "Why do people still say *national TV*? I'd think at this point, YouTube has better distribution."

"Samuel." Bree wasn't impressed. "Why?"

He ran his palm along the tips of her hair; then his expression turned serious. "I fucked up with an audience. Everything I apologized for was public. Even with you, the thing with Blaese, with—me encouraging you to be with me in public. I dragged you into that tornado. So I figured I owed you public atonement."

"It hasn't been so bad," she said, with a shake of her head. "A few unsolicited emails and texts? I can handle that. Not being with you—that was bad."

Sam's grip tightened on her, and she could see him force himself to relax his hold. "I'm sure it was worse than you're letting on. But . . . I didn't intend the sketch to be the end of the conversation. I just wanted to get the ball rolling."

"What do you need to say?"

"I'm sorry." As ever, he slayed her with simple truths. "I reacted badly to your news. Which is why you didn't tell me in the first place."

She slid her hands inside his jacket, letting the warmth from his chest soak into her cold skin. "Yup."

"If we're going to be together, I have to be better. I have to earn you."

"No," she said quickly. "There's no test. Nothing you have to prove. I fell in love with you just because you're you. Right here—like literally here. So there's no 'earning' involved, either way. It's just a decision that we have to make, to be together. But that's not . . ." She shook her head. "*I'm* sorry I didn't tell you the truth. You deserved to know about the job offer, before we got together and definitely afterward. That was . . . not well done on my part."

"Okay." Now that Sam had cooled down, things were that easy. He wasn't someone for tortured apologies or contrition. It worked, or it didn't. "Let's try again. I promise I can be reasonable. I can listen to you."

And Bree believed him. She knew they had work ahead of them, but she and Sam together were unlimited potential. They had beaten the odds, and they would keep doing it. But only if they had each other.

"Here's what hurt," she told him. "I was having what seemed to me like pretty normal—I mean, not even doubts. Just niggles. And I needed you to be able to hear that without going *kabloom*." She pulled one of her hands out into the cold and made a firework with her fingers.

"No more *kabloom*," he promised, wrapping her hand in his. "No more *boom-pow*."

"Oh, I liked some of the *boom-pow*."

She could feel his entire body come to tight attention at that, but they weren't done talking yet.

"This isn't easy for me, loving you out loud," she admitted. "I loved you in silence for so long. Just carrying this secret inside my heart, where nothing could go wrong. I couldn't say something stupid, or not say something. I couldn't make a mistake. You couldn't reject me or get annoyed with me. It was an *idea* of love. The real thing is different. It's messy. It's scary, because our friendship is love too. I meant what I said that night: being your best friend never felt like settling. If the rest had to stay a dream, that was okay, because I already had so much with you. I just can't lose you."

He slid his free hand up her back and into her hair again. "The thing is, now that I've had a taste, I want all of it with you. I want you as my best friend, I want you in my bed. I don't want to choose."

"It's hard for me that you didn't choose me from the start."

"But I think it's always been you," he said with conviction. "That's why I could pretend with other people but never really be all the way there. It's why I always, always hated the guys you dated. At some level, I knew I was too messed up to try for you. The thing is, though, you know every part of me—all the unwashed socks under the bed—and you haven't run away or stopped answering my calls."

Well, she *had* for a while. At least metaphorically.

She freed her hand from his and began to play with the zipper on his jacket. "Our past is . . . shared," she agreed.

"I need that. I have a big mouth, but I can't seem to talk about where I come from without making it a joke. With you, it can just be there." But she knew that it was really more than that. "All the other times, with everyone else, I have to be funny. Not just funny—brilliant, showstopping. Every part of my life except one: with you. You're the only person I can be myself with. Be real with."

"So it's about how I make you feel?" she teased.

"Only a little." He gestured around them. "It's about how you have the same foundation I do, but you don't want to grind everyone around you into dust just to show that you can. Instead, you want to make the world better. To give other people what we didn't have. You're a beacon in a dark world, Bryony Edwards. You're always drawing me home."

"I guess there's just one thing left to ask. Wanna drive to Michigan with me?"

"What?" His question wasn't angry. It was open and curious and everything she needed him to be.

"So I still have to go to Michigan. I have to start this job. I want to try something different, and it sounds perfect for me. I just . . . I'll always wonder if I don't." She'd started talking quickly, as if she were worried he was going to blow up. "I have lots of leave. I can see about working remotely. I think we can still make things work."

She hoped he was going to be on board with this. But she knew it was pretty fast to be putting their only-just-restarted relationship to the test.

Except Sam passed with flying colors when he nodded. "Bree, it's fine. I—understand. *Comedy Hour* is on hiatus for most of January."

Bree began drawing his head down. "You can stay on my couch."

"You sure about that?"

He kissed her then, deep and thoroughly. The tension and the fear and the ache in Bree's body evaporated, and all that was left was the peace. She had him back. Had him forever. It wasn't that she thought they'd never screw up again. But now that they'd managed to fix things once, she knew they could again. They'd always find their way back together because they were meant to be.

She pulled back. "So I guess we better head out if we want to get to Ann Arbor before dark. Let's synchronize our Google Maps."

Sam didn't get out his phone. He began towing her toward—Roxy's car. That was it, he'd borrowed Roxy's car. "Nah, we have a pit stop first."

"What are you talking about?"

"I got a suite at the Marriott. I still have to make some more things up to you."

And after a short drive, he did.

They finally left for Michigan three hours later.

EPILOGUE

One Year Later

"And then she forgave me—which made absolutely no sense. But I told you she's too nice."

The audience roared, as if the recorded Sam had said something hilarious. It was further proof, as if Sam needed it, that they didn't really understand him.

Bree was curled up in her pajamas on her couch—their couch—with a mug of coffee, streaming the Videon recording of his *All Apologies* tour on her laptop.

"Do we have to watch this?" he groused. It wasn't as if she hadn't already seen it from backstage a zillion times.

But Bree's glare was pronounced. "It dropped today! Don't you want it to break all their records? Every view matters, Samuel."

The tour had already sold out within minutes and been proclaimed "an instant classic" by those yahoos at the *Times*. In every city, hordes of people had lined up to listen to Sam talk about how he'd started therapy, tried to make things up to the people he'd hurt, and attempted to forgive himself.

Critics had written some truly rapturous bullshit about it, calling it serious, hilarious, and—most ridiculously—"important." How could comedy be "important"? Honestly, what crap.

But all the same, Roxy had gone viral with a series of TikTok videos in which she read the highlights of the reviews with increasingly absurd filters on. Gibson had apparently melted down about it, and Jane had invited him to leave *Comedy Hour*—which, good riddance.

Gibson probably had been finding the studio a bit empty anyhow since his nemesis, Sam, had left at the end of the previous season. Sam had been torn about it, but the show's production schedule was torturous, he didn't want to have to be in NYC for half the year if Bree wasn't there, and he had other projects in the works. Jane had actually told Sam she was going to miss him.

He was still recovering from the shock.

Hashing through the decision had given him more than a little sympathy for how hard Bree's own work crisis last year had been—and she'd had to go through her thing without his input since he'd been busy being a butthead at the time.

But in the end, he'd decided it was time for him to move on from *Comedy Hour*. When Videon had come crawling back to Sam, tail between their legs, Bree had joined Riaz in declaring herself not at all surprised. Videon had explained they'd only dropped Sam to appease Michal Blaese, but then the jerk billionaire had pulled his investment because of a spat over a documentary critical of self-driving cars, and well, they'd been only too happy to take Sam back.

He'd almost said no, but he'd settled for doubling his fee and forcing them to include a clause about how they wouldn't interfere with his content—either in the special itself or in the subsequent stuff he'd agreed to develop for them.

Riaz had been rapturous. The contract included filming this tour and Sam's next one, plus a curated series with up-and-coming comics he was putting together, *and* it had an option for the pilot he was writing. He hadn't crossed the sitcom event horizon, but it had its hooks in his gut. At least if he wrote the script, he'd know it wasn't complete dumpster slush. He still bristled at the title *executive producer*, but it got those Hollywood types hot and bothered.

No, things had worked out well. While Sam knew Videon was mostly trying to make a point to Blaese about how little they needed his money, Sam had told everyone who would listen that he had no problem signing a spite contract—which he thought represented growth on his part. In the past, he wouldn't have taken their call; now, he was sitting in the house he'd bought with their check. However on the ropes his career had seemed a year before, it was clearly thriving now.

He watched Bree check her phone. "Who's texting you?"

"Megan." Bree gave him a coy smile. "She wants me to tell you that you don't deserve me, but she's certain you'll continue to try."

He would've been annoyed, but he happened to agree with Megan. "Did you send her a picture of the ring?" He pointed to the third finger of Bree's left hand, which was weighed down by the very sparkly Christmas present he'd given her a few days before.

"That would be crass."

"I am assured if the ring costs enough, it's crass *not* to share." That was pretty much what the folks at Tiffany's had said, anyhow.

Bree just snorted . . . and then admired the rainbows the ring cast across the couch cushions. That—that made the rock worth every penny he'd paid for it.

On her laptop, Sam was wrapping up: "So despite everything, I'm still an asshole. I'm a better person, not a new person. Apologies aren't multilevel marketing."

That line always slayed, and with the taped audience, it was no different. As always, the most sincere and truthful things Sam said garnered the biggest, most inappropriate response. He could only shake his head.

Not wanting to let the audience's ignorance ruin his mood, Sam leaned his head back against the couch. Bree had spent several months in a short-term rental before persuading him to look at houses with her.

He didn't care for real estate one way or another—the term gave him hives—but he couldn't resist Bree's excitement over what she'd called *Craftsman-style bungalows*. So he'd bought one for her. Well, technically, *with* her. She insisted on contributing to the mortgage, and he understood she might not ever be able to let go of some of her fears about independence and money.

If the coffered ceiling in the living room didn't make his heart go pitter-patter, well, he was a well-known grinch. If Bree wanted a coffered ceiling, she got to have it. And seeing the way she'd made the house a home for him—that did make him melt. Made him feel cared for. He'd never thought he could've strung twelve months of relative calm together. But with her, he not only had but expected to keep doing so for the rest of his life.

It was the damnedest thing since George Carlin's "seven dirty words you can't say on television" sketch. Sam didn't deserve this happiness, but he wasn't letting it go now that he'd snatched it.

On Bree's laptop, Sam ended the show by saying, "I know what matters now, and it's loving the right person—and sticking it to billionaires."

When he'd written the first draft of the show, he printed out the pages and presented them to Bree with a big, awkward bouquet of flowers. He'd said, "This is what I've been working on. And if you never want me to perform a word of it, I won't."

Sam knew he was and would always be at the heart of his own material, but he also promised Bree he would never say anything about her or their relationship publicly that she hadn't signed off on. He gave the pages to Bree, fully open to shelving the concept forever if that was what she wanted.

Since he'd spent years presenting his flawed-ass self for public consumption, Sam thought it was only fair to make his self-improvement public too. Plenty of assholes like Michal Blaese had taken Sam's persona entirely wrong, and Sam's attempts to parody that (à la Rich

White) hadn't actually penetrated public consciousness. *All Apologies* was an attempt to be so direct, so dead-on, that no one could miss it.

Bree had read the pages. Then she'd reread them. Then she'd covered them with notes and color-coded stickies and returned them to him. "I mean, if you're going to do it, it ought to be good, right?"

He'd tossed the pages to the floor and made love to her on the couch.

On the screen, the audience was still clapping and hollering, and Sam pushed Bree's laptop closed.

"Hey, I would've thought that was your favorite part."

Sam craved the applause, and he didn't trust it. He lost his mind when it wasn't there, but it made him sheepish and embarrassed when it was.

He was an absolute fuckup.

"Nah, and besides, we have somewhere to be, Smoosh."

Bree's look was quizzical. "Where?"

"The Ann Arbor Mural Walking Tour."

Her jaw dropped open.

Sam knew Bree was happy with her new job. For all the stink he'd made, he could see that she loved managing a team. She loved the challenges and differences of a new place—well, really, many new places, since she and her team were currently working on stuff in six different cities. For years, she'd said she'd felt stuck. But now, he loved seeing how she was in constant motion, between Michigan and New York before he'd left there, and between the stops on his tour when she'd been able to join him. Between the different projects she was making better. Between the quiet, practical person she'd been, and the more confident, loud person she was becoming. He couldn't have been more proud.

The still part at the center was the same as it had always been: them. Sam and her.

In the last year, they'd both had to grow. Especially him, because he'd been particularly stunted emotionally—basically a human bonsai tree. But they'd both had to learn how to be in the kind of real relationship neither of them had let themselves have before. It hadn't been easy, it hadn't been boring, but it had always been worth it.

He grabbed her hand, running his finger over the ring. Over the last year, they'd talked a lot about what marriage looked like. Real marriage, not some crap on television. He would've dragged her down the aisle the second they'd gotten back together, but that would've freaked Bree out. Loving her, really loving her, meant giving her what *she* needed. While he didn't have doubts about them, that didn't mean he could toss her caution aside or take it personally.

So they'd talked about *why* they might get married, and how they could avoid becoming their parents, and what they needed to know to be good at being together. All of which made it sound as if they'd given each other homework, when it had really been more like . . . devotion.

You didn't accidentally nurture a relationship when you were both on the road a lot. Everything had to be intentional, but he'd come to see that could be sweeter.

In the end, when he had knelt in front of Bree and opened the ring box, it hadn't felt impetuous. It hadn't felt scary. And it definitely hadn't felt like he was playing. It had felt as if they'd arrived at the moment they'd been headed toward since they'd met in kindergarten. The sum of every decision, every mistake. The flowering of something good and inevitable, even from the hard soil of where they'd been born.

"It can be something we do tomorrow, or in a year, or never. It can be just for us," he'd said.

"Oh, don't you worry. I'm keeping you, Sam Leyland. For forever." And he knew she meant it.

"A walking tour?" she said as he pulled her toward their bedroom. "It's, like, ten degrees out."

"Yup, so dress warmly."

"Couldn't we do this in, like . . . May?"

"We've lived here for a year, and we haven't done it yet. We've got to make new memories. Learn new shit."

Bree started to peel off her T-shirt, and Sam lost his train of thought for a minute. "There's the Sam Leyland I know and love."

"In the flesh." But if he didn't get his mind *off* the flesh, they weren't going to get out of the house in time.

He turned away from her and began digging in his drawer for long underwear. That was a nice, cold thought—as was imagining how gleeful Bree would be once they got back home, filled with new ideas about this new home city.

Ann Arbor wasn't Leanver, in that it wasn't framed by shit memories. And it wasn't New York, in that it wasn't tattooed with his blindness in not seeing what was right in front of him: that he loved Bree. That he always had and he always would.

No, Bree had been right. They needed to start over in another place, one that could be all about them. And Sam was determined that, as they filled it up with memories, they would be happy ones.

"Oh, I heard back from Salem," Bree said.

"Yeah?"

"She's free on that date for the wedding. And she said if we don't hire her to sing at the reception, she's going to write another song about you."

Sam snorted. "A third one?"

Salem's latest single was called "Happy for You." It was about the sweet ache of your ex settling down with his soulmate.

It was totally, totally fictional.

ACKNOWLEDGMENTS

In 2018, after a lifetime of listening to and enjoying such music, I began to wonder what it would be like if your ex wrote a hit song revealing all your flaws to the world—particularly if you were a high-profile person who had to endure the negative attention in public. As I was contemplating how this might work in a romance novel, iTunes shuffled up Stephen Sondheim's "Not a Day Goes By," a song from the point of view of a woman who's hopelessly in love with her best friend. And I began to imagine this plot as a friends-to-lovers, forced-proximity scenario.

My first attempt to write this book was, well, bad, but I hope the second version is stronger. Whatever superficial resemblance the hook might have to persons living or dead, these characters are entirely the fictional creations of my own imagination.

I would never have finished *Funny Guy* without Genevieve Turner, who read those first few chapters in 2018, plus all the various false starts and drafts in 2022. I am incredibly grateful to her for wry, insightful notes and boundless support.

Olivia Dade, Jenny Holiday, and Ruby Lang beta read the book and offered invaluable feedback. I'm especially thankful for how much they all loved Sam, which gave me the confidence to believe in my righteous-asshole hero when I was doubting why I'd written this caustic romance and whether anyone except me could ever adore it.

Sarah Younger is an incredible agent. Fierce, protective, kind, and hilarious: I'm thrilled she's in my corner.

I can't heap enough praise on Lauren Plude, my editor. She believed in this story from its skeletal proposal form, and she's shepherded it, and me, so carefully and with so much skill.

This book reached its potential because of the editorial genius of Kristi Yanta, who instantly understood Sam and Bree and pushed me to write and rewrite until the book was worthy of them.

I am in awe of the team at Montlake, who are so kind, professional, and organized. The amount of work that happens behind the scenes on a book is mind boggling, and this one wouldn't be in your hands without them. I'm particularly indebted to Karah, Jenna, and Elyse for their production and copyediting prowess. Whatever mistakes remain are mine alone.

Finally, and perhaps most importantly, I must thank my family. You gave me the time and space to write, you listened to me blather about made-up people, and you honestly assessed my jokes. I love and appreciate you so much.

ABOUT THE AUTHOR

Emma Barry is a teacher, novelist, recovering academic, and former political staffer. She lives with her high school sweetheart and a menagerie of pets and children in Virginia, and she occasionally finds time to read and write. You can visit her on the web at www.authoremmabarry.com.